# Accusing Elizabeth

A Pride & Prejudice
Variation

Jennifer Joy

Accusing Elizabeth

"Accusing Elizabeth: A Pride & Prejudice Variation"

This is a work of fiction. The characters, locations, and events portrayed in this book are fictitious or are used fictitiously. Any similarity to real persons, living or dead, is purely coincidental and not intended by the author.

Published by Jennifer Joy

Blog: jenniferjoywrites.com

Facebook: Jennifer Joy

Twitter: @JenJoywrites

Email: contact@jenniferjoywrites.com

ISBN: 1-944795-99-5

ISBN-13: 13:978-1-944795-99-3

# TABLE OF CONTENTS

To Mammy, who instilled a love of reading in all of her kids.

# CHAPTER 1

Elizabeth Bennet clenched her hands, her nails biting the flesh of her palms until they hurt. She glared at Mr. Fitzwilliam Darcy, the man who dared insult her family in the same breath in which he professed his love for her. How dare he proudly admit to separating her sister from Mr. Bingley! And the disdain with which he spoke of Mr. Wickham, a man whose manners were so far superior to those of his own, set her in opposition to the overbearing, pompous man before her.

The more he spoke, the bigger the hole he dug for himself. When he insulted her father, that was the last straw.

Shaking in her ire, she said in no uncertain terms, "From the very beginning— from the first moment, I may almost say— of my acquaintance with you, your manners, impressing me with the fullest belief of your arrogance, your conceit, and your selfish disdain of the feelings of others, were such as to form the groundwork of disapprobation on which succeeding events have built so immovable a dislike. I had not known you a month before I felt that you were the last man in the world whom I could ever be prevailed on to marry." Her chest heaved in the passion of her disgust.

He paused, visibly grappling with the emotions he had said moments ago that he could no longer contain.

"You have said quite enough, madam. I perfectly comprehend your feelings and have now only to be ashamed of what my own have been. Forgive me for having taken up so much of your time and accept my best wishes for your health and happiness."

His speech, broken and forced, struck Elizabeth. She raised her fingers up to her hot cheek as he turned and walked out of the room. He had spoken in earnest. Then again, so had she.

Bereft of strength, she sank into the seat behind her. Drawing her legs up to her chest, she rested her face against her knees and measured her breaths. Charlotte and her younger sister, Maria Lucas, would return with Mr. Collins from their tea at Rosings soon. She must gain control of herself or risk being plied with questions she was unable to answer.

The crunch of wheels on gravel straightened her posture. It might be them returning from Rosings. She reached for the book she had been reading and sniffed back the tears threatening to spill.

Some minutes passed, but nobody entered the parsonage. All the better. Elizabeth's overactive imagination conjured up a scene where Mr. Collins chanced upon Mr. Darcy leaving his home, knowing that she was without a chaperone. Instead of releasing his indignation on the gentleman— she used the term loosely— Mr. Collins would sooner blame her for her lack of propriety and accuse her of attempting to ensnare Mr. Darcy as a husband by arranging a compromising situation. Mr. Collins' accusation, though not in reality uttered, and the ease with which he thought the worst of her, heaped fiery coals of anger toward Mr. Darcy and his unsolicited call on top of Elizabeth's already large list of complaints toward that particular gentleman.

That made two proposals within the past six months— both refused.

Before she could wallow in too much self-pity, the Rosings carriage brought the inhabitants of the parsonage home.

She touched her cold fingers to her eyes to relieve the swelling and hoped the Collinses would assume she was miserable from the headache which had prevented her from joining them— a headache which had grown significantly worse since Mr. Darcy's lousy proposal.

Cheerful chatter preceded the party to the door, but they fell silent as they crossed the threshold and saw Elizabeth sitting in the window seat. Charlotte stepped forward, concern on her face. Clasping

Elizabeth's hands and sitting next to her, she said, "Are you well? Your face looks feverish." To her husband, she said, "She is not well. Should we send for the doctor?"

The insides of Elizabeth's cheeks stung as she bit them to refrain herself from expressing her ire and the source of her heightened complexion. "I assure you, I do not need a doctor and thank you for your concern for my health. I thought a quiet afternoon would ease the pounding in my head, but perhaps a stroll around your garden would be of more benefit."

She rose, loosening Charlotte's hold on her hands. Mr. Collins' chest swelled at the mention of his beloved garden.

Before he could bless them with a lengthy oratory on the benefits of spending time out of doors in appreciation of God's creations, Charlotte stood beside her, looping her arm through her friend's. "I will join you. Let us walk in the orchard. It is quiet there, and we shall not disturb Mr. Collins in his book room. Lady Catherine had several opinions regarding his forthcoming sermon. He takes his duties to the people of Hunsford seriously, and he has much to investigate before next Sunday."

Mr. Collins, whose feet had pointed to the door with every intention of accompanying them outside, now shuffled his boots toward the hallway leading to his study overlooking the road.

"How often it is that we must put the needs of others ahead of our own. Thank you, dear Mrs.

Collins, for reminding me of the path I have chosen. How fortunate I am to have such a supportive wife, who seeks not her own selfish wants, but the benefit of others." He pointed his words at Elizabeth, who had refused his offer of marriage only months before. She had not regretted her decision then, and she certainly did not regret it now, though he used every opportunity to show her what she would forever fail to benefit from.

"Come, Lizzy. You are in need of some fresh, spring air." Charlotte stood by the open door.

Elizabeth needed no further encouragement.

The sweet breeze brought the best of spring's offerings to her senses. Her hair, free of a bonnet, swirled in her loose coiffure. The tree blossoms scented the air with the promise of succulent fruit. Bees hummed a low buzz, and birds chirped at the close of another busy afternoon's work.

Charlotte did not speak until they were a safe distance from the house.

Choosing a plum tree to lean against, she folded her arms and gave Elizabeth the same self-satisfied look she had perfected on her dearest friend over the years. "Mr. Darcy was not even present, so you might have joined us instead of shrinking away from his company and spending a dull afternoon here."

"I avoid one tea, and you accuse me of avoiding Mr. Darcy? Come, Charlotte, I have made no secret of my dislike of the gentleman to you, but I am not afraid of him... or his aunt." Lady Catherine had done her best to intimidate Elizabeth at their first dinner at Rosings. Her failure to cower had only irritated the lady.

"I still think Mr. Darcy holds you in high regard. Otherwise, why would he look at you the way he does? Mark my words, Lizzy, Mr. Darcy admires you."

If only she knew. But Elizabeth was not ready to tell her. It would only worsen her mood to recount the events of the afternoon to her friend who had predicted it so accurately.

"From the first moment of our acquaintance, Mr. Darcy has never once given me any reason to suspect…." Elizabeth could not bear to continue. She had seen the look on his face. She had seen the hurt. But the remorse she felt lasted only a brief moment. He had hurt Jane, and as the man responsible for the ruination of her happiness, he was undeserving of forgiveness. Continuing, she added, "If he were to ask, I would have to refuse."

Charlotte's firm gaze brought Elizabeth out of her thoughts to reality. In a soft voice devoid of judgment, Charlotte asked, "Why could you not accept Mr. Darcy? Surely his merits far outweigh his social deficiencies."

Elizabeth wished, not for the first time, that she could be more like her pragmatic friend. Charlotte had married for convenience, and the past month spent in her company had proved her to be content with her circumstances. Charlotte made the best of it, encouraging Mr. Collins to spend time in his study and in his beloved garden while she took solace in turning the cramped parsonage into a comfortable home which she took pride in managing well. Such a life was not for Elizabeth. She would sooner die a spinster than sacrifice her values for anything less than the deepest, truest love. But Charlotte would not understand.

"No, Charlotte, I am convinced that a man's character is defined by his actions, and I have seen nothing in Mr. Darcy's behavior to justify any tender regard for him on my behalf."

Charlotte propped her fists on her hips. "I know you too well. You have held a grudge against Mr. Darcy since he snubbed you at the Meryton Assembly. Admit it."

Elizabeth lowered her chin and grumbled, "If I have a grudge, he has earned it."

What frustrated her the most was that other than the all-important issue of manners, Mr. Darcy was the image of her ideal gentleman: tall, dark, mysterious, wealthy, and handsome in a way that should be painted and preserved in a museum for ladies of many generations to enjoy. She had hoped he might notice her at the Meryton Assembly where they first met. His charm melted away when he opened his mouth and revealed that he was nothing more than a puffed up snob. Though months had passed, she remembered his exact words: "She is tolerable, but not handsome enough to tempt me. I am in no humor at present to give consequence to young ladies who are slighted by other men." He had looked directly at her as he spoke. He had to have known that she could hear him. The memory of it made her angry with him all over again.

Charlotte reached her hand out to Elizabeth's shoulder. "Perhaps he earned it. But you cannot afford to refuse another proposal. Who would propose to you if it became known that you would refuse Mr. Darcy? Please, Lizzy, promise me that you will give the matter serious consideration should he make an offer. After all, what would your parents say if you did not?"

Indeed. What would they say if they knew? They must never know. Swallowing hard, she tried to remember how lovely the orchard had felt minutes ago. The birds chirped their gossip, scoffing at her in high-pitched shrills. A strand of hair swirled in front of her nose and poked her in the eye. The bees listened from the safety of their hive, ready to spread the news of her secret across all England at first light.

In hopes of evading this conversation again, Elizabeth said, "You ought not worry yourself too much, Charlotte. Is Mr. Darcy not engaged to marry Miss de Bourgh?" She knew it could not be the case. Mr. Darcy was disagreeable, but he was not dishonorable.

Charlotte harrumphed. "If Lady Catherine had her way, they would have married years ago. Nobody in Hunsford takes it seriously. The fact that he has not married her makes me think that he does not want to and is under no obligation to do so."

She looked at Elizabeth with an 'I-told-you-so' air.

In another attempt to change the subject away from herself, Elizabeth said saucily, "No man would choose to have Lady Catherine as a mother-in-law. In that, I will acknowledge his good sense. Now, tell me, my dearest friend: In what way is your household lacking, and how ought you to care properly for your poultry?" She threw her nose up in the air in her best imitation of Lady Catherine.

Charlotte chuckled as Elizabeth intended. "Considering how Mr. Collins takes her every word to heart, I admit to letting my mind wander when she shares her multitudinous admonishments. So intent is she to impart her superior knowledge, she does not bother to make sure I am listening."

They laughed heartily, and the orchard returned to the charming retreat it had been before any mention of Mr. Darcy had been made.

# CHAPTER 2

Fitzwilliam Darcy marched his battered pride the half mile back to Rosings. What a fool he had made of himself— laying his heart bare before a woman he found intriguing enough to spend the rest of his life with, only to have her refuse him with disdain. What was worse… as bitter as he felt, he could not hate her or see her any less favorably than he had before. He *had* been abominably rude at the Meryton Assembly. He had hoped that his other merits would have softened the insult he had directed at her in time. Alas, he had lost her good opinion.

Stalking into his aunt's house, he trudged up the stairs, ignoring the call of his cousin Colonel Richard Fitzwilliam until he reached his room and shut the door behind him. He was in no mood to talk, and Richard's cheerfulness would goad him beyond what he could bear.

With a singular purpose, he crossed his room to

the desk and pulled out several sheets of paper. Perhaps it was a foolish errand, but he could not allow Miss Elizabeth to continue to think so wrongly of him when it was in his power to enlighten her. Would it change her opinion? He could only hope. He would not give up so easily when his very soul knew that she was the only woman he could ever love. No other lady had altered the beating of his heart as she had. Ironically, it had begun with a refusal. Wispy curls of hair had caressed her rosy cheeks, an eyebrow arched over her gleaming eyes, and her curvy lips parted to rebuff him so politely and resolutely, he had determined to win her favor that moment. The intensity of his resolve was no less now than it had been that evening months ago, burning in his bones stronger than his pride.

He closed his eyes, and the mess of accusations against him ordered themselves into a neat line by order of the importance Miss Elizabeth placed upon them. Bingley and Miss Bennet were at the top of the list. How could he have known that Miss Bennet, with her tepid manners, was sincere in returning Bingley's affections? He had watched them closely and judged her indifferent. Apparently, he had been wrong.

Next was the ever-present thorn in his side, Wickham. Miss Elizabeth's appalling misjudgment needed clarification. To think that he came out the loser in a comparison against his enemy— a man so lacking in decency, he had nearly succeeded in eloping with Georgiana, his innocent sister. She was so shy in nature, he had never suspected that she had developed an attachment. Just like Miss Bennet and Bingley. Darcy groaned. Could it be that he had misread Miss Bennet's manners toward Bingley just as he had overlooked Georgiana's growing interest in Wickham?

Cursing himself for not seeing what was now blatantly obvious, he nearly dumped the ink on top of the paper as he jammed the quill into the pot.

A great deal on his mind, he wrote in a tight script. Soon he had filled several pages, front and back, with thick, black letters. The relief of sharing his locked-in secrets cast a burden off his shoulders. He felt confident that Miss Elizabeth would protect them as much as she did her sister's happiness. Her unwarranted prejudice against him aside, he had no reason to distrust her character. His confidence returned. The revealing pages beneath his fingers would cast a more favorable light on his behavior. Would her answer have been favorable had she understood? Had he forever lost her good opinion?

Quickly, not wishing to waste any more time, he penned a second letter. He would send it by a messenger so that Bingley would have it at first light.

Sealing the letters, Darcy looked out of his window to the darkness outside. He must have lit the lamp on the desk, but did not remember doing so. Nor could he account for the hours he had spent penning the letter on which all of his hopes depended.

He looked over at the vase of roses on the bedside table— the first of spring. He had plucked them earlier that morning. The soft pink petals reminded him of the color of Miss Elizabeth's cheeks after one of her walks. Reaching out, he touched the soft silk of the flower. He could not give them to her now. Nor could he deliver her letter at such a late hour.

*** 

Another day dawned, and Darcy tucked the letter into his coat pocket. With determination, he set out to find Miss Elizabeth. The morning looked deceptively pleasant with a few puffy, white clouds littering the bright blue of the sky. Rain would have been more welcome, more comfortable.

He reached the bottom of the stairs which led to the entrance hall. A figure paced back and forth across the marble floor, his hands clasped behind his back.

"Richard," Darcy called to his cousin.

Disrupted from his thoughts and his pacing, Richard looked up. "Ah, precisely the man I have been waiting for. I hope you rested well."

Darcy did not slow his pace, not wishing to be distracted from his mission. "I wish to leave today. I only have to deliver a letter, which holds some information for which you might be sought out to corroborate. We can leave this afternoon." He paused briefly, expecting Richard to ask about the contents or recipient of the letter and fall in beside him. He pulled the letter out of his pocket as he neared the front door, turning it over in his fingers.

"Good morning to you, too, my taciturn cousin. Not so much as a greeting or a polite inquiry to my health?" teased Richard in the maddening way he had of scolding Darcy with a laugh.

Darcy grit his teeth. He needed to try harder to be pleasant.

Turning back from the door, he said, "Excuse me. I forgot myself. Are you well, and why were you waiting for me?"

Richard shuffled his feet and crossed and uncrossed his arms. It perplexed Darcy to see his confident cousin, a colonel in His Majesty's Army, nervous. If anything, he looked more agitated that moment than before.

Gulping a large breath, Richard said in a rushed exhale, "I wish to stay at Rosings longer."

That was the last thing Darcy had expected to hear. Richard enjoyed Aunt Catherine's company as much as he did. Their yearly visits were made merely out of a sense of familial duty. Anything more would only encourage Aunt Catherine in her obstinate wish that Darcy marry Anne. Richard knew this.

"I see the reply on your face, but I must beg of you to reconsider. Please, Darcy, I so rarely ask favors of you. Let us stay for two more days. That is all I ask."

"Whatever for?" Darcy regretted having made the pact to stay together during their visits to Rosings. Richard had made it sound so honorable: something about never leaving a man in the hands of the enemy alone.

"I have a matter of great importance to discuss with Aunt Catherine." He stopped, leaving Darcy waiting for more details.

After an awkward silence, where it became clear to Darcy that Richard would share nothing more, Darcy slapped the letter he had toiled over against his hand. He felt certain that it would cast a kinder light on his actions. However, its impact would be greater felt in his absence. At least, that was the reasoning he used to justify leaving so that he might lick his wounds in the comfort of his home. He would have to wait to give it to Miss Elizabeth.

His heart sinking at his lost opportunity to raise her low opinion of him, Darcy tucked the letter back into his coat pocket. How he wished he could deny his cousin's request. The grin spreading over Richard's face at his resignation to stay brought only a small measure of comfort to his upset plan.

Slapping Darcy on the arms, Richard said, "I knew I could count on you. If all goes well, I will tell you everything. If not…. If it does not go well, then I hope you will allow me to spare my injured pride by keeping the matter buried."

Darcy shook his head at Richard's cryptic language. He had no intention of sharing the news of Miss Elizabeth's emphatic refusal, so he understood Richard very well. "Whatever your endeavor, I wish you success."

"Thank you, but now it is my turn to apologize. You mentioned something about me confirming the contents of a letter?"

"No mind. I pray you do not concern yourself over it."

He left Richard pacing at the bottom of the stairs as he continued out of the door. Over the past week, Darcy had grown accustomed to walking over the property. He justified it by telling himself that he did it to suggest improvements or repairs to Aunt Catherine's steward, but his eyes searched for a young lady walking without a bonnet. He knew it was foolish of him, but he wanted to erase the look of hurt and anger he had last seen on her beautiful face. He craved the sight of her smile.

Darcy walked for the better part of an hour, going to Miss Elizabeth's favorite spots, before he saw her coming around a bend in the road. Nothing could have prepared him for the clenching in his gut at the sight of her lovely figure gracing the path she walked upon. Tempted momentarily to shrink behind a tree, Darcy pulled his thoughts together and tried to catch his breath and keep his dignity. His fingers twitched to deliver the letter he had painstakingly written the night before. Why not? His absence was not necessary, only more comfortable.

Decided, he pulled it out of his pocket. Only, Miss Elizabeth was not alone. Miss Lucas was with her. He could not deliver a letter to an unmarried woman he had no right to claim an attachment to. Especially before a witness who would surely tell Mr. Collins, thus adding to Miss Elizabeth's misery and her worsening opinion of him. It was wicked of him, but he would not mind a forced marriage with her. If he were not convinced that she would hate him forever for taking her freedom away so cavalierly, he would be tempted....

He turned away into a small grove of trees to let the ladies pass by undisturbed. It would not do to startle them, and he did not want to give Miss Elizabeth any further cause to criticize his actions. The letter would have to wait.

Lengthening his gait, he returned to Rosings in short time with every intention of riding his favorite horse. He had not yet inspected the fences along the western edge of the property, and now was as good a time as any— even though Richard had undoubtedly seen to it by now. Richard rode the property every day to exercise his new mount— a handsome stallion worthy of the polished saddle on its back and the colonel.

Aunt Catherine's steward was a capable man, but he fought an uphill battle to see that funds which were used to support her lifestyle were not diminished by needed repairs or the welfare of her tenants. Rosings provided a comfortable living, but it was not enough for Aunt Catherine. She wanted more. She wanted Darcy's money.

A quick trip up to his room to change into clothes

more suitable for riding and he would be on his way. Slipping into the entrance hall, he was half-way to the stairs when Simmons addressed him. "Mr. Darcy, her ladyship wishes to speak with you. Let me accompany you to her drawing room." The butler extended his arm in the direction of Aunt Catherine's preferred room.

Preparing himself for another verbal skirmish about his marital plans, he straightened his shoulders and walked through the dark antechamber to her room.

Sitting in a gilded chair, her hair piled on top of her head like a silver crown, she did not motion for him to sit down, but let him stand in front of her as one accused.

Anne sat off to the side next to her loyal companion, Mrs. Jenkinson. Her pale hands clasped, Anne shook her head at Darcy with wide eyes.

Richard sat opposite them, avoiding eye contact with Darcy.

Aunt Catherine's voice cracked like a whip through the room, making Anne flinch and Mrs. Jenkinson reach out to calm her. "Have you disgraced our family by engaging yourself to another?"

# CHAPTER 3

Elizabeth walked with Maria into Hunsford, her bonnet swaying with each step she took from the ribbon weaved through her fingers.

Though not quite so large as Meryton, the trip into the small village afforded Elizabeth the chance to escape the parsonage, so when Maria had expressed a desire to walk into Hunsford, she had jumped at the opportunity to accompany her. Her friendship with the girl closer in age to Lydia than to herself had grown over the past few weeks as their stay in Hunsford progressed. Maria, though nearly the age to be presented at court and enter society, was excessively naive and tried too hard not to seem awkward in front of strangers. Once she found confidence in herself, she would fare well. In the meantime, her shy attempts to act more sophisticated than she was endeared her to Elizabeth.

Cutting into her meditations, Maria said, "How

exciting it will be to dine once again at Rosings tomorrow. Such grandeur and luxury! It is kind of Lady Catherine to condescend to invite us so often."

Elizabeth hid her scowl with a smile. "Indeed. The food is very good, and the addition of Colonel Fitzwilliam brings liveliness to the conversation."

Maria blushed. "His manners are charming, but he is not so handsome as Mr. Darcy."

Elizabeth felt Maria's keen eyes looking at her. Why was it that every conversation led to Mr. Darcy? Since she had refused him, nobody spoke of anything else! "I will not deny that Mr. Darcy is handsome, although his manners leave much to be desired. Let us not talk of him." She did not have many pleasant things to say, yet her own manners did not allow her to malign him in detail outside of the confines of her own thoughts.

Tying her bonnet on, she resumed walking. Her pace, no matter how fast it was, could not keep ahead of the invasive thoughts of Mr. Darcy. Someone had passed by in a carriage not long after he left the parsonage. What if someone had found out that he had called on her whilst unattended? What if she were forced to marry Mr. Darcy after refusing him? And what a refusal it had been. It had been one of those rare moments in time when the exact words flowed off the tip of her tongue to express the intensity and clarity of her sentiments.

After a few minutes, as the first thatched roofs

became visible, Maria called out, "Not so fast, Lizzy. Please, slow down."

Slackening her pace, Elizabeth turned to see Maria several strides behind her. "I apologize. My eagerness to send this letter to Jane increased my pace overmuch." She had written a lengthy narration of her activities since her last letter, carefully leaving out any mention of the offensive gentleman responsible for Jane's solitary exile in London.

Catching up, Maria said, "No matter. I only do not want to mottle my complexion before we go into the shop. Mrs. Baxter watches me like a hawk as it is."

Elizabeth laughed. "Mrs. Baxter has a son your age who watches you every bit as intensely as she does."

Maria looked down, her cheeks reddening. "Do you really think he notices me? I am not used to young gentlemen paying me any heed. They are all afraid of Father, and it is impossible to receive any attention with…" She stopped abruptly and avoided Elizabeth's amused gaze.

"… with my sisters around? Is that what you were going to say? If it was, my dear Maria, you would only be speaking the truth. Kitty and Lydia make no secret of their flirtations. Their need to be admired extends far beyond their want for sense." Elizabeth wrapped her arm through Maria's to assure her that no offense was taken.

Maria relaxed. "Sometimes, I do wish I could be

more like them. How lovely it would be to throw caution to the wind and act as one wished instead of always doing what is proper and expected. How I should like to do just one impulsive deed!"

Elizabeth squeezed her arm. "You must not take society's expectations too much to heart lest it rob you of your spirit. So long as you do not bend the rules too much, you will find that most people are forgiving of a few eccentricities." Like Mr. Darcy. Several times, he had caught her walking unattended and had engaged her in conversation. When she spoke her opinion freely, he openly debated a point with her. She had thought she had offended him with the freedoms she allowed herself— with the freedoms society would take away from her— but instead, it had won him over. She shook her head, still unable to understand how he could possibly have grown to love her as he said when she had done nothing to encourage him.

Maria unwound her arm from Elizabeth's, who only then realized how much she had been squeezing the poor girl. "I aim to live with more spirit, as you call it. Now that Father has returned to Lucas Lodge, I will have more opportunity to do so."

Elizabeth pulled Jane's letter out of her coat pocket. "Just promise you will *not* do anything that Lydia *would* do, and I think you will be safe. Freedom is precious, but if it is abused, it will be snatched away soon enough." The hair on her arms stood on end as an image of a forced marriage to

Mr. Darcy flashed before her eyes. Mother always assumed that, of all her daughters, it would be Mary who would be left on the shelf. Maybe they could share a small cottage together. Elizabeth preferred Jane's company, but she still held hope that Mr. Bingley would return to Netherfield Park to propose to her sister. How difficult it had been for her not to include Mr. Darcy's admission that he was the cause for their separation in her letter. But it would only add to Jane's sadness.

Maria chattered at her side, but Elizabeth heard little as she went through the motions of posting her letter, and they entered the shop to see if the past week had brought anything new and worth seeing to the shelves.

Mrs. Baxter smiled with her lips, but her eyes were alert and serious. "Good morning, Miss Bennet. Miss Lucas." She spoke in a clipped voice.

Over in a corner was her son— a tall, thin lad of sixteen years. He leaned against the broom in his hands, his eyes following Maria's every move.

"Matthew. Matthew." Mrs. Baxter cleared her throat. "Matthew!"

Losing his balance, young Mr. Baxter nearly tripped over his broom. "Yes, ma'am," he said as he righted himself and looked in Maria's direction to see if she had seen his blunder. As if she could miss it.

Mrs. Baxter took the broom away from him before he could poke himself or someone else with it. "I want you to move the bags of flour from the far wall in the storage room so that they are closer for me. This one here is almost empty."

From what Elizabeth could see, the bag of flour behind the counter was recently opened.

Stepping over to a shelf which held some magazines, Elizabeth looked through them, waving Maria over to join her. Mr. Baxter was in enough trouble already, and Maria's close proximity did nothing to improve his lot.

"Look, Maria, Mrs. Baxter has the newest edition of *Lady's Monthly Museum*. I think even Mr. Collins would approve, its focus being on the improvement of the mind and moral living." Elizabeth would rather read a novel than a magazine, but her purpose was to occupy Maria until Mrs. Baxter quit staring at her.

"I much prefer *La Belle Assemblée*." Maria pulled out the thick magazine and placed it on top of the shelf. "He would not approve of this. Nor would Father." In a lower voice, she added, "In Meryton, I admit to flipping through the pages when the shopkeeper was not looking to catch glimpses of the beautiful dresses inside."

Elizabeth looked up at Mrs. Baxter. The woman occupied herself by sorting cards of lace according to color in a neat box between glances toward the magazine shelf. "I do not think we could flip through half the magazine before Mrs. Baxter would take notice and complain to Mr. Collins. We had best take our leave."

Maria pouted. "What good is it to have a shop

full of lovely things when the customers cannot enjoy perusing?" She looked longingly at the magazine, her fingers trailing along the top of the cover as they turned to the front door.

A loud crash and a groan from the storage room startled Elizabeth. Mrs. Baxter charged into the back room.

The sounds of scuffles and grunts reached out to them.

Mrs. Baxter soon came out, brushing the flour off her hands. Elizabeth bit her cheeks to keep from laughing when she saw young Mr. Baxter standing in the doorway, covered in the white powder. He looked like a ghost.

Maria tugged Elizabeth's coat sleeve, "Come; let us go."

Bidding a good day to the Baxters, they left, walking a fair distance from the door before they burst into laughter. Elizabeth laughed louder and longer than she needed to, but the relief it brought her eased her turbulent heart.

When she could catch her breath, Elizabeth said, "Good. We have had our fun. Now, we shall return to the parsonage to hear the result of Mr. Collins' extensive research for his next sermon."

Maria chuckled and stiffly grabbed her ribs.

Concerned, Elizabeth asked, "Are you well?"

With a weak voice, Maria said, "I laughed so hard, my side hurts."

"It was quite a sight. I thought I should burst when I saw Mr. Baxter come out covered in flour. I imagine his mother was cross with him and made him sweep up the mess, though she very clearly was the cause of his unfortunate accident."

She was careful not to make Maria laugh all the way to the parsonage. The girl clutched her side and grimaced every so often.

Charlotte sat in her favorite chair, embroidering on a christening gown. Though her sewing box was in her sitting room, the lighting was better in the front parlor.

"Maria, are you well?" she asked as they entered. The girl still clasped her aching side.

Maria mumbled that she needed to lay down for a spell as she continued without a pause up the stairs.

"You will not guess what happened at Mrs. Baxter's shop!" said Elizabeth as she sat down on her perch in front of the window to relate a scene-by-scene description of young Mr. Baxter's woes.

# CHAPTER 4

Darcy stood in shock. Did Aunt Catherine know of his proposal to Miss Elizabeth? He kept his gaze level and his face neutral, but his heart hammered in his chest.

Aunt raised her chin and stabbed the cushioned arm of her chair with her pointy nails. "Tell me immediately why you have not yet offered for Anne."

Darcy glared at Richard. Over the years, he had taken great strides to time his visits and cut his stay short to avoid this very confrontation. What could he say that had not already been said? He had managed to escape in time before, but thanks to his cousin, he would not be so fortunate that day.

Standing tall and speaking with unwavering confidence, he replied, "We have not married because we do not desire to do so. There would be no love in our match outside of the familial bond we enjoy as cousins."

Aunt Catherine scoffed. "What does love have to do with marriage? You ought not place such importance on that fickle emotion. How many men have you known to marry for love who, after the passing of the years, can say with impunity that they still have affection for their wives?" She pointed her sharp nail at him. "I can guarantee you that the majority of them have taken on a mistress."

Darcy tensed in revulsion, but his pulse quieted slightly in relief. He had successfully changed the subject. Before she could continue in more detail, he cut in. "When I marry, I intend to be loyal to my wife because I love her. Though the examples in our family would attempt to prove otherwise, I believe my expectations to be realistic."

That brought a gasp from his aunt and he heard Richard suck in air through his teeth next to him.

Now that the insinuation of Sir Lewis de Bourgh's infidelities had been made, there was nothing left but to continue. "I know that a good marriage requires effort from both the man and the woman. When I find a lady whom I am willing to work for as hard as I must to ensure her happiness, a lady whom I am confident will value our love as much as I do by proving herself loyal, then she is the lady who will receive my proposal of marriage and my undying affection." A lady like Miss Elizabeth. No, not *like* her. Only her.

Aunt Catherine leveled her head and spoke through gritted teeth. "I thank you not to speak of the dead. Lewis was an exemplary husband and his sins, if indeed he had any, were washed away on his passing. He in no way acted contrary to the habits of most gentlemen in his position."

Darcy trod on dangerous ground, so chose his words carefully. "I cannot accept what others do as the norm by which I will live. The values I choose to live by form my very character, and I would no sooner lower them than lose all sense of respect in myself."

"What of your position in society? You have many responsibilities incumbent on you as one born into wealth, property, and prestige. You speak freely about honor and values. What of all the people who depend on you for their living? They hold high expectations for you too. Anne is suited to take on the role of the Mistress of Pemberley. She was bred for it."

Looking at Anne slumped over on the couch, Mrs. Jenkinson fanning her face, Darcy doubted that.

"I have no doubt but that Anne will make a suitable wife for a gentleman who will care for her and nurture her. As you recently said, I have too many responsibilities which would not suit her needs."

Aunt Catherine scrutinized him through the slits of her eyelids. "Is there someone else?" she repeated, to his chagrin.

He could not lie. Disguise of any sort was despicable to him, but he could not unleash Aunt Catherine's fury against Miss Elizabeth.

"Were I to share information of such an intimate nature, I would do so only with Georgiana. She is the one to be most affected by it, and it is of no one else's concern."

"Have you written to her of anyone in particular?" Aunt Catherine pressed, her nostrils flared and her eyes calculated. She knew him too well. Any flinch or hesitation would be noted by her and used against him in future conversations. She would find out somehow who his heart desired.

Putting on his coolest expression, the same one he used to discourage fortune-seeking mothers at balls and assemblies, he said, "I am through speaking of matters on which you have no authority over me. Now, if you will excuse me, I have some letters to see to in my room."

Leaning back against her chair, her claws retracted from the padded arm, Aunt Catherine inclined her head toward him with an arched brow. She conceded his wish for the moment, but he knew all too well that he would render account for it.

He reached the door when she spoke again. He ought to have known she would want the last word. "You will marry Anne," she hissed from between her teeth.

He turned back to the room to see Anne start to rise, but Mrs. Jenkinson clasped her hands and pulled her down, shaking her head.

"I do not love Anne, and she has given me no indication that she loves me. Why should we be forced to marry against our will? Ours would be a miserable union." It was the same argument over again. How many times would he have to repeat the same?

Aunt Catherine scoffed. "People do not marry for love. If that is what you wish for, you will die single. Do not think for one moment that you could ever find love. With your fortune and social status, it would be impossible to find a young lady uninfluenced by the name Darcy."

He had found one. Her refusal only confirmed her honest nature and heightened his admiration.

"If I am to be punished for my money, then I would rather not have so much of it."

Aunt Catherine's eyes widened, and her small pupils stared daggers at him. "That is an utterly selfish comment to make. Too many people depend on your income to live. Would you deny them their living as easily as you deny Anne her dignity? Your engagement is as legally binding as a contract."

"A contract which neither Anne nor I entered," he said, controlling himself to not throw his hands up in the air as he wished to do at her repeated, stubborn insistence for her vain demand.

"You would see your cousin suffer the scrutiny and gossip of society only to see how impossible your fantasy of love is? She would be ostracized."

Darcy stood his ground, but his voice softened. "I would never intentionally cause any discomfort to Anne."

"Then you must honor the agreement I made

with your mother and marry her before summer. Mr. Collins will read the banns."

"I cannot agree."

"That is what you say now. I trust that you will see reason."

With that, she turned her head, thus dismissing him, and engaged Mrs. Jenkinson in conversation.

The two elderly women spoke in a sanguine tone, as if nothing was untoward, although Mrs. Jenkinson had the decency to look guilty of overhearing their heated exchange. Anne's eyes glistened as she met his glance, but she was being watched. She could say nothing.

Richard stood from his chair to follow Darcy out of the room. His departure went largely unacknowledged.

With a curt bow, Darcy retreated from the room, feeling as if he had been squeezed in a vice.

Heading toward the hall, he turned to Richard. "We need to talk," he said, without breaking his stride.

He did not stop until he had reached the stables where the grooms bustled about to ready two horses as soon as they saw them coming. Darcy was happy not to have to give orders. He wanted to focus his full attention on his blasted cousin.

"Richard, is there any reason keeping us here? Is your business with Aunt Catherine complete?" he asked, hearing the sharpness in his own voice. He took a deep breath and tried to relax his shoulders. His quarrel was with Aunt Catherine and his own internal struggle to act more like a gentleman and less like the brute he had been at the Meryton Assembly.

"After your pretty conversation with Aunt Catherine, I wonder why you persist in being in such a hurry. Her pride would not let you leave with the upper hand, but your jab against Uncle Lewis should keep her quiet for a day or so." Chuckling and shaking his head, he said, "I cannot believe you made reference to his final hours."

Darcy shrugged. "It was his own fault that he died in the loving arms of someone else. That she had been hired as his nurse to give some justification to his treachery is something even Aunt Catherine cannot easily delude herself over."

"It took a lot of nerve to say, nonetheless."

"I see no reason why. Everyone in the room knew of it. Were there strangers amongst us, I would have kept my silence. However, it proved my point, and so I spoke. I will not be that kind of husband, and it disgusts me that Aunt Catherine would allow that sort of treatment to her own daughter."

Richard crossed his arms, his face serious. "I cannot find fault with that, Darcy. But I could not help but notice how smoothly you evaded her question." He bunched his eyebrows together and leaned forward. "Are you in love?"

Darcy gave him such a look as to squelch his meddlesome inquiries.

With a cackle, Richard leaned back and slapped his hand against his thigh. "Imagine that!"

"Imagine what? I have revealed nothing but distaste for your intrusive prying."

"You pride yourself on your ability to hide your reactions, but you lost your calm. There is such a look in your eye and a restlessness in your manner that I recognize all too well." Darcy wanted nothing more than to wipe the smirk off Richard's self-congratulatory face.

Damned no matter what he said, Darcy kept quiet and did his best to keep his gaze steady until the horses were ready. That would give him an excuse to look away. Where was the stable boy? How long did it take to saddle his mount?

Richard smacked Darcy's shoulder. "Fear not, my friend. I would no sooner betray you than you would me. Of course, you know I will make it my mission to find out who has caught your eye. It would be no small feat to win your heart. She must be quite the lady, and I hope to meet her someday."

"She would not have me anyway... even if I were to ask." Darcy was not ready to accept, much less admit to anyone else, that Miss Elizabeth would not agree to marry him. He cursed himself for saying too much, but for a moment, the need to confide in someone had been too great to resist completely.

Richard paused, holding his breath, looking intently at Darcy.

Darcy leaned against the entry to the stall and crossed one foot over the other in his best imitation at nonchalance. He knew he had failed when Richard burst out laughing.

Between outbursts, he said, "I will not ask because I know you will not tell me until you are well and ready. But this does shed a new light on the meaning of certain events. Is she why you insisted that we have our annual visit to Rosings two months early? Is she here?"

Darcy jutted his chin out and bit his lips together. The less he told Richard, the better. It had been a simple thing to learn that Miss Elizabeth was visiting her best friend, the newly established Mrs. Collins, at Hunsford parsonage. The casual opportunity it afforded Darcy looked coincidental, when in reality, it had been anything but a fortunate happenstance.

Richard laughed so hard, the horses the boy brought to them pranced at his excitement. "You do beat all. And here, I thought that my news would startle Aunt Catherine. You have not told her, have you?... No, what a foolish question. Of course you have not. All of Kent would have heard the threats and screams coming from her drawing room. Today's squabble would be nothing compared to the wrath she would impale you with if she believed your affections otherwise engaged."

Something Richard said piqued his interest. "You have news? What news?" By God, anything to change the subject!

"I see no need to share my news with you if you are unwilling to confess that you were refused by your mysterious maiden. Oh, how I would love to hear how that happened!"

Not for the first time did Darcy wish he had some of the charm and easy manners his cousin possessed. There was no doubt in his mind that, in a competition of character, he would come out the loser. Especially if Miss Elizabeth was the judge.

No, he needed to rally his thoughts. He needed to find a way to turn her opinion of him around, for he would never find another woman her equal. He was already hers. She only needed convincing that he was worth having.

"Do your plans, whatever they are, still require our prolonged stay? Aunt Catherine is unbearable." He held his breath, hoping Richard would change his mind. They could leave that same afternoon. He could trust the butler to see his letter discreetly to Miss Elizabeth through the maid. The distance would clear his mind, Aunt Catherine's threats would fade in their intensity, and he could decide how best to change Miss Elizabeth's mind about him. They could make it to London by nightfall if they left soon.

"I am sorry to disappoint you, Darcy, but it is impossible. You are not the only one in a bind," said Richard as he mounted his horse and took off across the yard.

What worries could Richard possibly have? Why did he believe Aunt Catherine would assist him?

# CHAPTER 5

Elizabeth looked at the view outside her bedroom window at the back of the house, overlooking the orchard. Unlike her home at Longbourn, the grounds at Rosings were well maintained and cared for. Mr. Collins, feeling it his duty to emulate everything deemed important by Lady Catherine, took pains to ensure that not a blade of grass was out of place at his home lest it reflect poorly on his patroness. Charlotte ensured he had plenty to keep him occupied: bees, poultry, the pig, his rosebushes in the carefully cultivated garden, and his orchard brimming with fruit trees.

A light knock at her door, followed by the entry of Maria, brought her thoughts back to the present.

"Are you feeling better?" Elizabeth asked, as Maria plopped herself down on the chair at the foot of the bed.

"Well enough, thank you."

Elizabeth had been thinking about Jane, wasting

away in London, waiting for Bingley to call when
Elizabeth knew that he would not go against the
advice of his most-trusted friend. Blast Mr. Darcy
and his presumptuous interference! The
disappointment she felt for her sister broke her
heart. Several times in her dreams, she cursed Mr.
Darcy's arrogance. How dare he interfere with the
happiness of her most beloved sister!

"I wonder why Colonel Fitzwilliam and Mr.
Darcy have not called lately," said Maria with a
pout.

"It has only been two days since their last call,"
she said, trying not to recall Mr. Darcy's visit the
day before.

"Yes, but they had been coming almost every day
between the two of them. Could it be that they have
grown tired of our company? I know that I am not
very interesting, and hardly manage to speak at all
when they do call." Maria picked at a loose thread
on the blanket she sat on.

Elizabeth struggled to keep her composure. She
was relieved that Mr. Darcy had not attempted to
call again. Of course, after her stern refusal, he had
every reason to avoid her as much as she avoided
him. She had seen him deviate from the path to
avoid meeting them that morning on their walk into
Hunsford and had been grateful. Aside from their
obligatory invitations to Rosings, she hoped never
to lay eyes on the man again.

"Perhaps they have departed." One could hope.

"Without so much as a farewell? No, they are too mannerly for that."

Elizabeth bit her cheeks. "I, for one, intend to spend the remainder of our visit enjoying the serenity the grounds at Rosings offer. Never in my life have I seen such an immaculately kept park, and I plan to walk in it every day until we leave in a week's time."

Maria slumped in her chair. "How I do wish we could stay longer."

Aside from Mr. Darcy's unwanted proposal, Elizabeth had surprisingly enjoyed her time. Charlotte was content in her home, and the surroundings were a welcome change to Longbourn.

"I am certain your sister will welcome frequent visits, and the distance is not so great that your parents would forbid it. Take heart, Maria."

"It is just that… Mother and Father watch my every move at home. It has been refreshing to experience the freedom other girls my age enjoy."

"So long as you do not abuse your freedom, their trust in you will grow. That is how it normally works." Not so in the Bennet family. Her younger sisters were afforded freedoms they should not be allowed. Elizabeth felt guilty that perhaps her sisters were the reason Maria's father, Lord William, kept such a tight hold on her.

"I can only hope. But we do have another week here, and I plan to use my time wisely. Lady Catherine has invited Charlotte, and has been gracious enough to include us, to practice the pianoforte at Rosings. Today, I intend to go."

It appeared that Elizabeth would be walking alone then. Only, the girl sat fixed in place, looking expectantly at her.

Not knowing what she was supposed to say, Elizabeth ventured, "Very good. Perhaps you shall play for everyone after dinner tonight."

The excitement in Maria's eyes told her that was precisely what she hoped for.

"Please come with me."

Elizabeth wanted to kick the floor and grimace like a fractious toddler, but she contained herself. It was bad enough that she had to endure a dinner there that night. She could not beg off with a headache twice in a row, though her temples already ached.

"You should ask Charlotte. It would make Lady Catherine happy for Charlotte to take her advice." Advice which she gave freely and exaggeratedly.

"Charlotte is going into the village today with Mr. Collins to visit some of the families in their parish. She invited me along, but I would much rather spend my time at Rosings."

"And you feel that you must go today? You could not wait until tomorrow when Charlotte could accompany you?" Elizabeth held her breath. It was her last argument.

"Dinner is tonight, and I should like to practice beforehand. You were asked to play last time, and I am certain that tonight I shall be asked. It would be embarrassing to stumble over the keys for lack of practice, especially when her ladyship was so insistent that we use the pianoforte in Mrs. Jenkinson's room."

Maria looked up at her with large, pleading, brown eyes. "Please?" she asked.

Elizabeth could not disappoint her. "Very well. I admit to being curious to see the rest of the house. We shall catch glimpses of the rooms so that we can report to our families of the fineries we saw whilst here." It was not in her nature to despair, though there were times she wished life would deal her a kinder hand.

They readied themselves, changing into their best dresses lest they cast a shadow on the opulence of Rosings with a sullied hem or simple gown.

Soon enough, and much too soon for Elizabeth's taste, they were following a maid up to Mrs. Jenkinson's room.

Elizabeth had not been upstairs before and took advantage of the prospect to take in her new surroundings. The number of windows in the house, and the excellent positioning of the building itself, lit up the interior with sunlight. Baroque paintings covered the walls with mythological creatures in rich colors and bold tones. Father would love this house, with the many philosophical opportunities it afforded. Elizabeth preferred simple elegance over gaudy luxury. Ascending the stairs to the private rooms, Elizabeth could not shake the sensation that the painted figures watched her. In a corner, a fat cupid pointed an arrow in her direction. She skipped up the last two steps to get out of its way.

Turning right at the top of the stairs, they passed several doors before they arrived at Mrs. Jenkinson's room. Elizabeth was relieved to see that her walls were papered with a modest floral pattern.

Mrs. Jenkinson welcomed them as she rubbed a liniment onto her knuckled hands, massaging it into her fingers and joints. Her room smelled of camphor, but the draft coming through the windows promised to chase the harsh odor away.

"How delighted I am to see you young people here. Her ladyship enjoys music, and it will please her to know that you have come to improve your skills on the instrument. Do you plan to play tonight?" the lady, who looked to be the same age as Lady Catherine, asked.

Maria smiled nervously. "I will not refuse if I am asked, but I dare not presume."

Mrs. Jenkinson's eyes crinkled up, and her cheeks dimpled. "Perhaps I shall presume for you then. I will suggest it to her ladyship before we dine. We cannot have you practice in vain. Now, I must attend to Miss Anne. Please, make yourselves comfortable. If you need anything, the maid will attend to it."

She closed the door lightly behind her, and Elizabeth and Maria turned to face each other.

"She is kinder than I imagined her to be. I was a

bit nervous coming here. I did not want her to think we wanted to impose," said Maria.

Elizabeth's impression being similar to Maria's, she easily agreed. "It is a pity she must attend to Miss de Bourgh to the exclusion of conversation with her patroness' guests. It must be difficult to take her dinner in her room when her mistress falls ill just to keep her company."

Maria crossed the room to the pianoforte. "If I were a lady's companion, I would want it to be for someone closer to my age, someone who travels extensively and has grand parties."

"That would be a glamorous life and hardly Mrs. Jenkinson's experience. I doubt she travels much." Elizabeth sat next to Maria on the bench, so that she might turn the pages for her as she played.

Following along with the notes, Elizabeth thought of the life of a lady's companion. If she were not so fortunate as to find her match, she would have to find employment. She refused to be a burden on her parents or fall under the protection of Mr. Collins should Father pass. Shivering, her hand trembled as she turned the page. Maria played on, not noticing. How frustrating that Mr. Darcy's character prevented her from accepting his offer. She shivered again as she remembered his atrocious proposal and his ungentlemanly disregard for social niceties.

As marriage seemed to be an increasingly less likely event, she focused on employment. Of all the ways a lady could earn a living— of which there were too few— Elizabeth thought that a lady's companion would serve her the best. Of course, it all depended on the lady. Oh, if only she could be content like Charlotte. She would marry Mr. Darcy without hesitation. He was pleasant to look at. Her aunt Gardiner, who grew up near his estate in Pemberley, spoke well of the family in general. Of him, Aunt Gardiner knew little. She had also described the estate, which was so grand as to be toured by visitors to Derbyshire. If it was half as grandiose as Rosings, it would be impressive indeed. Her every need would be provided for, and her family would benefit from the improved connection,… but her spirit would shrivel up and die if she denied her belief in a true love.

The music stopped abruptly, and Elizabeth looked up to see Mrs. Jenkinson standing in the doorway which connected her room with Miss de Bourgh's.

"Oh! I am sorry to interrupt. You were playing so well. Miss Anne asked if she might enjoy your company for a few minutes before you resume playing." Mrs. Jenkinson looked at her and Maria expectantly. As if they would refuse.

"Of course, Mrs. Jenkinson. We would love to spend some time with Miss de Bourgh," said Elizabeth when Maria said nothing.

On the other side of Miss de Bourgh's room was her sitting room. She sat in a window seat covered with more cushions than the entire parsonage contained.

"How good of you to come. My doctor is to arrive shortly, and your conversation will be a welcome distraction," said Miss de Bourgh as she indicated a tray of bottles near her. Elizabeth could not imagine having to take so much medicine. The thought of the revolting tonics contained in the dark bottles— What medicine ever tasted good?— churned her stomach.

The lady's maid opened the door between Miss de Bourgh's bedchamber and the sitting room and proceeded to look on every table and surface visible, as well as behind the cushions on the unoccupied couch.

"What is the matter, Hortense?" asked Miss de Bourgh as the ladies sat in the chairs before her.

In a lovely French accent, Hortense said, "I apologize, miss, but I cannot find your earrings. You will want them for the dinner this evening."

Miss de Bourgh leaned back against her cushions with a sigh. "I must have mislaid them again. Whatever would I do without you, Hortense? Those earrings have been in the family for many generations, and I despair to be the one to lose them."

Elizabeth and Maria looked about them. Elizabeth could not imagine being so careless with something so valuable. She had a set of paste earrings she guarded like the treasure they were to her.

Maria leaned forward to the foot of the window seat where a novel lay with its pages open. "Are these what you are looking for?" she asked, scooping them into her hand and holding them out to Miss de Bourgh.

"You have found them! How thoughtless of me. I frequently take off my earrings when I get a headache, and I must have been so engrossed in the story, I did not remember having done so. Please, Hortense, will you put them away for me?"

Elizabeth had not expected Miss de Bourgh to speak politely to her maid. It was refreshing and distinctly different from Lady Catherine's terse orders.

Hortense crossed the room and put the small diamond earrings into a jewelry case they could just see through the bedchamber door. How much fun it would be to have enough precious jewels to merit a case to put them in. It was probably lined with velvet or satin to keep them sparkling.

Returning her attention to the book the earrings were found on, Elizabeth read the title of book. *Camilla* by Frances Burney.

"Are you enjoying the novel? I have read *Cecilia* by the same author, but I have not had occasion to read this one," she nodded her head toward the book.

"Oh, it is every bit as good as her previous works. I adore her satire and wit. When I am done, shall I send it to the parsonage for you to read? I am a slow reader, as Mother insists I dedicate myself to books of a more instructive nature, but I will get it to you as soon as I can."

Elizabeth's opinion of Miss de Bourgh brightened by the minute. "I would love nothing more. Books feed the soul, do they not?" If only her life were more like a novel where the perfect, romantic hero would sweep her off her feet.

Miss de Bourgh smiled through her melancholy eyes. "For me, they are an escape. I pretend that I am the heroine of the story, and soon I can forget my own troubles."

Mrs. Jenkinson, who had been readying the table for the doctor's impending visit went to answer the knock at the door. An elderly gentleman with long, white whiskers stood there with a grave expression and a dark suit. He looked like he had come to a wake instead of a healing treatment.

"Miss Anne, might I see the ladies back to my room so that the doctor may proceed. Maybe their music will alleviate your discomfort?" Mrs. Jenkinson looked toward Elizabeth, who answered her unspoken plea with a smile.

They left the sitting room to the warnings of the doctor advising against company who would only agitate Miss de Bourgh's delicate state.

# CHAPTER 6

"Lizzy, will you play?" asked Maria, apparently having completed her exercises on the instrument before their visit to Miss de Bourgh's room.

"I suppose I should. We came here with the purpose of practicing, and I am not above the need to improve. But let us search for a livelier tune, something to bring joy to our hearts and cheer Miss de Bourgh."

She looked through the sheets of music until she saw one with fewer long notes and flat keys. After a few stanzas, she decided the tempo needed to be increased. So, she played the rest in her own manner. A music teacher would not have approved, but the tune sounded merrier. Maria hurried to turn the pages in time. With a flurry at the grand finale, Elizabeth rested her hands on the smooth ivory keys.

"Oh, do play that again!" begged Maria.

Happy to oblige, Elizabeth tore into the piece again, increasingly confident in the notes and placing of her fingers.

***

Darcy paused at the top of the stairs. Someone played the pianoforte. The sound made him miss his little sister, Georgiana. She was an accomplished musician, and she played beautifully. Had it not been for Richard, he would be half-way to Pemberley by now. Why had he insisted they stay in Kent? What was Richard about?

Following the melody, he soon found himself standing in front of Mrs. Jenkinson's door. Looks up and down the hallway confirmed that no one was there, so Darcy leaned against the opposite wall and let himself listen to her play. It could be none other than Miss Elizabeth. He recognized the tune as one that was written to be played slower, but in her jovial nature, she had turned it into a lively tune. He rather liked the change, and he respected her ability not to conform to the restrictions inscribed on the written page.

The song ended, and Darcy prepared to leave when she started in again. It was the same song, but improved by her confidence in having played it before. He stood enchanted, closing his eyes so that he could imagine her sitting in the music room at Pemberley. Georgiana would be seated next to her, and Elizabeth would encourage her to play something other than the melancholy dirges she had taken to since her disastrous stay at Ramsgate. Georgiana would play a song fit for dancing. He would happen by the door. Seeing his wife smiling by his sister, he would swoop her up into his arms and twirl her about the room. Georgiana would laugh and so would Elizabeth. He would do anything to earn her smile.

"Mr. Darcy?" she asked, so close he could wrap his arms around her for another spin about the room. Oh, why did she not call him William?

"Mr. Darcy?" she repeated, her voice cutting through his reverie.

Startled, he opened his eyes to see the very same woman who frequented his sleepless dreams.

"Miss Bennet,—" He bolted into a straight posture. "—you play well." He shuffled uncomfortably in place as he sought for the words to explain his presence. "I… I do hope you will honor us with a performance this evening after dinner."

Clutching at Miss Lucas' arm, she tugged her forward to stand beside her. "I thank you, sir. While I appreciate the invitation, I surrender all requests of hearing my mediocre attempts at musical entertainment to my friend, Miss Lucas. She plays much better than I do and has been practicing a great deal."

Had she understood his compliment to be sarcastic? He searched her face but she avoided him.

With a bow to Miss Lucas, he said, "I look forward to hearing your performance."

Miss Lucas blushed. "Thank you, Mr. Darcy."

Squeezing Miss Lucas' arm, Miss Elizabeth suggested they depart.

"I will see you out as I am going downstairs as well." He motioned for them to precede him, the hallway not comfortably wide enough for them to walk side-by-side lest he trip on the multiple furnishings with which his aunt cluttered her house.

Miss Elizabeth furrowed her brow before her normal pleasant expression returned. She must feel as awkward to see him as he did seeing her. Awkward and insecure— emotions he was unaccustomed to experience and ill-prepared to conquer.

Halfway down the stairs, they met Richard. Ugly, green jealousy consumed Darcy as Miss Elizabeth smiled sweetly at his cousin in a manner she never had toward him. His kingdom for a smile!

Polite words were exchanged, but Miss Elizabeth's desire to depart from his presence was more powerful than her desire to converse with Richard. He saw the ladies to the door and watched through the window pane as his anguish increased with each step she took away from him.

\*\*\*

There were no stars to light their way as they walked to Rosings. Even the moon hid behind black clouds. Elizabeth had made the trip more times than she had wished to since her arrival, but she still stepped lightly. Grass stains would not suit her cream colored dress. Her pale green slippers were more forgiving, but she prayed that the inky sky would not bring rain.

Mr. Collins marched a few paces ahead of them, every so often stopping to encourage them on with a wave. "Come, come. We must not keep her ladyship waiting."

The entrance hall, which had been bright during the day, was lit by an abundance of candles. It looked more like a cathedral's prayer altar than a home. Servants rushed up and down the stairs, fear overtaking their normally expressionless faces. Elizabeth's skin prickled with anxiety. She said a silent prayer as they entered Lady Catherine's drawing room. Something felt dreadfully wrong.

Though the artwork dated the space, with the extravagant baroque murals painted on each surrounding surface, every time Elizabeth entered the room she could not help but hold her breath at the exorbitance of it. Thick rugs covered the floors and hushed their steps. The room seemed more fit for the mythical gods which adorned the walls and ceiling of the entrance hall than for mere mortals.

She sensed Mr. Darcy before she saw him. She felt his look. No doubt, he searched for something to criticize, so that he could add it to his long list of objections against her and her family. She was happy she wore her best dress and Maria had taken special care when arranging her hair. She would not make it easy for him to find fault with her.

Lady Catherine's voice bit into her appraisal of the room and Mr. Darcy's intentions. "You arrived later than I expected."

Mr. Collins stood in the center of a yellow circle of gold in the rug before the great lady in the bowing stance he adopted whilst in her company. "I do apologize, your ladyship. The night is particularly dark."

Tilting her head so she managed to look down her nose at Mr. Collins, Lady Catherine said, "You should have requested the use of my coach. I always put it at your disposal for your return home, and it would have been no bother to me to send it to bring you here in a more timely fashion."

Elizabeth looked at the clock ticking against the near wall. They had arrived a quarter of an hour early. Not even Miss de Bourgh had descended to the drawing room as yet, though both of Lady Catherine's nephews were present. She felt Mr. Darcy's eyes linger on her, and she tried her best to calm the heat in her cheeks.

Gently raising her bejeweled hand to press on her temple, Lady Catherine added, "This afternoon has been most perturbing." She glared at Mr. Darcy.

The butler entered the room. His jaw was clenched and sweat beaded on his upper lip, betraying his agitated state through his cool facade.

He crossed the room and spoke quietly to Lady Catherine. Elizabeth strained her ears to listen, but she could not even distinguish one word. She looked at Charlotte, who shrugged her shoulders.

Lady Catherine soon appeased everyone's curiosity. At her violent reaction, both Colonel Fitzwilliam and Mr. Darcy stood from their chairs to stand on either side of her stout throne. Her face turned a startling shade of scarlet and her breath came out in puffs and gasps. Mr. Collins rushed to her assistance, tripping over his own feet. He would have landed in her lap had it not been for Mr. Darcy and the butler. They caught him by the arms and helped him to his feet.

The butler stood in front of her, awaiting instructions. Concerned expressions over Lady Catherine's health were uttered by all. Elizabeth hoped she would not suffer an apoplexy. She did not particularly care for the lady, but she did not want her to come to harm.

Smelling salts were procured, and Lady Catherine came to with her irritation of them being presented. She smacked away the well-meaning hand. "I am not a weakling that I require smelling salts! Get that horrid smell away from me, and tell Anne to join us immediately."

The butler escaped the room to see to his task.

Lady Catherine looked about the room, her eyes settling on Maria and Elizabeth. "You were here this afternoon, were you not?" she asked in such a way to make it sound like an accusation.

Maria cowed in her seat, so Elizabeth spoke. "We practiced the pianoforte in Mrs. Jenkinson's room, your ladyship." For good measure, she added, "Just as you had invited us to do."

"Humph. Were you only in Mrs. Jenkinson's room or did you look in other rooms of the house?"

Her spine stiffening at her denunciatory tone, Elizabeth answered, "Miss de Bourgh invited us to sit her in her sitting room until the doctor arrived."

Lady Catherine's eyebrow twitched and the side of her mouth jerked up into a snarl. "I see. So, you did not confine yourself to Mrs. Jenkinson's room. Interesting." She tapped her fingers against the arm of her chair. "Very interesting indeed."

Elizabeth did not mean to, but her eyes searched the others for answers— even Mr. Darcy. What was happening? Why did she feel she was being blamed for something? Their puzzled expressions revealed that they knew no more than she did.

Lady Catherine raised her chin, and looked over each new arrival with a scrutinizing glare. "There is a thief in our midst," she said dramatically. "Someone has stolen Anne's favorite diamond earrings."

Between her and Mr. Darcy, Elizabeth felt like she might catch on fire. When Lady Catherine stared at her, she returned the look. She had nothing to be ashamed of. *She* was not a thief.

After a long silence where everyone waited for more explanation, it was Mr. Darcy who spoke.

"Perhaps you could share more details. Are you accusing one of us in the room of stealing?"

Lady Catherine arched an eyebrow, unappreciative of her staring contest being brought to an end. "It would appear so, when during this same day, Anne's diamond earrings have gone missing."

"Shall I send to fetch the constable?" asked Mr. Collins, his body inclined toward the door in his eagerness to be of service.

Lady Catherine's eyes flashed. "The blacksmith? No, I would sooner do the investigation myself and avoid having a commoner poking around my home, asking questions of the servants, and setting tongues wagging. No, Mr. Collins, that will not do. I have always had a clever mind for seeing truth and shall conduct my own investigation with the help of my nephews. Once I have proof, I will see that the guilty person feels the full weight of the injustice done against me."

Elizabeth could not suspect Mr. Darcy or Colonel Fitzwilliam of theft, but she could not help but wonder why they were exempt from suspicion.

Bowing ever deeper, Mr. Collins said, "Of course, you are right. It was a foolish question, and I vow to do all in my capabilities, small though they are, to see that the criminal is brought to justice—"

Miss de Bourgh entered the room with Mrs. Jenkinson, effectively cutting Mr. Collins short. They looked wretched.

Mr. Darcy spoke as soon as they sat in their usual perch. "Please be so kind as to illuminate us, cousin. Do you suspect that someone stole your earrings?"

"My maid could not find my earrings in the jewelry box. I had told her that I did not intend to wear them this evening, but she understood me to mean that I would rather wear a different set. When she opened the jewelry case, she noticed that they were gone and immediately set to looking for them and alerting half the household in the process," Miss de Bourgh said in a faint voice.

To Elizabeth, she sounded more upset at her maid's reaction than for her lost earrings. Perhaps she had mislaid them again? Though that would be odd since only that morning they had been replaced in the jewelry case. Why would she remove them only to mislay them again?

"When was the last time the earrings were seen?" she asked, directing her question to Miss de Bourgh.

"This morning when they were found in my sitting room. My maid put them away then." Her eyes flickered over to where she and Maria sat. Elizabeth was grateful she had left out their names. It was plain to see that Lady Catherine already suspected them.

Said lady's sharp voice cut in. "Your sitting room? Who was in the sitting room when they were found?"

Maria shrunk back into her chair, her face white. Elizabeth lifted her chin and squared her shoulders when Miss de Bourgh looked toward them with a painful expression.

"If it pleases your ladyship, I should like to answer that question," Elizabeth said to spare Miss de Bourgh from having to reveal what she clearly did not want to. If the truth was to be found out, the truth needed to be spoken. Elizabeth was not about to let Miss de Bourgh's hesitancy make her or Maria look guilty.

"Miss de Bourgh's maid searched for the earrings while Miss Lucas and I were present in the sitting room. Miss Lucas found them lying on top of a book at the foot of the window seat. The maid put them away in the jewelry case visible through the open door in Miss de Bourgh's bedchamber. We all saw her put them there."

Colonel Fitzwilliam, pinching his chin in thought, said, "You do have large windows facing out over the lawn. Is it possible that someone could have entered there?"

Elizabeth thanked the good colonel in her heart for drawing the stares away from her.

Miss de Bourgh's eyes grew large. "It is possible, I suppose. So long as they were quiet enough not to disturb Mrs. Jenkinson or alert the servants. I do not think I would have heard, feeling out of sorts after the doctor's treatment."

It was too complicated. Besides, one look outside at the wall and the ground beneath Miss de Bourgh's window would reveal if someone had attempted to enter through her bedchamber window. "Is it possible that someone inside the house, a servant perhaps, snatched them when no one was looking?" asked Elizabeth.

Mr. Darcy cast an angry glance at her, though everyone else looked pensive.

Lady Catherine said, "Never in all my years have I had difficulties with my servants. They know their place well and lack the intellect to do so."

Mr. Darcy said, "You do have a great amount of servants. Could it be that one of them harbors a grudge against you or is in desperate need of money? You must not exclude them simply because you do not feel them intelligent enough to carry out such a task."

"It is true, Aunt. You have as many servants as there are inhabitants in the village of Hunsford. I will make inquiries," said Colonel Fitzwilliam.

"As will I," said Mr. Darcy. His eyes narrowed at Elizabeth. Did he think she stole them? Would he use this as an opportunity to revenge himself against her for refusing his hand? If the accusations Mr. Wickham had against Mr. Darcy were only half true, he was capable of it.

Lady Catherine kept looking between Maria and Elizabeth. She believed the servants too stupid to effect a crime against her own household, but she did not extend the same courtesy to the guests of her rector. The unfairness of her misjudgment struck Elizabeth as unjust, and she determined in her heart to find out where the diamonds had gone.

She looked up to see Mr. Darcy still

contemplating her, undoubtedly plotting his revenge. She would show him. She would seek the truth and find Miss de Bourgh's earrings before he or Lady Catherine could imply anything more against her.

# CHAPTER 7

The air grew heavy in the room as everyone looked about them suspiciously.

Just when Elizabeth felt she could not stand their questioning glances any more, the butler entered to announce that dinner was ready. As if she could eat.

Silently, they filed into the dining room. The draft running through the space sent chills down Elizabeth's arms as she took her seat between Colonel Fitzwilliam and Maria. At least she was in good company and far enough down the table not to have to suffer the immediate conversation of Mr. Darcy and his snobbish aunt. She wondered how Colonel Fitzwilliam had escaped the family characteristic of pride.

Mr. Collins sat on the other end of the table. He was so pleased with the honor bestowed upon him by his generous patroness that he sat as tall as the peacock pie which would most likely make an appearance at a later course.

Maria leaned in to whisper to her. "I hope they do not think that we did it. I never set foot inside Miss de Bourgh's room, but we were practicing on the pianoforte next door. Do you think we will be accused?" Her voice trembled, and for a moment, Elizabeth thought the girl might cry.

"We are innocent of any crime. Do not forget that." Her determination to find out who the real thief was became stronger as she looked at the scared girl next to her.

"I know that, but sometimes mistakes are made."

Patting her hand and determining to end their whispered conversation before Lady Catherine demanded to know what they were talking about so secretively, she said, "Do not worry. I will find out who is behind this, and everything will be all right. You will see."

During the evening, she often felt Mr. Darcy's scheming eyes upon her. Her opinion of him worsened as the evening progressed.

Elizabeth tried to focus on the beautiful spread before her, but her appetite did not cooperate. It was a long dinner. Conversation was halted and every second passed as slowly as an hour before the meal concluded. Finally, Lady Catherine ordered that her carriage take her guests home.

\*\*\*

After a tiresome day, and an even worse evening, Darcy slept little. The only silver lining had been Miss Elizabeth. He tried to keep his attention elsewhere, but too often, his gaze wandered down the table more often than he could help. She wore her hair differently, and her dress shimmered in the candlelight.

Like a dark raincloud set on spoiling their dinner, his aunt had determined that one of Mr. Collins' guests was responsible for the stolen jewelry. Her mind was made up, and there was little he or anyone else could do or say to alter her opinion. All he could do was buy time until he found the culprit.

Anne did her best to calm her mother, but she had quickly grown weak and had retired early. Richard supported Darcy's endeavor to prevent Aunt Catherine from making premature accusations or reacting before anything was fully known.

It was ridiculous to accuse both ladies of a crime when the only proof against them was that they were in the adjacent room, playing Mrs. Jenkinson's pianoforte hours before it was found out that the earrings were missing. Only when he recommended that she give him and Richard a couple of days to look into affairs in order to keep down the gossip did she calm down.

Darcy had much to think about, and many plans to make. Waking before his usual time the following morning, he went outside to clear his mind in the fresh air and to order his thoughts. He would need some sort of plan to effectively find out what had taken place. He needed information.

He started toward the rose garden.

The soft spring breeze carried snatches of conversation to his ears. It came from the opposite side of the garden. Darcy slowed his pace, not wanting to interrupt nor to eavesdrop. The voices sounded vexed. He delayed at the corner of the house, but only for a moment. If someone was having an argument outside where anyone could hear them, perhaps it would do more good for him to interrupt it.

Stepping around the corner, he found himself looking at his cousins. Anne sat on a bench, her skin as white as the lace trim on her dress. Richard ran a hand through his already tousled hair and shoved the other one into his pocket. He paced in front of Anne until he froze in place when he saw Darcy.

Proceeding cautiously, Darcy asked, "Is all well?"

Richard said, "It is nothing to trouble yourself with, Darcy. It is only that our cousin and I do not see eye to eye on the development of recent events."

Darcy looked between the two of them, still confused.

Anne said, "You see, I would not have said anything. Only Hortense, when she saw that the velvet pouch I keep the earrings in was empty, made such a fuss as roused the entire house."

Furrowing his brows, Darcy asked, "You would have said nothing. Why?"

"Do you not see? How are we supposed to catch a

thief, if indeed there is one, when he knows that we are on to him?"

She made a good point, but he had to ask, "You doubt that your diamonds were stolen?"

Shrugging her thin shoulders, she said, "We searched my room thoroughly, but something as tiny as a set of earrings could easily have dropped somewhere. And I have been known to take them out during the day when my head aches. There is the chance that I mislaid them again."

Darcy doubted that. "With a household staff of nearly one hundred, it is not likely. And I do not think you so careless as to mislay your diamonds twice in one day."

Richard nodded vigorously. "That is what I tell her."

She gave Richard an annoyed look. "Let us not quarrel anymore, please. I have enough on my hands with Mother being so upset as it is."

Richard grumbled, "If only I could have spoken to Aunt Catherine before all of this took place…"

Darcy snapped, "You have not spoken to her yet? My God, Richard, what is taking you so long? After you begged me to stay another couple days… Now, we will have to stay as long as it takes just to keep her from calling the constable for Miss Bennet and Miss Lucas."

Speaking in a tone just as strong as his, Richard answered, "Thanks to you, Aunt Catherine has been in such a foul mood as to prevent me from doing so. The nature of my business with her is so delicate as to require that she be in a good humor."

Consumed with frustration, Darcy grumbled, "If that is what you seek, we shall have to remain here indefinitely."

Holding up her hand, Anne said, "Stop quarreling, I beg you. Richard, I think it wise not to disturb Mother any more than she already is. Your business with her will have to wait. Darcy, Mother will soon speak with you about it, so I had best warn you that she wants us to marry by the end of spring. She thinks that I must have done something to discourage you and has been lecturing me daily since your arrival to encourage you to pursue your suit."

Darcy heaved a sigh. He did not want to marry Anne. He wanted to marry Miss Elizabeth. Her soft brown eyes appeared like a vision before him, then they flashed in anger as her refusal played in his mind. She chose not to marry him despite all that he could offer her— a choice Anne had never been offered by her mother... by him.... by anyone. It occurred to him that in all of their adult years, he had not once asked Anne what she wanted. How selfish he had been!

Taking a step forward, Darcy lowered his voice and asked, "Anne, what is it that *you* want?"

She looked startled to be asked. She opened her mouth to speak, but her thoughts slowed her. Finally, she placed her hand over her mouth and something like a chuckle escaped.

Darcy and Richard looked at each other. What was funny?

"Do you know, *that* is what I want."

Not understanding her meaning, Darcy shuffled his feet uncomfortably. Could it be that she did want to marry him? It would be an escape from her overbearing mother... Oh, please, no. "What is that? Please, explain your meaning."

A scoff escaped her lips. "I want to be given a choice. Everyone around me feels they have the right to order me around and make plans for my future without so much as a consideration as to what I want. I would like for others to ask me what it is that I want."

Richard broke in. "What do you want?"

She looked at him steadily before shifting her gaze to Darcy. "I do not want to marry you. I will not allow myself to be a tool for Mother to use so that she might continue in her extravagant ways. What is more, I do not love you, and I know I never shall."

Darcy could have kissed her hand then and there, his relief was so great.

"Very well. Thank you for the warning. I will do my best to deal with Aunt Catherine, knowing that your feelings are similar to my own. And, Anne,... I am sorry."

She rose from the bench with a smile that reached her eyes. "I must return to the house before I catch a chill. I am still fatigued from yesterday."

Richard extended his arm. "Let me assist you. I

have some letters I need to see to, so I should return as well. Are you coming, Darcy?"

"I will see you as far as the door, but I feel the need for a long walk. I have much to ponder."

Giving little thought as to where his feet took him after passing the front door, Darcy continued past the large oak tree in the middle of the lawn in front of the house.

In his mind, he created a list of everyone who had the ability to steal Anne's earrings. Any of the household staff who knew where she kept her jewels had to be added. He would talk to her maid again. Maybe she had thought of something new since he had spoken with her the day before.

He had been looking at the ground as he walked, kicking the occasional pebble on the path. When he looked up, he saw her. She was walking alone.

She looked as if she might turn around to escape meeting him, but then thought better of it.

Darcy looked about and realized the mistake he had made. He had let himself wander without any thought as to his whereabouts and had unwittingly walked to her favorite path. Had he been paying attention, he would have chosen to go elsewhere, but his feet had realized a conspiracy with his heart. The damage was done, and he decided to do his best to act the part of a proper gentleman— though there was hardly anything proper in encountering a lady with no chaperone.

He bowed, nervous she might hear the pounding of his heart when he opened his mouth to speak.

"Good morning, Miss Bennet. You are out early."

"As are you, I might add," she said with a shallow curtsy.

"Are you on your way back to the parsonage?" he asked. He patted his empty pocket. Now that he had the opportunity to talk with her alone, he wished he had brought the letter he had written. It sat in a drawer in his desk, waiting for her to read it. Blast! He had carelessly left his best defense behind when the ideal situation to give her the letter presented itself. He would put it in his pocket where it would stay until he next saw her.

"Yes. It is time for me to return. The other residents should be awake and breakfasting by now." She took a step forward, then paused before taking another.

"Miss Bennet, please allow me to be honest with you. It seems that the harder I try to avoid you, the more frequently we cross paths. It is not intentionally done, I assure you." Not entirely intentional, only partly.

She looked at him for what felt like an eternity. Finally, she nodded and continued down the path. He followed. She did not tell him not to.

"Mr. Darcy, I meant what I said the other day, but my heightened emotions led me to speak with too much feeling. It was never my intention to hurt you." She added hurriedly, "Though it does not change my reply." The roses in her cheeks brightened her eyes considerably.

"You made yourself perfectly clear. You need not

repeat anything said that day. It is forgotten." Not that he could forget, but he did hold on to the hope that she might forget her poor opinion of him, as well as the revulsion she had expressed that fateful day.

They walked in silence for some minutes. Darcy tried to think of something clever or interesting to say. He wished he had the ease of speech Richard was gifted with, but he had always experienced difficulty with casual conversation— especially so with Miss Elizabeth.

# CHAPTER 8

When the silence grew unbearable, he said, "My sister is at Pemberley at the moment." There was no genius in the words, but he hoped that they might lead to a pleasant conversation. He had a sister. She had several sisters. It was something they had in common.

"Oh. How nice for her," she said, looking at him with an odd expression. Then, relaxing her shoulders, she added, "Please, tell me about her. I know that you think poorly of my sisters, but I do miss them so. What age is she?"

He bristled at the mention of her nerve-grating siblings, but kept his thoughts to himself as he should have before. "Georgiana is fifteen. There was a brother between us, but he died when he was just a child." He had not meant to share that detail, but he found that, when he could speak, he often said things he did not mean to say while in Miss Elizabeth's company.

"I am sorry for your loss. That must have been painful for your parents and for you."

Darcy could only nod. It had devastated Mother especially. She never returned to her normal, happy manner after it happened.

"I was too young to remember, but it devastated my parents. It is the worse fate a mother can suffer, I think. By the time Georgiana was born, Mother's sadness had weakened her heart so much that she could not continue much longer. We lost her within a month of the birth."

Miss Elizabeth's face lost its joyous aspect, and Darcy felt foolish for making her sad. This was not going how he had anticipated.

"I am sorry, Miss Bennet. I did not mean to share my sadness, but rather to talk of my sister. Sometimes I think she would benefit from the company of other young ladies closer to her age. She only has Richard and myself to keep her company... besides her companion."

***

Elizabeth tried to imagine what it would be like to have someone like Mr. Darcy as a guardian. It was such a disagreeable thought, her pity for Miss Darcy grew.

"Does she prefer to stay at Pemberley rather than visit her aunt with you?" If it were her, she would prefer to avoid the company of her supercilious aunt, as well as her proud brother at every chance.

Darcy smiled. "It is a challenge to visit my aunt Catherine. She has an overbearing personality from which I would rather protect Georgiana. She is a shy girl, and the company here only makes it worse."

His response surprised Elizabeth. Could it be that he thought of the comfort of his sister more than his own? "That is selfless of you, Mr. Darcy. Often, I have wished to have Jane here with me to offer her gentle support. She is far kinder than I am, and she would find many positive things to say about those whom I do not." She bit her tongue. It was one thing for Mr. Darcy to call his aunt overbearing. He was family, and as such, had the freedom of speech to say what he very well pleased about them. She did not have that same luxury.

With a smile, Darcy said, "What you tell me of your sister is similar to Georgiana's character. I had not seen it before." His smile vanished.

Elizabeth had revealed Jane's shyness of character to him when she refused his proposal. Though she regretted speaking so forcefully to him, she did not regret a word of her accusations against him for separating Jane from Mr. Bingley.

"Is that why you would rather Mr. Bingley marry your sister?" she asked. It was a bold question, but she needed to know why Mr. Darcy had seen fit to interfere with her dearest sister's happiness.

Stopping abruptly, Mr. Darcy gawked at her with his mouth wide open. "That is what you think? That

I cultivate Bingley's friendship out of self-interest for my own sister?"

His shock stunned her. It was too genuine. Her cheeks burned at his reaction and blunt statement of her equally blunt opinion. Still, she would not back down. "It is what I thought when Miss Bingley made it perfectly clear to both Jane and me that her brother was set apart for Miss Darcy. After it was revealed to me that you were the cause for their separation, it was as good as confirmed."

"Nothing could be further from the truth. Bingley is my friend. I have never singled him out to be my brother."

Still unwilling to believe Mr. Darcy to be in possession of any good qualities, she said, "Of course, his connections in trade would rule that out."

"You think that, do you?" he asked, clearly annoyed. "My sister is too young, and I would be the last person in the world to attempt to match make when I have suffered the effects of a supposed arranged marriage most of my life."

"You are not engaged to Miss de Bourgh?"

Mr. Darcy's eyes widened in horror. "You think that I would propose to you if I were engaged to another?" Shaking his head, he added, "You must think I am the worst class of gentleman to believe me as selfish and unfeeling as you claim."

At a loss for words, Elizabeth clasped her hands together in the hopes that she could find some way to justify her opinion of him. It all sounded so much worse coming from his mouth. Could it be that she had mistaken his character as badly as he had Jane's? Her mind flooded with doubt.

Her confidence shaken, she said, "You have given me every reason to think poorly of you, and I do not understand why my opinion of you is of any import." Especially when she felt unsure what that opinion was.

Mr. Darcy breathed in sharply, the muscles on his jaw tensing. After a long exhale, he said, "Though I cannot explain my reasons at this moment, I can assure you that your opinion is important to me. I have promised that I will speak no more of the subject, so let us change this current one. How are you enjoying your stay at Hunsford?"

It was a safe question, and one he had asked her several times since his arrival to Rosings.

"I am enjoying it as much as the last time you asked," she said, tongue in her cheek. She could not help it. She peeked up at his face to see his reaction.

Did he really roll his eyes? She had not thought him capable of such a common gesture. She bit her lips together to keep from laughing. Then, she remembered that she did not like him and willed her face to reflect the intensity of her dislike. She forced herself to focus on Mr. Darcy's negative traits— cloudy though they were. His greatest and most unforgivable fault stood out as clear as crystal: he had ruined Jane's chances of making a loving and advantageous match with Mr. Bingley, even sounding proud of having done so.

Busy trying to justify her appraisal of his character after what he had revealed, she was startled when he spoke again.

"What do you think happened to my cousin's diamonds?" He looked at her intently. Unlike the previous evening, his manner held no accusation. Or had she misread him then? What she had seen so clearly before muddled into a confusing mess, so that she did not know what to think about the man walking beside her.

"Your aunt has already decided on the guilty party. She made it quite obvious. My only defense is to prove who the real thief is before she decides to call the village constable." She tried to sound confident, though she trembled. There was no humor and nothing ridiculous about facing an accusation from a lady respected in society.

Mr. Darcy's shoulders stiffened. "She can be unreasonable. Please let me reassure you that I intend to get to the bottom of this. Have you learned anything thus far?"

"I have only made a list of everyone who could have stolen the jewelry. I even went so far as to include Miss Lucas and myself. Next to their names, I have attached a motive. It could be anything as simple as the need for money to a lifelong grudge against Lady Catherine."

Darcy nodded. "It is a good start. A growing suspicion has taken root in my mind... Do you not think that someone with a grudge against my aunt would have stolen an article of importance to her?

Why would they steal Anne's earrings?"

Elizabeth, disappointed he had not shared what his suspicion was, but knowing better than to ask, thought for a while. Normally, any harm done to one's offspring would be a cut against the parent. But Lady Catherine and Miss de Bourgh did not seem to have that kind of relationship. On first seeing Anne, she had even mistaken Mrs. Jenkinson for her mother when they had crossed in front of the parsonage in her pony and cart. Mr. Collins had corrected her, and later that same day, they had met Lady Catherine.

"Perhaps you are right. What we need are some facts. It could be that a servant, one of the multitude at Rosings, was in need of money. I have no way of conversing with them, nor do I think Lady Catherine puts much store in that theory."

"No, and I tend to believe her, though my reasons for doing so are different to hers. Rosings is the largest estate in Kent. It employs a great number of people, as you have seen, and I do not think that one of her servants would be so simple as to think that they could get away with stealing property from her residence without drastic consequences. Contrary to her views, they are too intelligent for that. If they fall into Aunt's disfavor, not only would they lose their employment at Rosings, but they would be unable to find work elsewhere." He relaxed as he spoke, and their conversation felt strangely comfortable.

"I see. Do you really feel that someone else is

responsible then? Someone who was present at the dinner?"

"I cannot say for certain, but I cannot rule out the possibility."

Stopping to face him directly, she asked, "Do you think I did it?"

He looked straight at her, locking eyes. "No. I do not."

They stood thus for some time, the weight on her shoulders lightening. His eyes had flecks of gold surrounding his pupils.

Catching her breath, she said, "Thank you." She was not prepared to think kindly toward the gentleman. Not yet. He still had sins against her family to account for.

The parsonage was now in view, and it was the perfect time to depart from Mr. Darcy.

He must have thought the same thing, for he said, "I should leave you here. Have a pleasant day." With a bow, he turned to cross the lawn leading to Rosings.

Elizabeth watched him retreat. Then, with a sigh, she walked to the parsonage.

She was met at the door by Mr. Collins. He stood rubbing his hands together, his customary layer of sweat covering his forehead.

"Cousin Elizabeth, we have been waiting for you to return for some time now. It is time to begin my investigation, and my first order of business is to go through all the belongings in your room." He said it like he would take great pleasure ruffling through her things.

Elizabeth looked behind him to where Charlotte sat in the parlor. She raised her hand to her temple and shook her head with her eyes closed.

"Am I the only person in your household to have this honor?" Elizabeth asked with sarcasm.

"Certainly not. All members of my family shall be treated equally. Even Mrs. Collins' room has been searched thoroughly. Only you and Miss Lucas remain." He slapped his hands together, and rubbed them again. "Come in, cousin. We have work to do," he said with the same glee Lydia had when she had informed her family in Longbourn of the arrival of officers in Meryton.

# CHAPTER 9

Elizabeth opened the door to her bedchamber. There was not much to see other than a stand with a wash basin near the door, a chair in the corner by the window, the bed against the wall to the right, and the trunk with her possessions at the foot of it.

Mr. Collins walked in, telling the ladies to stand on the opposite wall to observe while Betsy, the housemaid, sorted through everything under his watchful eye. Elizabeth could only imagine the disorder her cousin would make in his home during the course of the day. She looked at Charlotte, who appeared tired. As much pride as she took in the orderliness and comfort of her home, it must distress her greatly to have it disarrayed so badly by her own husband.

Starting in the corner with the chair, Betsy ran her fingers down the curtains, checking every fold and seam in the fabric for hidden diamonds. Elizabeth folded her arms and leaned back against the wall.

This would take some time. How fortunate for her that she had missed everything except the ransacking of two bed chambers.

Betsy flipped the covers off the bed, meticulously checking each blanket as she had the curtains, pausing on occasion to look to Mr. Collins for instructions. The feather pillow, of which Elizabeth was grateful she only had one, was flattened and squished inch by inch.

Looking at them from under his moist brow, he said in a disappointed tone, "Nothing thus far."

She stepped away from the wall, but one look at Charlotte silenced the retort on the tip of her tongue. Grumbling to herself, she leaned back, resuming her position against the floral paper. Just because she had refused his hand and insulted his pride did not mean that she was a thief!

Mr. Collins turned his attention to the trunk. It was not large, nor did she have many possessions in it as her wardrobe consisted of the minimum assorted dresses a gentleman's daughter should be in possession of. Since a pair of earrings could only be placed in a book if a hole were cut in it, the two novels she had brought with her had been spared a page by page inspection. Still, it did not stop him from thumbing through the pages.

After removing all the contents so that Mr. Collins could ensure that no secret compartment existed in the trunk, Betsy kindly arranged everything back in the order in which it was found.

One more look around the room confirmed that

there were no other hiding places available, and ended the search.

In an official sounding voice, Mr. Collins declared, "The earrings are not here. Let us continue." He could not hide the disappointment in his tone, and Elizabeth glared at his back as they followed him to Maria's bedchamber.

Maria's room was slightly larger than Elizabeth's, but it held no more furnishings nor hiding places than hers. The search proceeded in the same manner, and Elizabeth occupied herself with counting how many insects buzzed past the window outside.

Maria shuffled her feet back and forth. She clasped her hands together and unclasped them, then wiped her palms against her morning dress.

Charlotte, who stood next to her observing Betsy's progress, placed her hand on Maria's shoulder. "You are making me nervous. Calm down."

Maria looked anxiously at Elizabeth, a pleading look in her eye. It was the same look her younger sisters gave her when they were about to get into trouble. Not that they got into trouble often. It was not so much for want of trying, but rather due to Father's indifference to their silly actions and Mother's nerves which refused to confront anything not to her liking.

Mr. Collins finally got around to the trunk. Elizabeth wondered at her young friend. She had obviously hidden something she did not want him to see. Surely, she did not steal the diamond earrings?… Or did she?

Elizabeth considered the day they had gone together to Rosings. Not once had Maria left her side. Maria would have had no opportunity to take them. Besides, she was a good girl. In Elizabeth's recollection, she had never done anything to draw unnecessary attention to herself.

The trunk lid opened with a squeak. It embarrassed Mr. Collins greatly to see a pair of lady's stockings— so much so that Charlotte joined him as Betsy removed the rest of the personal effects.

They reached the bottom of the trunk, and all but Betsy froze. Charlotte placed her hands on her hips and stood erect, facing her sister. Mr. Collins' face took on a stern aspect as he continued to stare at the object at the bottom of the trunk.

Elizabeth heard Maria suck in her breath and hold it. Wringing her hands in front of her, she resumed her shuffling.

What had they found? Elizabeth chewed on her lip, and was sorely tempted to walk the few steps to the foot of the bed to see for herself. As it was, the silence in the room only made Maria's now shallow breaths sound too loud within the small space.

Finally, when Elizabeth did not think she could stand another second of ignorance, Mr. Collins reached down to gather the offending item.

***

Darcy sat in the library overlooking the topiary garden. He had not had an opportunity to speak with Richard since he had returned from his morning walk. Richard had ensconced himself in his room— no doubt to tend to the letters he had mentioned.

Needing a place where Aunt Catherine would not bother to enter, he felt safe in the library. Unlike the other gaudy rooms in the house, the walls in the book room were lined with volumes of tomes, rather than murals and tapestries. Darcy did not like the painted figures in his aunt's home. Dozens upon dozens of eyes watched his every move, and it made him crave the simpler, more elegant design of Pemberley.

A man walking across the garden toward the front door caught his attention. It was not the gardener. Aunt Catherine made sure that every servant in her employ wore garments easily identifying them as such. This man, at first glance, looked like a dandy with his coat cut in the latest fashion and satin breeches. The buckles on his shoes shone. But he was no gentleman. Of that, Darcy was certain.

The man walked tall— like he had every right to be there. Like a man with a score to settle.

Darcy listened by the glass. Aunt Catherine would send any unwanted or uninvited visitors away without the slightest consideration.

"I am here to see Colonel Fitzwilliam. Be so good as to announce that Mr. Badger has come to collect what is his," the visitor spoke loudly enough to the butler, Darcy had no difficulty hearing him.

Of course, the man was not allowed entry, but was left to wait by the front door as Simmons went upstairs to Richard's room.

After a short time, Simmons returned to the entry and Mr. Badger.

"The colonel is away at the moment. Are you staying in the village where he can contact you, perhaps?"

Mr. Badger affirmed and stated his location, as well as a warning. "Tell the colonel that I expect a visit very soon. My employer does not take kindly to delays."

Darcy watched Mr. Badger depart.

Intrigued, Darcy went to pay his cousin a visit. As he suspected, he was in his room.

"Richard, what is going on?" Darcy demanded. "First, I see you in an argument with Anne, and now I could not help but overhear a man demand to see you. Are you in trouble? Is there something I can help you with?" His concern grew as he watched Richard shove his fingers through his hair and down to squeeze the back of his neck.

"It is not what you think, Darcy."

# CHAPTER 10

Massaging the nape of his neck, Richard invited Darcy to pull up a chair to sit by him.

"You are aware that I recently had to buy a new horse because Ebony, may his soul rest in peace, broke his leg when he stepped in a hole and landed in such a way to put paid to my saddle. In a series of unfortunate events with no merciful ending, I had to replace my horse, my saddle, and a few other items essential to my profession. All of this happened suddenly, and I had to take on a great deal of debt."

"What about your father? Could he not spare the funds?" asked Darcy, angry that he had been unaware of his cousin's difficulties until that moment.

Richard ground his teeth together, clenching his jaw. "Let us leave my father out of this. He and I are not on speaking terms at the moment— his choice, certainly not mine."

"What has happened? You get along with everyone." Darcy was appalled. Richard's jovial nature and charming manners put him in a good light wherever he went. He was the favorite in the family— except with Aunt Catherine, who only favored Darcy for his fortune.

Richard choked out a cold laugh. "The loss of a pretty piece of the family's fortune in a bad speculation has strained our relationship, though I had advised him against it. To make matters worse, last season I was hunted by a young lady from a wealthy family. I say 'hunted' for her family endeavored to put her in my way at every opportunity. They even went so far as to arrange for me to fall into a compromising situation and, thus, force me to marry her."

Darcy hated the scheming ways some families had of marrying off their daughters. But, in Richard's case, he needed to marry into a fortune.

"I can understand your loathing, but would not such a marriage benefit you?"

Shaking his head emphatically, Richard said, "Not this one. You know that I would prefer to have some level of respect for the woman I choose to marry. We would need to have at least some common interests. I see marriage as one of the most important decisions a gentleman can make in his life."

"Who was this lady? Was it someone of my acquaintance?"

"I should say you know her. Or rather, you know her dearest friend."

Curious, Darcy waited for Richard to continue.

"She is none other than Miss Louisa Dawson, Miss Bingley's closest friend. Her parents have been unable to rid themselves of her after four unsuccessful seasons."

Darcy shivered. Any friend of Miss Bingley was someone he would run away from as quickly as his feet could carry him. Miss Dawson would make any man miserable in marriage if she was anything like Miss Bingley. No fortune could account for the misery she would put her future husband through. He was glad Richard had escaped.

"I take it that Uncle wanted you to agree to the match?" It always came down to money. Those who had it lorded it over those who did not. Those who had none resented those who did. Friends were easily made when one possessed a fortune, but how many of them really cared for the man more than his possessions?

"My father was furious. He felt that it was not my place to refuse to make an offer when the lady was obviously willing to accept it. He is so much like Aunt Catherine, it is disturbing. Both of them refuse to live within their means— not that their means are difficult to live within, quite the opposite. Did you know of Aunt's latest plan to hire an architect to improve the already perfect gardens in the park?" Leaning back in his chair and running his hands through his hair, he continued, "So, I was in the position of owing a good amount of money I had no means of paying. I did what most men in my position do. I borrowed from a lender."

Darcy winced. "Why did you not appeal to me for help? I would gladly have given you the money."

Richard's stance softened. "I know it, Darcy. And I thank you for it. However, you had just dealt with Wickham, and you had your hands full with Georgiana. I could not burden you with my problems too."

Richard did not need to say it, but Darcy sensed that his pride would not let him ask for help when it was so desperately needed.

"Was that what you wanted to speak to Aunt Catherine about?" he asked.

Richard shifted his weight in his chair, and kicked the heel of his boot against the floor. "Essentially." Kicking his boot heel against the floor again, he added, "Have you seen Anne's arms?"

The change in direction of the conversation caught Darcy off guard. "No. She always wears elbow gloves or long sleeved gowns. Why?"

Richard leaned forward. "I think her doctor is a charlatan. I only happened to see because one of her gloves slipped down. She is so thin... Well, I shall never forget the cuts I saw on her arm. I suspect the other one is just as bad. I know that bleeding is an accepted treatment in the medical profession, but I saw with my own eyes what a loss of blood did to the men on the battlefields. It killed them, Darcy."

Darcy exhaled in disgust at the doctor and pity

for Anne. She was weak as it was. "Aunt Catherine calls him in from town, does she not?"

Richard scoffed. "She personally selected him and pays for him to travel the distance here so that he may bleed Anne once a week. I suppose he applies leeches to her temples for her frequent headaches as well." He threw his arms up, then crossed them in front of him, a scowl on his face.

Darcy tensed as well. He had never been close to Anne. His efforts to discourage Aunt Catherine's desire for their union guaranteed that. But he did not want her to be mistreated in any way. She was his family, and if her own mother would not protect her, then somebody should. Could he risk speaking to Aunt about Anne's health? Or would she twist his concern for her into unmerited interest in their imagined engagement?

"Richard, would you be willing to suggest a different doctor? I would be happy to pass on the name of mine in town."

"Someone needs to say something before the charlatan bleeds our cousin to death."

Darcy sat contemplating for a good while. This new information about Richard cast a new light on the disappearance of Anne's jewelry. He had nearly convinced himself that Aunt Catherine had contrived it to keep him at Rosings, but the unraveling of recent events pointed to Richard. He rebelled at the thought, rejecting it as false before it could poison him.

"I know what you are thinking, Darcy, and I

cannot blame you for it. The evidence against me is damning."

Measuring his words carefully, Darcy said, "I admit that the blame could easily be placed on you. If it became known that you were in debt to a lender, you would move up in the list of suspects. Does Aunt Catherine know about this?"

"Do you think I did it?" Richard asked, looking intently at Darcy.

Without hesitation, Darcy answered, "No, I do not."

Richard relaxed in his seat. "I am not a thief. But the reason I wanted to stay here for a couple more days was to ask a special favor of Aunt Catherine, and thus clear my debt. Mr. Badger had promised to give me until the end of the month, but he must have grown impatient. I am sure it brought him great pleasure to show up here."

"I saw him walk up to the front door. I heard him say that he will stay in Hunsford until you pay."

"Of course he will. He will make sure everyone in the village knows my business, and Aunt Catherine will know by the end of the day."

"We cannot allow that. What is the sum you owe? I will give it to you, so that he can depart this same day."

"I cannot accept your charity. My pride will not allow it."

Darcy had nothing to say against his reasoning. His own pride would not have allowed it either had he been in the same situation as his cousin. Stupid pride. He must tread lightly.

"Would you accept a loan? I will loan the money to you, and you may pay me back in installments over a reasonable period of time."

Darcy could see the war in Richard's mind. On one hand, he needed the money so badly, he had been willing to fall on the good grace of Aunt Catherine— if such a thing existed. On the other hand, he would be indebted to another. Worst still, to a relative. It was a difficult position to be in, but Darcy prayed he would make the sensible choice.

"All right. I accept your terms."

"Good. Let us go into Hunsford directly so the man can be on his way."

They stood and crossed the room together.

Reaching out to the door, Richard paused. His eyes full of gratitude, he said, "I want to thank you."

Darcy held his hands in front of him to keep him from having to say more, but Richard continued, "No, Darcy. It is not just the money. Thank you for not believing me capable of stealing property and dealing in a traitorous manner toward our relations."

"Let us hope that we can find out who is responsible before Aunt Catherine draws the wrong conclusions."

"I know it. It is between me and the visitors to the Hunsford parsonage. You do not think Miss Bennet or Miss Lucas could have...?" Richard asked, letting the rest of his question dangle in the air.

Darcy knew in his heart that Miss Elizabeth could not have stolen them, but he had no explanation nor any reason outside of his instincts to excuse Miss Lucas from suspicion, so he kept his thoughts to himself. "It is what I aim to find out."

With determination, the gentlemen left Rosings toward Hunsford in search of Mr. Badger.

# CHAPTER 11

"What is this immoral magazine doing in my home?" insisted Mr. Collins, his left eye twitching in his fury.

Elizabeth's breath came out in a rush. It was nothing more than a magazine. She read the title. *La Belle Assemblée*. And that was when she understood Maria's apprehension.

Maria bowed her head, too overwhelmed to speak.

Charlotte reached an arm out to Maria. "You know that not even Mother and Father allow you to purchase this magazine. It is frivolous and only encourages excessive vanity. Where did you get this?"

Indeed, where did she get it? Looking closer at the cover, Elizabeth saw that it was the same edition Mrs. Baxter had in her shop. Only, Maria had not purchased it. What was it doing in her trunk?

"I only wanted to look at the dresses. They are so lovely. I even found a design similar to one of Miss de Bourgh's gowns." Maria looked up, hope in her eyes. No doubt, she thought the mention of the great lady de Bourgh's daughter might soften Mr. Collins. It did not appear to work. The disapproving rector pinched the magazine between his fingers and held it out from him as if it were a snake.

Charlotte shook her head slowly. "You know that you are a guest in our home. As such, you must live in accord with the rules of our home. Mr. Collins has expressed his distaste of the magazine, and so we must remove it from the premises. I daresay you only fell victim to the follies of youth and will not do so again. Otherwise, I would have to speak to Mother and Father."

Maria shook her head vigorously. "No, you need not say anything. It was an impulse, nothing more, and I have learned my lesson."

Elizabeth narrowed her eyes at the girl. She was leaving out a lot of information. How did she acquire the magazine in the first place? She reserved her questions. She would not embarrass her further by asking them in front of her sister, but she would ask Maria how she had acquired the magazine as soon as they were alone.

Reaching out to Mr. Collins, Charlotte said, "Please let me have the magazine. I will see that it makes its way back to the shop in Hunsford."

Looking at Maria, she asked, "I take it that is where you purchased it?"

Maria nodded her head but said nothing. Her face flushed a bright red and, once again, she wiped her hands against the muslin of her dress. Yes, she was hiding something. And Elizabeth knew very well what it was.

Mr. Collins, still holding on to his righteous indignation, said, "I am disappointed in this turn of events. What would the members of my parish think of me if it became known that my sister by marriage entertained frivolity in my house?"

Charlotte, who had already got over her shock and now stood with the magazine in her arms, said, "At least, you can reassure her ladyship that a proper search was done, and the diamonds are not here. Unless you have somewhere else you wish to search?"

Mr. Collins shook his head gravely. "No, that is all."

"Then, might I suggest that you go to your book room or out to the garden. It will calm your nerves, and you will soon see how best to proceed."

They left the room, and Elizabeth closed the door softly behind them as she heard their shoes descending the stairs.

"When did you buy the magazine, Maria? Did you walk back into the village later?" she asked, hoping in vain that the girl had a reasonable explanation.

Collapsing onto her bed, Maria let the tears fall.

Elizabeth sat beside her, rubbing her back as if she were one of her own sisters, waiting patiently until the words could come.

She talked soothingly and handed her a handkerchief to dry her eyes and nose. And she waited some more.

After some time had gone by— sufficient time, really— Elizabeth repeated her question, albeit in a quieter tone. "Maria, how did you come to bring that magazine here?"

Looking up with a trembling chin and a red face, Maria said in a whisper, "I took it."

It was what Elizabeth deduced, but she had not thought Maria capable of doing something so remiss. "You took it? Why? How?"

"Do you remember when Mrs. Baxter went into the back to check on the crash in her store room?"

Elizabeth nodded for her to continue.

Sucking in a breath, Maria said in one long sentence, "I have always wanted to possess such a beautiful magazine and, in front of me, I had the chance. So, I tucked it inside my pelisse when she went away and you were not looking. I am so sorry for what I have done, and if I could go back in time, I would not do it again. My guilt has been so great, I have not been able to enjoy the magazine. I have not looked at even half of it. And now it is gone." She wiped her hot cheeks with the handkerchief and sniffed.

Elizabeth had not believed Maria capable of defiling her family's good name, and her own standards of right and wrong, so easily. It bothered her even more that it had happened while in her company. How did she not realize? "How did you keep the magazine under your pelisse the entire walk home?"

"I had to walk with my left arm pinned to my side. I thought I would die when you asked me why I moved so rigidly."

"You lied easily enough." Elizabeth pitied the girl, but she would not make the mistake of consoling her too much. After all, what she had done was horribly wrong— especially in the light of recent events. What would Lady Catherine think if she found out? This was bad. Very, very bad.

Maria's lip trembled. "I was so scared, I did not know what to do. You cannot guess how many times during our walk home I was tempted to return to Hunsford and put the magazine back."

"Why did you not? I would have accompanied you gladly."

"How could I have done so without drawing more attention? Mrs. Baxter would have wondered why we had returned so soon, and I would have had to explain what I had done."

"Do you not think it preferable to the situation you are in now? I could have helped you. I would not have had cause to doubt your motives as I do now. As it is, you will have to explain to Charlotte what happened. Otherwise, she might hear Mrs. Baxter's version of the story before you have had opportunity to explain what happened... Not that your version helps much. Do you not realize what this means? You look guilty, Maria— like a thief!"

The red in Maria's face spread down her neck, mottling her skin. Her hands trembled as much as her lower lip did. Elizabeth hated being so stern with the girl, but she could see no other way out of it.

"No, I cannot tell her. I am not so close to my sister as you are to yours. She will think that I am not mature enough to visit her on my own, and she will never invite me back. She will tell Mother and Father of what I have done, and any freedoms I had before will surely be taken away. I will end up like Miss de Bourgh— frail, thin, and trapped indoors. I will die a spinster!" She burst into hysterical fits of weeping.

Elizabeth did her best to shush her, but this was not the time for dramatics. It had been plain for all to see that Lady Catherine had laid the blame on them for the theft of Miss de Bourgh's earrings. Were it found out that Maria had stolen a trifling magazine, it would guarantee her guilt before Lady Catherine and everyone else in Hunsford who had heard the news. By now, everyone knew about the missing earrings. It was only a matter of time before they heard about the magazine.

"Maria, listen to me." Elizabeth put a hand on each side of Maria's tear-stained cheeks. Wiping her disheveled, soggy hair off her forehead, she said, "You must calm yourself. It is unfortunate, but you have to take care of the damage done from your impulsive action. Would you prefer for Mrs. Baxter to attack Charlotte for something you did? Or worse yet, for Charlotte to hear the accusations against you before you have the opportunity to defend yourself? You simply *must* tell her. What is more, this puts you in a bad light because of the theft of Miss de Bourgh's diamond earrings. What if people begin to reason that you are a thief, first stealing a magazine, then moving on to bigger rewards? People must not be allowed to make that connection, and you can prevent it by confiding in your sister. She understands the danger you are in, and she will help you." Charlotte was reasonable and incredibly practical. Elizabeth's confidence that she would assist her sister out of her predicament was absolute.

Maria did not share her confidence. Shaking her head emphatically, she said, "How I wish this would just go away. What I would give to turn back the hands of time."

Elizabeth felt like Charlotte when she said, "You must see what is practical to your situation right now. It does you no good to lament the past. It is done. Now, you must deal with the consequences of your choice. It will be difficult but, in the end, you will have an honest conscience and your punishment will be far less severe. Do you not realize the penalty for stealing jewelry from a family such as the de Bourghs? Were they to accuse you of the theft of their valuable property, you could spend the rest of your days in a prison. Or worse." Elizabeth shivered. Life was not valued as highly as a prized possession from a wealthy family. They could end Maria's existence if they chose to. Elizabeth would never place her trust in Lady Catherine's ability to be fair and just. Maria should not either.

"I need more time. Please, I need more time," Maria repeated. "I cannot face Charlotte in this state."

Elizabeth could see that Maria was in no condition to talk to anybody at that moment. She really did need some more time.

Biting her lip at what she was about to suggest, she took a deep breath and said, "I think I have a plan which might allow you a little bit more time."

Maria latched on to her with an embrace. "Thank you! Oh, thank you!"

Elizabeth hugged her, but then pulled her away so that she could see her face clearly. She would not have any misunderstandings. "*Only* a little bit more time. It does not mean that you are free from admitting your wrong to Charlotte. You must still speak with her. I only offer you the advantage of an hour or so. I can buy you some time, but you must speak to her before she walks into Hunsford this afternoon. Do you understand me?"

The girl placed her hand over her heart like she was making an oath. "Yes, I do understand. I will tell her. I will talk to Charlotte," she said, trying to convince herself.

Elizabeth looked into her face. Maria's eyes and

nose were swollen and red. She did not waver in her determined expression, so with one final look, Elizabeth nodded. "Then, we have a deal. I will do my best to delay Charlotte's trip, but you must confess today."

# CHAPTER 12

The tavern in Hunsford, which boasted the name, Hearty Lion, had much to offer the villagers after a hard day's work in the way of good food, refreshing drink, and abundant conversation. Darcy and Richard left their horses at the stables opposite the tavern to begin their search for Mr. Badger. The Hearty Lion had a couple of rooms upstairs and was their best guess at finding the man. If nothing else, the innkeeper, Mrs. Shepherd, would know where he could be found. Nothing happened in the village without her knowing about it.

"Mr. Darcy, Colonel Fitzwilliam! How good of you to stop by for a visit. Do you care for a tankard of my best ale?" she asked, with a large smile and rosy cheeks.

It was impossible not to smile back at Mrs. Shepherd. "Yes, a tankard would be much appreciated. Thank you," replied Darcy as Richard looked about the room.

"Let me set up my special room for my special guests. I will only be a moment," she said as she disappeared behind a curtain between the bar and the stairs leading to the rooms above.

Richard whispered to Darcy, "I do not see him. Do you suppose he might have gone back to London? The distance is not too great."

"That is nothing but wishful thinking on your part. If Mr. Badger is anything like the moneylenders' men I have heard of, he will be like a bulldog sniffing for a bone until he gets his master's money. He will go nowhere until his purpose is accomplished."

Richard tugged his sideburns. Darcy watched his cousin's attempts to keep his confidence in the face of his debts. He did an admirable job of it, but Darcy knew him too well. Richard had taken great pride in his ability to live off his army salary. For years, he had asked no favors of anyone. Darcy knew he often suffered want and there were times when he would invite Richard to dine with him when he was in town just so he could ensure that he enjoyed a fine meal and a warm room every so often. His family, who rarely came to town, were more preoccupied with their own financial burdens with their extensive, and unnecessary, renovations at Matlock.

Bustling out from the private room, Mrs. Shepherd said, "Come this way, please, gentlemen." Once they were inside the room, she said, "I will call the man who has come for you from London. The sooner I get him out of my tavern, the better. I do not trust men of his sort." Without another word on the matter, she left Darcy and Richard alone in the room to wonder how much she knew. Probably more than they were comfortable with.

A few minutes passed by. Richard must have pulled out his pocket watch half a dozen times while they waited.

Darcy, who did not want to lose any advantage they had over the money collector, tried to calm him. "Do not show any anxiety, Richard. He will get his money today, and your business with him will be done."

"It is not Mr. Badger I worry about. He is only a minion. Who I worry about is the man he works for." Richard shuffled uncomfortably in his chair, crossed one ankle over a knee, decided against it, then crossed the opposite ankle over his other knee.

Darcy intended to ask who Mr. Badger worked for and what kind of hold he had over Richard, but just then, Mr. Badger sauntered into the room. He swayed from side to side, his head held high and his shoulders erect as if he owned the place. It was the same posture Darcy had seen at Rosings. He knew he held the upper hand, but why?

"How good of you to come to me, Colonel Fitzwilliam. And I see you brought your cousin, Mr. Fitzwilliam Darcy of Pemberley."

The hair on Darcy's arms stood straight up. He had not been presented and, while his family name was well-known, it was a breech in common courtesy to assume knowledge before it was presented to him.

"Since you presume to know who I am, let me speak plainly, Mr. Badger. We have come to cancel the colonel's debt in full," said Darcy through his tense jaw.

Mr. Badger sat opposite them, taking his time to pick a piece of lint off his coat, roll it into a ball, and watch it fall to the ground. "If only our business were that easy. You see, the man I work for is a powerful man and used to getting his way in business. When the good colonel approached him with his scheme, he gladly obliged." His smile revealed pointy teeth.

Richard tensed, but kept his composure as steady as a card player.

"I see no need to draw this interview out any further than necessary." Darcy pulled out the bank notes required to cancel the debt. "This covers the amount borrowed, as well as the interest." Reaching into his pocket, he pulled out another bank note and placed it on top. "This extra should see to your expenditures and safe return back to London, bringing our business to its conclusion." Darcy moved forward in his chair in order to stand.

Mr. Badger, in a low, menacing voice said, "Mr. Volante will be most pleased with his payment. And I thank you for my share." He grabbed his portion from the top of the pile of bank notes and shoved it into his pocket greedily. The rest, he folded carefully and put inside his breast pocket.

"However, this does not conclude our business together. My work is to know everything about the people who come to borrow money from Mr. Volante. The question I will ask you, Mr. Darcy, is this: What secrets do you have that you would pay a tidy sum to keep quiet?"

Darcy never winced and, through many years' practice, he controlled his complexion and breathing. "I have nothing to hide, nor do I give any credibility to your threats. You are speaking to the air." He moved to rise again.

Richard leaned forward, his open hands on the table so that his knuckles turned white. "Your business was with me. Now, it is done. You will leave my family alone."

Mr. Badger chuckled. "I see that I have touched a nerve."

With that, Mr. Badger stood. "Gentlemen, our business is far from done. I thank you, Colonel, for introducing me to your relative. It will be a prosperous encounter— for me, at the least." He turned to leave the room, and Darcy put on his haughtiest expression. He would never let on that the greedy man's threats shook him to the core.

Just before he reached the curtain, Mr. Badger said, "Until we meet again, Colonel Fitzwilliam. Mr. Darcy."

He disappeared through the curtain, and Darcy sat in silence for some time before he turned to Richard, who had his hands on his temples.

"What kind of a man is this Mr. Volante, and why

did you involve yourself with him?" asked Darcy.

"He is the worst sort of man, but the only one who would risk giving me a loan. My parents have put off paying too many debts for too long in their efforts to renovate Matlock Estate. In doing so, they have blemished our family name. Nobody else would give me money, and I was in a desperate situation."

Darcy leaned back and tugged at his hair. "Why did you not speak with me?"

As soon as he said it, he wished he had not. Richard looked miserable enough and accusations would only worsen the problem by causing tension between them.

"Never mind, Richard. We must focus on the present and what harm Mr. Badger can do to Georgiana. If he found out about Wickham, the damage they would scheme together would be irreparable."

Richard's eyes shot up, and he clenched his hands together. "I never thought he would involve her. Do you think he knows about her near elopement with Wickham?"

Darcy nodded. "He certainly knows something. We must continue on the assumption that he knows enough to ruin her reputation and cast a shadow on our family's name. I will not risk Georgiana's future."

"I am sorry, Darcy," said Richard, his face downcast for the brief seconds before his jaw set with determination. "I will not allow any harm to come to her."

Sitting taller, Darcy clasped Richard on the shoulder. "I trust you. What is done, is done. We must think of a way to get Mr. Badger out of our lives and keep Georgiana's name clear."

Richard nodded, his shoulders tense. "All right. Where do you suppose we start?"

"You are the military man in the family. What do you suggest?" Darcy had some ideas, but he wanted to know what Richard thought.

With a smile, Richard said, "One benefit of my profession. Did you notice Mr. Badger's wording just before he left. He said it would be a prosperous meeting for *him.*"

Darcy nodded. "Do you think he is acting alone?"

"If my instinct is to be trusted, he is. If we catch him seeking to profit without the involvement of Mr. Volante, we could secure his silence in exchange for ours."

"He will have to strike soon. My guess is that he will attempt to extort money from Aunt Catherine."

Richard chuckled. "I should like to see him try!"

Darcy stood, and together with Richard, they left the private room for the open space of the front of the tavern. Mr. Badger was nowhere in sight, and only a few villagers remained, talking at their tables with their tankards of ale in front of them.

Mrs. Shepherd called them over to the bar where she wiped the rims of her newly washed mugs with a clean, white towel. "I forgot to mention earlier that

Mr. Collins came in before you did. He was overly interested in your business here, if you ask me, and has been up in Mr. Badger's room for some time. Take care of him," she said in a voice low enough to keep her words unheard by others.

Darcy exchanged a look with Richard. That was all they needed. Aunt Catherine's overzealous rector informing her of Richard's debt. It would only make his precarious situation worse.

"Thank you for the warning, Mrs. Shepherd." With a bow to the kind woman, Darcy and Richard left the tavern.

As they went across the way to retrieve their horses, Darcy could not help but feel that they were being watched. The impression that someone tracked their every move was unnerving.

They mounted and followed Hunsford Road out of town. Unable to shake the sensation that someone watched them, he turned. Mr. Collins stood half-hidden behind the side of the tavern.

# CHAPTER 13

"Lizzy, Maria, I am walking into Hunsford. I cannot wait another moment for Mr. Collins if I am to deliver this basket to the Thatcher family and return the magazine." Charlotte stood by the gate, her shawl protecting her from the moist air and a basket with the provisions she could spare in her arms. In her time at Hunsford, Charlotte had made several trips to visit the parishioners in and around the village to help alleviate their needs. Her practical views and no-nonsense manners made her popular amongst the poor families. She could be counted on for sensible provisions outside of merely expressing her sympathy and giving suggestions to help them improve their lot.

At the top of the basket, Elizabeth, who was enjoying the warm afternoon sun in the front garden, could see *La Belle Assemblée* poking out.

Maria sat inside the house by the window seat which overlooked the garden. Elizabeth glanced at her with the unspoken question in her mind. Had she talked with Charlotte? Not even an hour had passed.

The wide-eyed look of terror she saw in Maria's face was answer enough. She had not said anything, and now Charlotte would surely find out from Mrs. Baxter that Maria had not purchased the magazine— that it was, indeed, stolen property.

"Wait, Charlotte. Are you certain you cannot wait just a few minutes longer? Mr. Collins might be cross," she suggested, knowing full well that Mr. Collins only concerned himself with the whereabouts of his wife if it inconvenienced him or, God forbid, Lady Catherine.

"Do not be silly, Lizzy," Charlotte clucked at her and reached her hand out to undo the latch on the whitewashed picket gate. That one simple action jolted Elizabeth with inspiration.

With one look of appeal to Maria, Elizabeth jerked her head toward Charlotte. If Maria wished to speak, now was the time. She prayed she would, or else Elizabeth might regret what she was about to do.

Large, teary eyes looked back at her.

As Charlotte left the house accompanied by the housemaid, Elizabeth marched to the back of the house and down the sloping lawn to the pig's pen. Elizabeth had not experienced the flight of said animal, but she knew that Charlotte lived in terror of it escaping again. Every commotion Mr. Collins caused was followed by the question, "Did the pig escape again?" from Charlotte.

Walking quickly, before her sense of reason could catch up with her and stop her, Elizabeth raised the latch which secured the door to the pen. She flung open the gate and clapped a few times to set the animal in motion. It needed no further encouragement.

Squealing with the joy of its newfound freedom, the pig ran as fast as its four pink legs could carry it, its ears bouncing and its tail swishing through the air as it cut through the lawn with Elizabeth chasing after it, trying with all her might to keep up so that she might encourage it to go toward the front of the house where Charlotte could hear it.

"Charlotte! The pig is loose!" she yelled.

Charlotte, who had not walked far down the road, shoved the basket into Betsy's hands, picked up her skirts, and ran toward the house. The look of determination on her face was a fierce thing to behold.

"You block it from that side, Lizzy. I will make sure it does not come through the gate. Maria!" she yelled.

The girl, not understanding what all the fuss was about, but observing it tranquilly through the front window, came outside.

Charlotte made no explanations, but she gave orders rather well. "See that the pig does not get into our garden."

Maria ran to the opposite side of the house to

stand guard, but Elizabeth knew that the pig must already be there. Its squeals of protest at Maria's attempts to shoo it out of the garden confirmed its location.

Charlotte threw her hands up by her face. "Oh, no! It will uproot and eat everything. Lizzy, I need your help," she called from over her shoulder as she ran toward the garden.

Elizabeth did not remember the last time she had run so much. Not since she was a child.

Maria was in some sort of deadlock with the offending animal. It stood with a carrot hanging out of its mouth, chomping at the greens contentedly and daring anyone to draw near.

"Maria, you get at him from the far side. I'll go from this side. Lizzy, make sure he cannot escape through the front," Charlotte instructed as she closed in.

Betsy, having freed herself of the basket, joined them.

With a wicked glint in its eye, the pig finished chomping on its carrot, then charged at Elizabeth. Widening her stance so she could grab the animal as it passed, it ran straight between her legs, catching her dress and pulling her down backwards. Charlotte and Betsy were quick to run to her, but the pig masterfully untangled himself from her dress, stepped over her, and continued squealing toward the open fence.

"I suppose I deserved that," said Elizabeth to herself as she tried to get back on her feet.

Thankfully, the pig was small and it had not hurt much when he stepped all over her in his haste.

Dashing across the lawn to the front of the house, they watched as the pig headed toward the open gate.

"Do not let it get out!" cried Charlotte.

Elizabeth ran with the women after the pig, wiping her loose hair out of her face.

"It must not cross into Rosings. Mr. Collins would be mortified," insisted Charlotte.

Chasing the tireless, pink beast down the Hunsford Road, Elizabeth's lungs burned for breath. After all this effort, Maria had best confess to Charlotte!

Down the road, two gentlemen on horseback appeared. Elizabeth gritted her teeth at the sight of Colonel Fitzwilliam and Mr. Darcy. It embarrassed her for them to see her in such a state. A great deal of her hair was loose, and her dress was covered in dirt and muddy hoof prints. But it had all been of her own doing, and she must see Charlotte's pig safely back to its pen.

Charging through her shame as she continued in the chase, she kept her focus on the pig, waiting for her opportunity to pounce. One quick look over her shoulder confirmed that she was on her own. Maria and Betsy lagged behind her. Charlotte had slowed to a walk, having grown tired.

As the runaway animal neared the horsemen, Mr. Darcy handed his reins to Colonel Fitzwilliam and dismounted. Elizabeth had expected him to observe piously from the comfort of his seat. When he rushed the pig, turning it back to trot toward her, she could not have been more surprised.

Unfortunately, the pig must have figured that its odds were better against one man than against four resolute women, who now stood closer together. It promptly turned back to Mr. Darcy, picking up his pace.

Elizabeth, her limbs as tired as her spirits, yelled, "Please do not let the little devil past."

Mr. Darcy took her seriously. He leaned down to grab the pig as it neared, but the pig had anticipated his move. Veering to the side just outside of Mr. Darcy's reach, he squealed in delight at what he thought was another victory in his escape. What the pig did not count on, nor anybody else, for that matter, was for Mr. Darcy to pivot in place and pounce on top of it. He circled his arms around the squirming animal.

Colonel Fitzwilliam had his hands full with the nervous horses that did not much like a small pig darting about near their feet. He laughed so loudly, it echoed down the lane.

Without losing his hold, Mr. Darcy's eyes shot up to glare at his audacious cousin. "Stop your cackling and make yourself useful."

Seeing that the colonel would not be of much help with two skittish horses in his care, Elizabeth knelt down next to Mr. Darcy so that she could hold the pig's feet and allow the gentleman to stand.

"Thank you," he said, a scowl on his face.

Wrapping his arms around the pig's middle, he asked, "Where does this thing belong, Mrs. Collins?"

Rushing forward, Charlotte said, "Oh, no. Please, Mr. Darcy, we will make sure it gets back into its pen. You need not trouble yourself."

Elizabeth shook her head at her overly polite friend.

Mr. Darcy, scowl still in place, said, "Nonsense. If I loosen my hold, this ingrate will only escape again."

"Very well," said Charlotte as she led the way back to the pig's pen.

They walked in silence back to the parsonage. Elizabeth did not remember running that great a distance, but the pig had covered a good deal of ground.

When the house was in view, Elizabeth chanced a glance at Mr. Darcy. She expected to see a trickle of sweat running down his brow, but there was nothing. Only a deep furrow.

As a giggle bubbled up through her throat, she wished she had not looked at him. It was ridiculous that such a fine gentleman who took himself much too seriously should be carrying a pig like it was a small child.

The pig's ears flopped with each step, and it looked like it was having a jolly time in Mr. Darcy's arms. It even looked like it was smiling.

That was all Elizabeth could bear. No longer able to stifle her laughter, she looked at Colonel

Fitzwilliam, whom she knew she could rely on for understanding, and laughed with such delight that her stomach soon hurt.

She avoided looking at Mr. Darcy again, lest the sight renew her laughter and upset the gentleman more than she already had. But the pig joined in with its grunts and snorts, and Elizabeth peeked up through her lashes to see Mr. Darcy in the height of a large grin.

The sight almost stifled her laughter. It certainly was not what she had expected to see. Mr. Darcy's eyes lit up and his lips curled up in the corners so bewitchingly that she had difficulty looking away from. Disarmed by his smile, she focused on the happy pig bobbing up and down in his arms.

They filed through the gate, the colonel waiting just outside with the horses. Elizabeth was grateful that at least he had laughed with her. He was a merry sort.

As Charlotte closed the latch to the pig pen and gave an accusatory glare to its resident, she turned to thank Mr. Darcy. He brushed off the front of his white cravat and cream colored waistcoat, but nothing short of the talents of his valet would remove the dirt stains running from his cravat down to his buckskin breeches. Even his boots were scuffed.

Looking back up to him, Elizabeth jumped when their eyes locked. He had caught her inspecting him. Oh, she hoped he did not take that as encouragement. One rescue of an escaped pig would not change the inclination of her drumming heart.

He lifted his hand as if he would touch her cheek or pull a twig out of her hair, but stopped himself short. She let out her breath.

With a curt bow, Mr. Darcy left for the gate.

Elizabeth felt that she should say something. Following him up to the gate, she hesitated while everyone else went indoors. She caressed the soft velvet muzzle of his horse as he mounted.

"Thank you, Mr. Darcy," she managed to say through her embarrassment. She felt her ears burn and she hated her complexion for showing him her feelings.

Looking at her with an intensity which made her wish the ground would swallow her whole, he said in a soft baritone, "Think nothing of it, Miss Bennet." The tenderness in his voice released something inside her, and she relaxed. She did not know Mr. Darcy well, but she understood that he did not think any worse of her. Smiling feebly back at him, wanting him to think well of her, but not so well that he might propose again, she bid him and the colonel good day, and they rode in the direction of Rosings.

Charlotte had rearranged her hair and looked none the worse for their chase. The exercise cast a healthy pink glow to her cheeks.

Maria sat next to her by the window in the front parlor facing the garden.

"How fortuitous that Mr. Darcy showed up when

he did. Otherwise, we would have chased that horrid pig all the way into Hunsford." Charlotte fanned her face with her hand and sunk back into her chair.

Elizabeth hurried upstairs to change her dress. She could not sit on Charlotte's impeccable furniture with a dirty derriere.

When she returned downstairs, Charlotte and Maria were discussing the possible means the pig had of escaping. Elizabeth sat quietly, careful not to add her opinion nor draw unnecessary attention to herself.

After some minutes, Charlotte said, "You are uncommonly quiet, Lizzy. If I did not know better, I would think that you know something you are unwilling to share." She said it as if it was a dare. Her eyes defied Elizabeth.

Elizabeth looked at Maria and said, "Now would be a good time."

Looking back and forth between the two, Charlotte asked, "A good time for what?"

Maria, her eyes tearing and her face reddening, sat forward in her chair, wringing her hands in her lap. "You see..." she began.

Just as she started to speak, Mr. Collins burst through the door in an agitated state. "I think I know who took Miss de Bourgh's earrings!" he said in triumph.

# CHAPTER 14

Darcy endured Richard's teasing all the way back to Rosings. Not that the distance was great from the parsonage, but it felt like it.

While he did not particularly like being laughed at, it had brought him great pleasure to cause a smile to pass Miss Elizabeth's lips. Knowing he was the reason behind the smile and her bubbling laughter helped him endure the taunting of his cousin and his own embarrassment at participating in such an undignified chase.

Tiring of Richard's comments, Darcy said, "I noticed how you stood by, sitting comfortably on your horse. Why did you not help?" It was more an accusation than a question requiring an answer.

"And miss the fun of watching you tackle that feisty beast?" Richard burst into laughter again. "There is nothing on this earth which would cause me to miss such entertainment. Never in my life have I thought you would do such a thing. I am in awe, Darcy!"

Darcy still could not believe it himself. What had possessed him? As soon as the question passed through his mind, he knew the answer. Miss Elizabeth had needed his assistance. She had come running toward him in pursuit of an animal she could not hope to gain in her tired state. Her cheeks were flushed, strands of hair fell around her face and down her back, her dress would have caused Miss Bingley to go into fits at the dirt which ran down the front and back. Not unlike him, he thought as he looked down at his stained cravat. His valet would not be pleased.

"Let us hope that we can sneak past Aunt Catherine lest she sees me in disarray. We have been out all morning, and she will demand to know where we have been." Darcy handed his horse over to the stable boy, and together with Richard, he walked into the house, aiming for the stairs so that he might change before anyone saw him.

"Darcy! Is that you?" a shrill voice sounded from the drawing room. Simmons, who stood silently by the door and had seen the state of Darcy's clothes, raised his finger up to his lips and motioned for him to continue upstairs.

Darcy took the stairs two at a time. The butler would give some excuse for his delay, but Aunt Catherine would not wait long.

Richard, the good nephew that he was, waited downstairs in case she should require him as well.

Darcy's valet said nothing about the state of his clothes. He only pursed his lips as he held them out to inspect the damage. With gratitude, Darcy donned the clean clothes he promptly laid out and hurried downstairs to see what Aunt Catherine wanted.

She sat in her favorite room, holding court from her gilded chair.

"Darcy, what took you so long? I have been waiting," she complained.

"I do apologize, Aunt. I went into Hunsford with Richard earlier this morning and had to change clothes to make myself presentable." Unless it came from Richard, she would never hear about the pig incident. He was certain the residents of the Hunsford parsonage would guard their silence.

She huffed like a spoiled child and extended her arm out to the chair in front of her.

Inclining her head over to the couch to acknowledge Mrs. Jenkinson's presence, she continued, "I want to discuss Anne's future with you. Every year you allow to pass weighs on me, Darcy. Anne is getting older, as are you, and yet, you have not married."

She expected an answer to a question she never asked. Darcy knew very well where the conversation was heading, and he would do nothing to make it easier for her.

With another huff, she continued, "I have called

Mrs. Jenkinson here as my witness to hear you declare when you plan to announce your engagement to Anne. Like me, she has Anne's best interests at heart, and I feel that it is time that we let Mr. Collins read the banns so that you can marry before summer."

Mrs. Jenkinson nodded her agreement, looking every bit as presumptuous as his aunt. Of course, she was paid to follow suit. Darcy could not blame her for that.

Sitting stiffly in his chair, Darcy said, "I do not agree to have the banns read, for I have not entered into a commitment with my cousin. This engagement that you conjured up with my mother is as distasteful to Anne as it is to me."

Raising her chin and flaring her nostrils, Aunt Catherine said, "You dare defy the wishes of your superiors? You would cast Anne off as if she had no worth? How dare you, Darcy!" Her eyes were icy gray and as hard as sleet.

He felt his body tense. In no way was he in the wrong. Not once had he been consulted about his future plans for marriage. Neither had Anne. When he had asked Anne what she wanted, she had been clear that she did not want him. Still, his manners would not allow him to openly offend Aunt Catherine while he was a guest in her home. He would do what he could to preserve peace, but he would not give in to her wish that he marry Anne.

"Have you asked Anne if she would even have

me as her husband? Do her wishes mean so little to you?"

"Anne does not know what she wants. She relies on others to guide her for her benefit. As her mother, I know what is best for her interests. I am surprised that you do not place more respect on the wishes of your blessed mother."

That was a low blow, and it cut Darcy more than he would let on. He had loved his mother— respected her even. But where Darcy's happiness was concerned, his mother had been dreadfully wrong. She had been content with her arranged marriage, but Darcy could never consent to a lifetime of insipid conversation and dullness. He craved to feel things to their fullest— the desired happiness, love, passion... even the anger, hurt, and disappointment that naturally came along with a life lived fully. He wanted Miss Elizabeth with all her excited conversation and refreshing impulsiveness.

"Mother was an exceptional lady, and I respect the values she inculcated in me, but if I were to agree to marry Anne, it would go against the very ideals she worked so hard to instill. It would be a lie. I could never make Anne happy in the way she deserves, and I am convinced that I am the last man in the world to make her happy. If you place any importance on her happiness, I encourage you to speak with her. She does not want me."

"What do you say, Mrs. Jenkinson? Has Anne

said anything implying that she is unwilling to marry Darcy?"

Mrs. Jenkinson spoke without hesitation. "No, your ladyship. All these years I have been her companion, she has never expressed any opinion contrary to yours."

Aunt Catherine looked triumphantly at Darcy. "You see? Anne is agreeable. I will send for Collins and have him read the banns this week."

"No. This is my future you are talking about, and I thank you to leave any decisions concerning it to me," Darcy said as calmly as he could. How many times would they have the same conversation?

She narrowed her eyes and looked down the slope of her nose at him. "You have not betrayed Anne by falling in love with someone else, have you?"

Unable to answer the question honestly, and resenting being asked yet again, he replied, "How could I possibly betray Anne if I have not agreed to marry her? I have never encouraged her affection, and she made it clear to me when I asked that she reciprocates my distaste of the match."

"You did not answer the question, nephew. Are you in love with another?"

"If I were, would it free me of your insistence that I marry Anne?"

"No. You are under obligation to your family. You must seek the benefit of your family over your own selfish desires."

Darcy clenched his jaw so hard, his head ached.

He was more determined than ever not to give in. He was not acting selfishly as she accused him. Her wish to continue in her extravagances at the sacrifice of her own daughter and himself was deplorable, and he would take no part in it.

"I am under no obligation to you," he said, his voice steady.

"You have until the end of the week, Darcy."

He rose to leave before he lost complete control of his tongue. How dare she threaten him. Did she not realize that he could simply leave?

Calling after him, she said, "Do not forget, Darcy. You are to help me find proof against Miss Bennet and Miss Lucas. I want an arrest to be made soon."

Darcy froze in place. He forced his shoulders down, though they had crept up close to his ears. It was only by his persuasion that she had not already sent Miss Elizabeth and Miss Lucas to the constable. He had to find out who was behind the theft of his cousin's earrings— to find out what tricks Aunt Catherine employed— or else risk losing the one woman he loved forever. That took precedence over everything.

With renewed determination, Darcy crossed the entrance hall to go outside. He was more convinced than ever that Aunt Catherine only used Anne's earrings as a ploy, and he wanted to sort through the facts he knew to test the strength of his theory before presenting it to Richard.

# CHAPTER 15

Elizabeth stared in disbelief at Mr. Collins. Unless someone walked up to him and said, "Here are the diamond earrings. I stole them," she could not imagine a circumstance where he would be the one to solve the crime before anyone else.

Charlotte must have had similar inclinations. She asked, "What? Has someone confessed?"

Stepping into the room and asking the maid for a little something to calm his nerves, he sat down with them. He slapped his hands together, wrung them, and slapped them again, as if he were trying to figure out the most dramatic way to tell his story.

"It all began when I went to call on her ladyship to inform her of my findings in our humble home. I knew it would please her greatly to hear how seriously we take the matter and of the thoroughness of my inspection. It so happened that as I crossed the lawn from one side, I saw another man cross from the other end. He is not the sort to be allowed entry to her ladyship, and his presence at the threshold quite shocked me. Uncertain as to how to proceed, I promptly hid behind a bush. I do not think he, nor anyone else, saw me."

"That was quick thinking," thought Elizabeth.

Reveling in his cleverness so long, she thought it would take the rest of the afternoon to hear his story, Charlotte came to the rescue. She asked, "Then what? Who was the gentleman?"

"I had hoped you would ask," he said, rubbing his hands together. "I had not thought that Lady Catherine would allow such an individual entry into her dwelling. His coat was cut in the latest fashion, but was made of inferior fabric. So, suspecting that her ladyship might be in some kind of danger, I took it upon myself to ensure her safety when he was left standing outside."

Elizabeth kept her mouth shut, but she could not control her thoughts so well. "You protected her from behind the bush? How very brave."

Charlotte gave her a look that made her determined to behave. What a pity her friend knew her so well. It was almost as if she were reading her thoughts. She stifled a laugh, pursing her lips together and nodding in attention to the noble protector of his patroness, Lady Catherine de Bourgh.

"He did not remain long at the door before he was denied entry, so I took it upon myself to follow him into Hunsford. He is lodged at Mrs. Shepherd's tavern."

Charlotte gasped, "You went inside the tavern?"

Mr. Collins had the decency to blush and fresh beads of sweat covered his forehead. Nodding in a most grave manner, he said, "I felt it imperative upon me to do so. These are a special set of circumstances, and I could not have the man threaten her ladyship when there is a thief about."

That made the second time Mr. Collins cast an unfavorable light on the man. Elizabeth asked, "What was it about the man that made him appear threatening?" A coat made of inferior fabric was not enough to judge a man.

"He dressed the part of a man seeking to look greater than his born station. From the little I know on the subject of fashion, he seemed to be dressed in it. He is not from here, as I have never had occasion to see him before."

Elizabeth wondered when Mr. Collins had occasion to know anything at all about men's fashion, but she decided against pressing for more information. He had yet to reveal who he thought the thief was. By all rights, he suspected the man he had just described.

"Do you believe him to be the thief?" asked Charlotte, leaning forward in her chair.

"No, indeed, though he did look the part. But I will get to that. I must beg your patience as I continue. I do not want to forget even the smallest detail, lest it be of the utmost importance."

Elizabeth sat back in her chair. They would be

there for a while, and she might as well make herself comfortable.

Rubbing his hands together yet again to restore his memory, he picked up where he left off. "Ah, yes, I followed the man into the tavern, and learned through discreet questioning that Mr. Badger is his name. I asked him politely what his business was at Rosings. At first, he did not want to confide any details in me, but I condescended to inform him of my position with the family de Bourgh. He must have been impressed because he spoke openly and, I believe, honestly of his business with Lady Catherine's nephew."

Elizabeth sat up in her chair, all ears. Maddeningly, he did not continue, but sat there with a sardonic smile as if he would say no more, but leave them with half of the story.... and just when it got interesting.

Maria, who had been silent, broke the silence, "Surely, you do not mean Mr. Darcy. What business would he have with someone like the man you described? But I cannot think that Colonel Fitzwilliam would either." She rested her chin in her hand on her knee, contemplating the conundrum revealed before them.

Slowly, savoring the effect each word had on his listeners, Mr. Collins continued, "Mr. Badger's business is with Colonel Fitzwilliam. Apparently, the colonel owes the gentleman Mr. Badger works for a great deal of money, and he has come to collect it. How the mighty do fall." He looked at

Elizabeth with a haughty glee she knew was intended more for her than for Colonel Fitzwilliam.

Elizabeth's heart sank for the colonel. He was a charming man, and his manners toward them had been impeccable. What would Lady Catherine think of her nephew when she found out that he had incurred debts?

Mr. Collins sat with a pleased expression at his revelation. "So, you see, Colonel Fitzwilliam must be the thief. He is in need of a tidy sum of money, and it is no coincidence that the diamonds went missing during his visit." Folding his hands, he sat back with a self-satisfied look on his face.

While Mr. Collin's finding certainly gave the colonel a motive to commit the crime, Elizabeth could not justify it in her mind.

"What do you plan to do with this newfound knowledge?" she asked, curious to see if Mr. Collins had the audacity to accuse Lady Catherine's own nephew of the theft.

"I took great care to verify his story. While I was at the tavern— the topic being of such a delicate nature and myself feeling uncomfortable on the premises, Mr. Badger was so good as to attend to me in his room— who do you think arrived but Mr. Darcy and Colonel Fitzwilliam? I was able to hear bits of their conversation through the curtain at my position at the top of the stairs. I felt at liberty to do so since the matter concerns her ladyship, who preoccupies herself with all things related to the good people in and around Hunsford, as well as her family. It was enough for me to verify that what Mr. Badger had said was true. Mr. Darcy paid him in full and practically threatened the man to make him leave."

Charlotte said, "I can imagine so. Just think if word was to get back to Lady Catherine. You cannot tell her what happened."

Mr. Collins shook his head gravely. "Oh, I do agree with you. What insight you show, Mrs. Collins. It is for the reason you so sagaciously expressed that I agreed to meet with Mr. Badger at Rosings tomorrow. I could never be the one to reveal confidential information. But if it came from him and Lady Catherine knew how it was found out, then I think it would bring her great comfort to know that it was me who discovered her nephew's secret and tactfully revealed it to her in the most delicate way I could arrange." He looked so pleased with himself, Elizabeth could only gape, astonished at the delight he took in his egotism. Surely, Lady Catherine would not appreciate him meddling in her family's affairs in the least— no matter his intentions. Nor would she appreciate him bringing Mr. Badger into her home. Elizabeth had the presentiment that whatever happened tomorrow, it would not end well— for Colonel Fitzwilliam or for Mr. Collins.

Charlotte spoke warily, "It sounds as if you have already made arrangements with the man and you must see it through." She swallowed hard and looked nervously at Elizabeth.

"Yes, all will be taken care of on the morrow. Her ladyship will be most pleased, I think." He pressed his fingers together in front of his chin and smiled greedily.

She had to try to stop him. "If the debt was paid, then why do you consider him a suspect?"

He looked at her like she were a simpleton. "My dear cousin, were the earrings not stolen before the debt was paid? Perhaps he sold them and used the money to cancel the amount."

Trying again, she asked, "Did you not say it was Mr. Darcy who covered the debt? He would have no need to sell an item of value to help Colonel Fitzwilliam."

Mr. Collins waved her concerns away. "I am thankful to have married a lady who understands my reasonings, instead of putting them to question. Your lack of comprehension astounds me, cousin. Are you not known in your family as the clever one?"

Elizabeth cringed at his insults, but they did little to harm her since she cared little of his opinion. She did care about the harm he could cause his own household, as well as the residents at Rosings. She did not know how she would manage it, but she had to warn the colonel. She could not send a note to him. That would be inappropriate. What else?... How could she send word?... Of course! Mr. Darcy. Many times she had chanced upon him during her morning walks. She would go out as normal in the morning in hopes of seeing him again. She would walk the entirety of the park if need be. Mr. Darcy and the colonel were not only family, they were friends. She could trust him to set matters straight.

Mr. Collins, his news delivered, went into his book room to contemplate the glorious moment which awaited him on the morrow.

The moment he shut his door, Charlotte spun around in her chair to face Elizabeth. "How did the pig escape?" she asked.

It was not what Elizabeth had expected to hear. She would have been more prepared for some comment on her husband's plan for the morning, not the pig.

Taking too long to respond, Charlotte repeated, "Lizzy, how did the pig escape? It could not have been on its own, for I checked that the latch was secure after the last time. There were no holes in the fence." She looked expectantly at Elizabeth.

Elizabeth looked at Maria, who had grown remarkably quiet. She shrunk into her chair, making herself as small as she could.

With a sigh, Elizabeth said, "I let it out. I am sorry." She would not lie.

"What? Whatever for?" Charlotte asked, thoroughly exasperated.

Elizabeth looked at Maria again, but got no reaction.

"It was a foolish thing to do, but Maria can explain the matter fully. I cannot tell you what crazy series of thoughts led me to do choose that particular means of delaying your walk into

Hunsford, but I regret it very much." Trying to find a way to lighten the judgment on Charlotte's face, she continued, "How fortunate we were that Mr. Darcy came to our rescue." With a laugh that started out forced and ended real, she said, "I will never forget the contented smile on the pig's face as Mr. Darcy carried it back to its pen. Nor the dirty stains on the gentleman's otherwise perfectly white cravat."

Charlotte chuckled despite her ill-humor moments before. "I do believe I saw the pig smile." She laughed some more. "Lizzy, I am still cross with you for what you did. Sometimes I think I will never understand why you act the way you do, but the pig was safely restored to his pen to grow fat in time for the winter. I shall laugh every time I eat a bite of ham in memory of this day."

Charlotte went upstairs to rest, apparently having forgotten to ask Maria for a better explanation. So many things had happened so quickly since their returning to the house, she must have been quite fatigued.

Maria, as quiet as a mouse in the room, looked questioningly at Elizabeth. "You let the pig loose for me?"

Elizabeth raised her arms to the heavens in a dramatic gesture. "Do not ask me why, but yes, I did. Maria, you simply must speak with your sister this day. She will try to go into Hunsford tomorrow, and there are no more animals I can set loose for you. Nor would I do so again. Chasing after that pig was horrid." She looked forward to her bath. Her unmentionables stuck to her skin until it chafed. If Mr. Darcy thought ill of her before, he certainly thought worse of her now after seeing her in a dirt-stained dress and disheveled hair.

Maria nodded her head. "I will," she said before Mr. Collins opened the door of his book room.

Standing in the hall, he said, "Cousin Elizabeth, there was one matter of business so insignificant, it almost passed my mind entirely. There is a letter waiting for you in the village. Having hurried out on my mission for Lady Catherine, I did not have the necessary coin to retrieve it for you."

Of course he did not. Mr. Collins would no sooner spend his precious money on another than miss a dinner with Lady Catherine.

Forcing a smile at his false generosity and importance, she replied, "Thank you for telling me. I will walk into the village tomorrow." She suspected that the letter was from Jane, but did not say so aloud just to annoy Mr. Collins. He looked at her expecting more information, but she only smiled back at him politely.

Maria escaped from the room the moment Mr. Collins retreated back into his study. That was fine with Elizabeth. She had suffered enough drama for one day, and she much rather preferred to spend her spare minutes thinking about her dear sister Jane. Poor, heartbroken Jane, who paled away in London on the hope that Mr. Bingley would call. Oh, that horrid Mr. Darcy— sticking his nose where it did not belong. Why did he see the need to meddle with her sister's happiness?

All of a sudden, she was not looking forward to her walk in the morning. Their recent conversation and the incident with the pig had softened her attitude toward him, but now that she remembered her grudge against the gentleman, she repented. He did not deserve her compassion. Only the amiability Colonel Fitzwilliam had shown during her stay near Rosings would make her seek out his company, so that she might save him from any embarrassment with his aunt. Only that. Nothing more. She never wanted to see Mr. Darcy again. And so it became a great source of frustration when the image of his friendly eyes and crooked smile invaded her mind time after time. She swatted the picture in her mind away like a pesky fly, but like the persistent insect, it would circle back around to assail her thoughts.

# CHAPTER 16

Elizabeth had no reason to think that Mr. Darcy would choose to walk the same paths she preferred after their last encounter, but she could think of no other way to cross paths with him or the colonel otherwise. What a happy coincidence it would be to run into the colonel instead. Though the only times Elizabeth had seen him on the property outside the house had been on the back of his horse, she held onto the prospect with determined desperation.

Elizabeth had as much desire to see Mr. Darcy as he probably did to see her. What would he think if he saw her? Would he turn and disappear into the trees? Was it very wicked of her to want him to be pleased to see her when she struggled to dislike him as her curiosity about him grew?

Setting out early in the dewy morning, she smelled the damp earth and fresh blossoms in the air. In spite of the tension she carried due to the task at hand, the soft, perfumed breeze calmed her.

Untying her bonnet, she let the sun soak into her from top to bottom and felt her worries melt away.

She lost track of time surrounded as she was by the pleasant day. She began thinking of other ways to send some kind of warning to Colonel Fitzwilliam. Though she had determined to do so, she could not wander around the park all day. Perhaps she would have to arrange to practice on Mrs. Jenkinson's pianoforte with Maria after all. She had hoped to use that as a last resort, knowing full well where Lady Catherine's suspicions lay.

Turning toward the road to Hunsford to retrieve the letter waiting for her, she saw a figure in the distance. She recognized him immediately. It was not merely his height which gave him away, but the confidence in his posture, and the slight slant to his hat.

She held her breath when Mr. Darcy saw her and his gait slowed.

Elizabeth stood in place, weighing her words in her mind and willing her pulse to calm itself. Her stomach full of nervous knots, she braced herself to face his disapproval at her news.

"Miss Elizabeth," he said with a bow. He stood up tall, looking about him as if he would dash away now that polite formalities had been seen to.

"Mr. Darcy," she said with a curtsy. "I have something of great importance to tell you," she said before he could depart.

His brows creased, and he looked at her searchingly.

Taking a deep breath and continuing, she said, "It concerns Colonel Fitzwilliam."

The worried expression on his face deepened, but he said nothing.

Taking another deep breath, she said, "Mr. Collins overheard his conversation with a man he saw call at Rosings. Mr. Badger was what he said the man's name was. Given the purpose of Mr. Badger's claims, Mr. Collins feels that Colonel Fitzwilliam has sufficient motive to have stolen Miss de Bourgh's diamonds." Leaving out the worst details against her cousin, she focused on the colonel. "I daresay you will think even worse of my family on hearing this, but my concern for the colonel outweighs my own pride and your propriety."

Mr. Darcy shook his head, his mouth pinched in annoyance. "If Mr. Collins had taken greater care to listen well, he would have heard that my cousin covered his debts with the man, who I hope has returned to London by now. His business with the colonel is through."

It struck Elizabeth as odd that Mr. Darcy gave Colonel Fitzwilliam the credit of covering his own debt when Mr. Collins had said that it was Mr. Darcy who had gone with him to lend the money.

"If only that were the end of the matter." She clasped her hands together, knowing how her news would dishearten the gentleman in front of her. "Mr. Collins is so convinced that Colonel Fitzwilliam is guilty, that he arranged for Mr.

Badger to meet him at Rosings so that together, they might reveal the state of the colonel's finances and his motive. Charlotte tried to dissuade him, but he is determined to find favor with your aunt by being the one to solve the mystery of the theft."

She heard Mr. Darcy's sigh. "What time were they to meet at Rosings?" he asked, leaving out any cutting remarks against Mr. Collins.

"They arranged to call at ten this morning."

Mr. Darcy's chest heaved up and down.

"Very well. I thank you for speaking to me about this."

Feeling the need to justify her warning, she said, "I do not think the colonel did it."

Shaking his head, his eyes piercing her through, he said, "Your warning is proof of that. Like you, I do not believe that even the worst want of money would cause him to act thus toward his own family. He is too honest for such treachery."

Elizabeth smiled contentedly in agreement. It pleased her to know that the colonel had a friend in Mr. Darcy.

"Miss Bennet," he said reaching into his pocket and pulling out a thick letter. "You expressed some concerns when I last called at the parsonage. Would you do me the honor of reading this letter?"

She reached out to take it, confounded when her fingers shook.

Before she could think of what to say or how to react, he had turned toward Rosings, walking in the long, purposeful strides she had grown accustomed to see.

"Thank you," she called after him, uncertain if he heard or not. She did not know what else to say, but she did not want him to think her impolite.

*\*\**

Darcy turned away from Miss Elizabeth. Her flushed cheeks and parted lips tempted him more than he could ever let her know. She was not his to caress, though he had been sorely tempted to brush the strand of curly hair away from her temple and rest his cold fingers against her hot cheeks so that his touch might cool her.

Ugly, bitter jealousy had struck him with all its force as she warned him about Mr. Badger out of her concern for Richard. Did she love him? Did Richard love her? He had called at the parsonage several times, with and without Darcy. Had his motive been to spend more time in Miss Elizabeth's company? They had much in common. Both laughed easily and conversation flowed between them. They had many interests in common. How had he not seen it before?

Now, he regretted having recommended that Miss Elizabeth verify the contents of his letter, and the facts he shared about Mr. Wickham and Georgiana, with Richard. Darcy's sense of honor would never do anything to prevent their match if they truly loved each other, but he certainly would not do anything to promote it. How would they live? Richard could hardly maintain himself on his limited salary. How could he support a wife— especially one who did not have a large dowry to recommend her? Would Richard be so irresponsible as to make an offer for Miss Elizabeth? Darcy would make it his business to find out. If Richard did intend to propose to Miss Elizabeth, Darcy would have to think of a way to tactfully see that they had enough to live on. He would stay out of their life permanently. It would be torture knowing that he loved another's wife. She would forever be out of his reach. But he would hate himself more if he thought that she might suffer want when it was in his power to prevent it.

His stomach clenched as he neared the house.

First things first. He needed to warn Richard about Mr. Collins and Mr. Badger's intended meeting with Aunt Catherine. They would arrive soon.

*\*\*\**

Elizabeth turned the letter over in her hands, contemplating what it meant. It was thick and heavy. She tucked it into her pocket to read after getting Jane's letter. No doubt, it had multiple accusations toward her family, Mr. Wickham, and justifications of his behavior toward Jane and Mr. Bingley. No doubt, he would chastise her behavior toward him. Only... his manners were not accusatory toward her. He had not seemed defensive in his behavior— certainly not so defensive as she had been toward him.

The stump of a tree beckoned for her to end her misery wondering over the contents of the letter and sit down to read it. Who was she to argue against nature?

Finding a comfortable position, she broke the wax sealing the pages together and read. It was several pages written in small, neat handwriting on the front and back of the paper.

She held her breath until she reached the end of the first paragraph, then she devoured the entire letter. Her pulse quickened as line after blessed line answered the questions which had haunted her and explained away behavior she had once thought abhorrent and offensive. Pausing to catch her breath, she began again at the beginning, this time reading slowly and deliberately. Her heart filled with joy and sorrow as she continued.

Every fault of Mr. Darcy's which she had exposed so ruthlessly four days ago was explained in clear, rational terms. He wrote in detail about his past with Mr. Wickham, as well as his recent dealings with that officer. It was not flattering— to Mr. Wickham especially, but also to Mr. Darcy. He shared information with her that, were it known by others in society, would cast his sister out of favor and denigrate his family name, which he held in such high regard. That he trusted her enough to share his family's secret humbled her beyond

151

measure. How foolish she had been to trust Mr. Wickham when he had done nothing to earn her confidence.

He gave examples of occasions when her family had acted indecorously, thus giving him an unfavorable impression. Her face felt hot as she remembered how her father had allowed Mary to embarrass herself on the pianoforte at the Assembly, how her mother had imbibed too much punch and had made assumptions about Mr. Bingley and Jane in the hearing of many, how her younger sisters, Kitty and Lydia, had shamelessly flirted and encouraged the attention of anyone wearing breeches. She even thought of her own attitude toward Mr. Wickham. How easily she had believed him when he had shared his tragic story of woe against Mr. Darcy, a tale which, had he any discretion, he should not have shared with such a recent acquaintance as she.

Her eyes stung at the truth set out before her in Mr. Darcy's script.

Looking about her, remembering that she was alone at the edge of a forest of trees on Rosings property, she began walking slowly into the village. She had much to think on. Mr. Darcy's letter had opened her eyes in many ways, but clouded it in others. How could he have fallen in love with such a contrary being as herself? Surely, by now, he detested her. She had felt uncomfortable at the thought of seeing him after her refusal. Now, she could imagine how he must have felt at the prospect of seeing the woman who had accused him so unjustly of things of which she was increasingly convinced that he was entirely innocent. Stunned by the range of contrary emotions surrounding her, her limbs felt so numb she did not know how she stood.

Walking through the village in haste, she paid for the letter and hurried away before anyone saw her. She did not feel like conversing. She would have been poor company in her present state. Clutching Jane's unopened letter next to Mr. Darcy's, she set out for her reading stump.

So enthusiastic was she to read Jane's letter, she almost tore through the paper on opening it.

Her eyes savored each word.

*April 11, 1812*
*Gracechurch Street, London*

*Dearest Lizzy,*

*I write this letter with the best of news. My heart is so full, I hardly know how to express my thoughts. Mr. Bingley has called at last. Apparently, he did not know that I was in town and the moment he found out, he came to present his card to Uncle Gardiner, who received him gladly.*

*Oh, Lizzy, I had thought that perhaps my memory had glorified him in some way with the passing of time, but he is everything I remember him to be.*

*He said that he will call again soon, and I believe that*

*he will. I will write to you with the details when I am able to.*

*I wish you were here so that I might share my joy with you. Though I do not like to speculate on these matters, I have hope that he will propose eventually. I know that I can share this news with you, though I dare not write so to Mother.*

*Would that you were as happy as I am at this moment, my dearest sister. Then, my happiness would be complete.*

*He tells me that he plans to return to Netherfield Park soon. He said that it was unexpected business which took him away, but I suspect it was the work of his pernicious sisters. It was only when he received a message from Mr. Darcy that he became aware of my presence in town and came to call the same day. If I were not so in love with Mr. Bingley, I would be tempted to kiss Mr. Darcy for the favor he has done me in reuniting me, albeit indirectly, with the gentleman I would marry.*

*I am,*
*Ever your devoted sister,*
*Jane*

Elizabeth grasped the letters to her chest, her breath coming out in sobs and cries of happiness. As her joy for Jane increased, so did her shame in the manner in which she had treated Mr. Darcy. She had misjudged him entirely and assumed that he was proud and as pretentious as Lady Catherine, when, in fact, he was a loyal friend and had been incredibly patient and understanding to offer for her when she had so little to recommend her.

Her heart squeezed in her chest as she realized the gravity of her error. How many times had she cursed Mr. Darcy for his appalling conduct toward Jane and Mr. Bingley when in every other way, he was the man of her dreams? And she had refused him.

She returned to the parsonage in a blur of mixed emotions. Charlotte met her at the door, her basket with *La Belle Assemblée* on the top, and a shawl wrapped around her shoulders.

"I had hoped to walk into the village with you, Lizzy, but it seems that you started out earlier than I did. Did you hear from Jane? Is she well?" asked Charlotte.

Elizabeth embraced Charlotte, allowing a couple of happy tears to escape down her cheek. "Jane is well. She is perfect!" she said with a triumphant smile she hoped would cover her wretchedness.

"You have had good news?" asked Charlotte.

"The best. Mr. Bingley has called on her."

"I am so glad to hear it. I was wrong when I suggested that she encourage Mr. Bingley in his affections. It appears that she did not need any help." Her eyes crinkled up.

Elizabeth released Charlotte from her grasp, righting the basket she had bumped against. "You only sought her best interests, Charlotte, and I shall never forget your kindness and the good intention behind your counsel. Nothing has been said yet, but he has called on her in London and plans to return to Netherfield Park soon. It is a happy ending."

"It *is* a happy ending. Now, we must focus on you, Lizzy. When will you allow yourself to fall in love?" asked Charlotte, as she looked askance at her best friend.

Elizabeth felt the smile on her face fade. Now that she had no excuse to dislike Mr. Darcy as she had before, she realized how dangerously close she was to falling in love with him. The very man she had forcefully pushed away was now the man she most admired. "I fear that I may have ruined my chances, Charlotte." She suffered no disillusions of Mr. Darcy repeating his offer. His good opinion, once lost, was lost forever. And she had done everything in her power to lose his good opinion. Scraping together what pride she had left, she added, "Let me rejoice in Jane's happiness and your contented match before I worry about my own."

# CHAPTER 17

He found Richard in the library, looking aimlessly out of the window, a book in his hand. He started when Darcy cleared his throat behind him.

"Some soldier you make, Colonel," he teased as he joined Richard by the window.

"It does not come naturally to me, Darcy. You know that," said Richard in a melancholy tone.

"Are you well? You sound out of sorts." It was not normal for Richard to be sad. He played the part of the dashing soldier very well. It was a rare occasion when he let his guard down.

Smiling halfheartedly at Darcy, Richard extended his arm to the seating area nearby. Sinking into a chair as if his weight was too heavy for him to bear, he said, "I am well enough. These events of the past few days have me a trifle out of sorts is all."

Darcy understood the feeling all too well.

"I fear that I have news which will do nothing to

alleviate your concerns. During my walk this morning, I chanced upon Miss Bennet. She told me that Mr. Collins followed us into the village yesterday. He overheard enough of our conversation with Mr. Badger to convince himself that you are responsible for the theft of Anne's earrings." He paused.

Richard rested his hand against his head. "Mrs. Shepherd suggested as much, but I had hoped he would not involve himself. Just what I need. More problems. I do not know Mr. Collins well. However, I heard him declare to Aunt that he would find out who had stolen the jewelry with such enthusiasm, I would not put it past him to accuse me before her in an attempt to gain her favor."

The audacity of Mr. Collins never ceased to surprise Darcy. He was so intent on pleasing his patroness, he did a good many things that, if she had condescended to understand, she surely would have frowned upon.

"That is precisely what he intends to do. He is not so preposterous as to believe that he can accuse you without providing proof. So he arranged to meet Mr. Badger here to present his case before Aunt Catherine."

Richard dropped his hand. "You do not think I did it, do you?" he asked, sitting up rigidly in his chair.

Darcy hesitated at his worried response. "No. Neither does Miss Bennet. Otherwise, she would not have taken pains to warn me on your behalf."

He watched Richard closely. Was the shift in his manners a result of his regard for the lady? Or was it relief that he was believed innocent?

"Miss Bennet is a fine lady, if ever I met one. I will have to thank her for her consideration," Richard said as he sat back in his chair.

Darcy wanted to ask the question which burned in his heart, but he could not without revealing his own ardent affection for Miss Elizabeth. So, he remained quiet and brooded.

After some moments in silence, Richard asked, "What do you think we should do about Mr. Collins? Aunt will admit him. She shows an odd favoritism toward him which can only be explained by her incessant need for praise and devotion. Will she listen to you?"

Darcy doubted it. She had ignored him for the most part since their quarrel the day before.

"I think our best chance is to speak with the butler. Simmons is reasonable, and if we tell him that Mr. Badger is not the sort of man to be allowed into the company of Aunt Catherine, he may deny the man entry. Can you imagine what a man like that would do if he saw the luxury Aunt lives in and thinks he has a way to blackmail her?" He had seen the greed in Mr. Badger's eyes at the tavern and he did not trust him.

"The same thought had occurred to me. I woke this morning praying that he had returned to town. If he has any discernment at all, which I suspect he does, he will sense Aunt's aversion to gossip. He would use me to get what he wanted from her unless we can get him to admit that he acts on his own behalf." His distress was worse than before.

"Let us speak with Simmons directly. We do not have much time."

Darcy accompanied Richard downstairs. Simmons stood ready, at the bottom of the landing, as if he expected them.

"Simmons," said Richard in a hushed voice. The high ceiling and marble floors made any voice echo in the entry hall. "Mr. Collins is to call this morning on Lady Catherine along with a gentleman we feel is not suitable company for her ladyship. Our concern is that the man— Mr. Badger is his name— will seek to cause division in our family."

The butler nodded slowly. "He is the same man who came for you yesterday?" he asked.

"One and the same," answered Richard. "We feel it is in Lady Catherine's best interest that he not be allowed an audience with her. My business with him is done, and there is no reason for him to stay in Hunsford."

Simmons nodded again, pursing his lips. "Normally, I would make him wait on the front step whilst I gave a description of the man to her ladyship. That would be enough to send him off without a word. However, Mr. Collins has proved himself very astute. He sent a message earlier this morning to her ladyship."

Darcy sucked in his breath and held it. He had not counted on Mr. Collins' forethought.

Simmons continued, "I do not know the contents of the message, but I received orders from her ladyship to admit both Mr. Collins and Mr. Badger when they come. I cannot go against her direct order." He looked genuinely displeased. "I am sorry."

Darcy looked at Richard. They had no other option than to spend the morning with Aunt Catherine in her drawing room so that they would be present when the men called. Maybe, if Mr. Collins had any sense, their presence would discourage him from speaking against Richard. One could hope.

Addressing Simmons, Darcy requested, "Please be so good as to inform us when Lady Catherine is ready for visitors. We should like to be present when they call."

"Of course, sir."

Having too little time, for Aunt Catherine would descend to her drawing room at any moment, they went back to the library.

Sitting in front of the window with a view of the lawn leading to the front door, Darcy asked Richard, "Who do you think stole Anne's jewelry? I have talked to most of the servants, and the more I hear, the more confusing all this business seems." He would not mention his suspicion of Aunt Catherine until he heard Richard's thoughts.

Richard, oddly, would not look at Darcy. Rather,

he looked all around him until he finally settled on Darcy's boot atop the plush peacock blue and red carpet.

"Let us not talk about that. I, for one, think the whole thing is a misunderstanding which has been blown out of proportion."

"What? How can you say that when, indeed, Anne's earrings are not in her jewelry case? Her room was searched and they were not found. You do not think she has made the story up, do you?" Darcy looked incredulously at his cousin, his growing suspicions toward him warring against his inner struggle with his brotherly loyalty. Richard was not only his cousin— he was his friend. He would never believe him capable of thievery, but Richard's own actions and words made him appear increasingly guilty.

"No. Anne is not a liar." Shoving both of his hands through his hair and pinching the back of his neck, he continued, "I do not know what to think, Darcy. I just wish that this whole mess would go away."

"It is unfortunate that life comes with so many obstacles to one's happiness, but it pains me to hear you speak thus. You have never been one to shrink away from a confrontation when necessary." Where was the fight in Richard? Looking at him massaging his neck, his shoulders slumped— out of defeat or sheer weariness, Darcy did not know— was disconcerting.

"You have no reason to concern yourself further

about this," Darcy said, knowing that it was only true if Richard was innocent of the crime. "Your debt has been paid in full and, with the debt gone, you have no motive to commit any crime."

"They will argue that the crime was committed before the debt was canceled. No, Darcy, I do not trust them. Mr. Badger will sniff out something else to make me lose favor with Aunt Catherine. There is a reason he works as a collector for one of the worst moneylenders in town." Dropping his face into his outspread hands, he moaned. "Oh, why did I go through with it? It was a foolish decision made out of desperation, and I have never regretted anything more in my life. How could I be so stupid?"

Struggling with his own emotions, Darcy tried to reassure him. He could not think his cousin guilty unless the evidence against him was overwhelming. As yet, there were only accusations and presumptions. Darcy determined to discover the cold facts and reserve his judgment until the real thief was found. He hoped with all his heart that the evidence would not point to Richard.

"Richard, you must not despair. You made a hasty decision, something which precious few men escape from doing at least a couple of times in their lifetime. It cannot be undone now, so there is no use lamenting it. We will do the best we can under this new set of circumstances. Trust that you have my full support as we face Mr. Badger."

Richard rubbed his face against his hands one last

time and slowly sat up. "I know how things look for me, Darcy. I am not a fool. Even you must have your doubts."

Darcy could not deny it, but he did not have to own to it either. His gaze never wavered from Richard. "I do agree that your case looks bad from the outside, but my instincts fight against it. I do not believe you guilty."

Richard fell back against the cushioned chair. "Let us hope that Aunt Catherine sees things as you do. I do not want to lose her favor. It is important to me to remain on good terms with her... just as I do with all in our family."

"That is the difference between you and me. I do not care to keep her good opinion— even though she is family. I will not allow her to have any influence in my life. Otherwise, I should have married Anne by now."

Richard opened his mouth to speak, but Simmons appeared in the doorway to announce that Lady Catherine was in the drawing room and the time for Mr. Collins' and Mr. Badger's call was fast approaching.

# CHAPTER 18

Aunt Catherine was not pleased. Darcy did not know what Collins' note said, but it must have been enough to set her against Richard.

"I would not have thought you would give me cause for grief, Fitzwilliam," she said to Richard. For once, Darcy was happy to escape her notice and sharp comments. Not that he wished them on his cousin, either.

Richard stood before her, his arms clasped confidently behind him, as if he was speaking to the general. "I would much rather you hear the news from me than from anyone else. The means of it having been overheard shows a distinct disregard for those superior in station, and I will not stand idly by while I am accused of something of which I am innocent." He tailored his words to appeal to Aunt Catherine's highborn values.

"Smart maneuver, Colonel," thought Darcy.

Arching one eyebrow, Aunt Catherine nodded for him to continue.

"I incurred several debts in a short period of a time. None of them were due to the vices common to those of my age and station. Rather, they were the result of unforeseen circumstances. My horse, as I am certain you heard, broke its leg and it was incumbent upon me to secure another mount which measured up to the high standards of my profession. Such horses are not come by cheaply. This, as well as the replacement of some of my equipment, put me in a position I have never been in before. I was in debt. If that is a sin, then I daresay that there are many others, better than I, who are worse sinners." He stuck his chin up, his stance wide, ready to receive whatever blow Aunt Catherine would strike him with.

"Did you not appeal to your father?" she asked with a bite in her voice.

"I did," was his curt reply.

"Hmm. I see. The rumors I hear about my brother must be true, then," she said with an unhealthy glee common in siblings who competed with each other.

"Why did you not appeal to your other relations?" She nodded her head in Darcy's direction.

Darcy could not help but notice that she had not offered to be a source of help.

Richard answered, "My pride prevented me from doing so."

"Pride? Or foolishness? Darcy would have given you the money," she insisted.

How easily she spent others' fortunes!

"I did not want to trouble him, though I know he would have given me the funds without any questions or rebukes," said the colonel, kindly leaving out any mention as to why he felt it would be a trouble. The truth was, Darcy had had his hands full with Georgiana. Helping a girl of fifteen pick up the pieces of a broken heart while dealing with that scoundrel Wickham had been almost more than he could handle. Though he had chastised Richard for not asking for a loan sooner, he understood his reasons and he was thankful.

"Who is this Mr. Badger, and why is he coming to my home?" asked Aunt Catherine.

"He is the collector for Mr. Volante." That was all he needed to say. Aunt Catherine clutched the arms of her chair and stiffened her spine. She knew very well who Mr. Volante was. Most people did.

"You put yourself under the thumb of a man such as he?" she asked in shock.

Richard's hands clenched behind him, but it was the only display of faulty confidence he outwardly showed. "It was not the wisest decision, but I had no other alternatives at the time."

"Do you not realize that he will take it upon himself to find any bit of gossip he could use against our family and use it to exploit us for fear of exposure?" The color drained from her face, and her fingers looked like icicles stabbing the padding on the arm of her chair.

Richard kept his silence, there not being anything

to say. Aunt Catherine despised gossip when she was the object of it. She feared what people would think of her, knowing that there were those who would mock her.

Darcy stepped forward to stand next to Richard. The thickness in the room was so dense, he felt like a dull knife trying to cut through it.

"Richard, understanding the implications of doing business with Mr. Volante, appealed to me. We covered his debt with Mr. Badger. It is only through the interference of Mr. Collins that he wants to speak with you today. I strongly advise you not to see Mr. Badger. If you accept an audience with him, it will only fuel the fire. As you have said, he will seek out anything that could be used against us. Converse with Mr. Collins, if you must, but do not allow Mr. Badger to cross the threshold." He prayed that Aunt Catherine would see reason.

When she inclined her head back so that she might look down at him despite his looming height, his hope shattered. "You dare tell me what to do in my own home when only yesterday you defied me in this very room? I am shocked at you, Darcy, and will see that you are put in your proper place."

Darcy grit his teeth. She was the worst fool if she thought any good would come of listening to the poison Mr. Badger and Mr. Collins would administer to her. He looked at Anne, who sat quietly on the settee beside her mother's seat of command. Mrs. Jenkinson pulled out the smelling salts and hovered them below Anne's nose. She did look shockingly pale, and Darcy hoped that the conversation to come would not overwhelm her.

The door opened and Simmons announced their visitors. "Mr. Collins is here to see you, your ladyship. He has a Mr. Badger with him." He stood waiting for a response hoping, no doubt, that he would be told to inform them that she was not in or accepting callers.

"See them in," she ordered between pinched lips.

As Darcy and Richard sat, Mr. Collins waltzed into the room with an air of importance to which he had no right. Behind him, taking in every detail of the grand room, was Mr. Badger. Darcy heard him whistle as he stepped over the threshold and saw the murals and gilded furniture.

"Stand before me, Mr. Collins, and be quick about stating your business," Aunt Catherine demanded.

Mr. Badger hesitated to join Mr. Collins in the center of the circle on the rug covering the floor. Darcy had always thought it looked like an archery target, so he understood the man's hesitation. Mr. Collins waved him over from his half-bent position, making sure to only look at Aunt Catherine from the corner of his eyes as he cocked his head up to see from his bow.

"Lady Catherine, I want to thank you for your kind condescension in permitting Mr. Badger to see you this morning. As I mentioned in my message, he is in possession of information which, if known by the public, would set the tongues wagging against your esteemed person. As the leader of the parish of Hunsford, and one who enjoys your patronage, I could not in good conscience allow your name to be slandered when it is in my power to assist you."

Aunt Catherine waved at him to hurry up, bunching up her cheeks in impatience.

Addressing Mr. Badger, Mr. Collins said, "Be so good as to inform her ladyship of your reason for coming to Hunsford."

Only then did Mr. Badger think to remove his hat. The butler must not have been able to pry it away from him. He ought to have left it on, but he managed to smooth over a few strands of hair with his fingers. The rest stuck to his head, matted down.

Standing up to his full height, shuffling his hat between his hands, he began. "Colonel Richard Fitzwilliam borrowed a tidy sum of money from my employer, Mr. Volante. The agreement was for him to pay in full in a month's time, along with a small amount of interest."

Darcy knew the interest to be anything but small. These men took advantage of those who needed a sum in a hurry.

"After three weeks had passed, Colonel Fitzwilliam requested that he be given two more weeks to acquire the necessary amount. Now, Mr. Volante does not normally make exceptions, but with the colonel being the son of an earl, and it being known that he is kin to other wealthy relatives, he went along with the request. However, when he found out that Colonel Fitzwilliam had quit London for Kent, he sent me to follow until he was able to pay."

Aunt Catherine leaned back in her chair, a disgusted look on her face that made Darcy's knee bob up and down so that he had to force his heels to stick to the ground.

After a long pause, she said, "That is all?"

Mr. Collins jumped in, "All, your ladyship?" His complexion deepened against his somber black coat.

Mr. Badger shrunk in stature, the haughtiness he had displayed earlier deflating like a hot air balloon. He must have figured out that Aunt Catherine was not one to be intimidated by the likes of him.

"I do not see why you have desecrated my home by bringing this... man... here to tell me something that families with good names do all the time. So my nephew needed a little money. What of it? He could not pay in a month, so he asked for another week? Let me ask you, Mr. Badger: Is my nephew still within his allotted time to pay off his debt?"

Nodding more vigorously than necessary, Mr. Badger said, "Yes, your ladyship."

She pinched her lips together and gave them a stare as sharp as an arrow. "Then I fail to see what you are doing here, Mr. Badger. You have no business in my home. You have no business in Hunsford. My nephew has paid his debt within the time agreed upon. Now, I must ask you to leave."

Mr. Badger did not move quickly enough for Aunt Catherine's taste. He plastered a smile over his face and opened his hands out to speak.

"Mr. Badger, did I not speak plainly enough? I have asked you to leave, yet you still stand before me. Must I inform Mr. Volante of your visit? I suspect he would not take kindly to the news of his man taking advantage of a highly regarded family for his own benefit."

Aunt Catherine's words had a blanching effect on Mr. Badger, verifying what Darcy had been inclined to think earlier. Mr. Badger's threats at the tavern were of his own making and independent of his employer. Aunt Catherine had called his bluff.

"No, please, there is no need to inform Mr. Volante. He need not know of this. I will leave and I beg your pardon." He backed toward the door.

"I certainly hope so, not that I am under obligation to extend my pardon unless I wish it." Clutching the arms of her chair, she raised her head and said, "And know this, Mr. Badger. If I hear of your continued presence in Hunsford or if it comes to my attention that you persist in persecuting my nephew, you will regret it." She paused long enough for all present to appreciate the absolute silence in the room. "Do you understand my meaning, Mr. Badger?"

"Yes, your ladyship," he said to the hat he still held in his hands. He was afraid to look at her.

Thankfully for him, the door opened, and he rushed through it like a dog skulking off with its tail between his legs.

Darcy would have laughed in triumph, but such expressions went unappreciated at Rosings. He would have hugged his dear aunt and felt generous enough to forgive her snobbery and unbending ways, but she would have been appalled at the affectionate gesture.

The door closed behind Mr. Badger, and everyone turned their attention to Mr. Collins, who still stood in the center of the rug in front of Aunt Catherine.

"How dare you bring that filthy man here! You implied in your note that you had found Anne's diamonds and that it was in my interest to see that man or else suffer gossip. The only gossip I will suffer is when it is known that a lowly collector was received here. Pray that nobody associates his visit with my name." The veins in her neck popped out against her flushed skin. The only other time Darcy could recall seeing her so irate was when he refused to marry Anne yesterday.

Mr. Collins wiped his forehead with a handkerchief. Darcy felt little pity for Mr. Collins. His own presumption had put him in the position he undoubtedly wished he was not in.

Stuttering, Mr. Collins said, "I... you see, your ladyship... it is that..."

"Stop your mumbling and speak clearly," said Aunt Catherine impatiently.

Surely, Mr. Collins would not lay bare the connection between the theft of the jewelry and

Richard's need for money. He would not dare!
Darcy sat on the edge of his seat.

Fortunately for Mr. Collins, he spoke no more of
Mr. Badger and his connection with Richard.

Like Mr. Badger had done moments ago, he
seemed to shrivel in place, his posture ever more
humble and subservient. "I do apologize, Lady
Catherine. I had thought that I was doing you a
service, as I am always looking for opportunity to
do. I assure you that I will never again bring up this
subject, if you will be so gracious as to forget my
grave error."

Aunt Catherine let him sweat for a moment. "I
trust your discretion, Mr. Collins, as, outside of this
unfortunate incident, I have no other complaint
against you. Need I remind you that your living
depends on me as your patroness?"

He energetically denied the need for any such
reminder. "Nay, your ladyship. I am grateful for
your patronage and only aim to please you."

There was no doubt about his sincerity. Darcy,
who tended not to like the gentleman at all, was
convinced of it.

Evidently, Aunt was too, for she dismissed him.
"Very well, Mr. Collins. You may leave now."

So practiced was Mr. Collins in backing out of the
room at half-mast, he wove through the chairs
toward the door and only brushed the tall vase near
the doorway. All the time, he thanked Aunt for her
generosity and praised her name to the high
heavens for her forbearance and forgiveness.

# CHAPTER 19

With a click, the door shut behind Mr. Collins.

Darcy sat back in his seat and took the first full breath he had taken since he had entered the drawing room. His aunt had effectively dismissed Mr. Badger in such a way that he was unlikely to return. She had put Mr. Collins in his place, allaying his interference and dismissing his implication that Richard was behind the theft of the diamonds. He would try harder to think more kindly toward Aunt Catherine. She had done them a wonderful turn. Perhaps, after the reasonableness she had displayed that morning, he could convince her of the folly of her wish that he marry Anne. It was worth a try.

Feeling cautiously hopeful, Darcy made to rise out of his chair.

"Darcy, sit. You too, Fitzwilliam," Aunt demanded, her voice toward them just as frigid as it had been toward Mr. Badger.

It had been too much to hope for. He ought to have known.

"Imagine my disappointment when I hear from my rector about your doings. Why did you not come to me sooner?" she asked.

Richard, who sat next to Darcy, said, "I did not think it necessary. Had Mr. Volante honored our agreement, Mr. Badger would not have set foot in Hunsford."

Aunt Catherine's eyes snapped at him. "But you know very well that money lenders, especially one such as Mr. Volante, are not honorable. Why would you trust him with your problem over me?"

Darcy had assumed that Richard had hoped to appeal to their aunt for a loan. Knowing what he knew now, he wondered what other business he had with her. Richard would never say what Darcy thought at that moment: that it was because he knew she would only refuse him, just as his own father had done. Nor did he have the confidence that she had the sum available. Aunt Catherine had grown accustomed to using her name as credit once she had overspent her income.

Richard said, "I did not want to burden you. I know how much you despise vulgarities, such as speaking of money."

Aunt Catherine raised her eyebrows at him. "True. We are of noble birth, and the mention of common worries is beneath us."

Thus placated in that area, she turned to another. "You do realize what the implication against you was? You ought to take better care of your finances. You are not in a position to spend wantonly and must take care that every coin is accounted for. Your irresponsibility makes you look guilty of stealing from your own cousin."

Richard bobbed his head. Everyone in the room understood the implication. Darcy had thought that Aunt Catherine had glossed over it masterfully. For a moment, he had even thought that she would make no mention of it.

"I understand fully. Mr. Collins would not dare accuse your own nephew of committing a crime in the home of his dear patroness, but he had no qualms about letting Mr. Badger suggest a motive." He held her gaze steadily.

"I am ashamed to think that a member of my family could act deceitfully in my home. I do not think you are responsible for the theft of her jewelry, Fitzwilliam, but you have to realize how guilty you look to others. How will I manage the gossip and idle talk you have caused if it becomes known?" Her face, which until now had been stone cold, deepened in color.

"I doubt much will be heard outside of the village. Richard is a favorite there, and as he is your nephew, few would dare speak against him lest it became known to you," suggested Darcy.

Aunt Catherine slapped a hand against the arm of her chair. "That is where you are wrong. People love nothing more than to speak against their superiors. They feel that it elevates them somehow and puts them on a level plane with our social class. They will revel in the opportunity to slander me, and it will not take long at all for word to spread as far as town— if it has not already." Silence ruled in the room while everyone waited for her to swing down with her ax. "You know how I detest being the subject of others' idle talk, yet your irresponsibility has made me the brunt of their criticism."

Darcy wondered how she could twist everything so that it was about her. Was she not concerned with Richard's welfare at all? Or only so much as it affected people's opinion of her? Darcy took back all his earlier kind thoughts toward her. She was just as selfish now as she always had been and always would be. More than before, he believed her capable of staging the robbery to suit her wants.

"I apologize for causing you any disturbance, Aunt Catherine, but it is done now, and I do not foresee it happening again. I thank you for ensuring that Mr. Badger leaves me and our family alone, but I do not know by what power I can prevent people from talking if it is their wish to do so." Richard spoke in a clipped voice, but he remained civil. Darcy bit his tongue, not trusting himself. He did not have the smoothness of speech that Richard possessed. He could insult in such a way that the offended would thank him for the compliment. Darcy, on the other hand, offended without intending to.

"You owe me, Fitzwilliam. Do not forget it." She

raised her chin and looked between her nephews with a scary sense of satisfaction that set Darcy even more on edge.

"How may I repay you, Aunt? I do not like to be beholden to anybody and would just as soon repay my debt to you as soon as possible."

A sly smile twisted the corners of her mouth up.

Past Richard, Darcy watched as Anne stood shakily on her feet. Her pale face had red splotches covering her cheeks. The sight of his sickly cousin in a state of high tumult made him want to rush to her side before she fell over. Fortunately, Mrs. Jenkinson stood beside her, grasping onto her arm before she swayed too much.

"Mother, this must come to an end. You ought to be happy to have helped Fitzwilliam rid himself of that horrible man. You advise him to take better care of his spending so as not to fall into the same situation, yet you would have him indebted to you? Do you not see the contradiction?"

"Sit down, Anne, before you topple over. You have nothing of value to add to this conversation, as one who does everything in her power to prevent Darcy from proposing, and I thank you to remain silent."

Anne plopped her free arm on her hip, her fist clenched. "And I thank you to stop forcing both me and Darcy into something that neither of us is agreeable to. I do not want to marry him, and he does not want to marry me."

Darcy felt like applauding Anne's boldness.

Never before had he seen her speak against her mother's wishes.

Waving her off, Aunt Catherine said, "Stay out of this Anne. I know what is best, and I will see it done. You will thank me later."

"No, Mother. And what is more, my diamonds never were stolen! It was all a giant misunderstanding."

Anne's words caused a hush in the room. Hope flashed before Darcy. If there had been no robbery, Richard and Miss Elizabeth were safe from accusations. He could join Bingley at Netherfield Park, for surely he would return there so that he might be closer to Miss Jane Bennet. In time and with the opportunity to know him better in friendlier surroundings, perhaps Miss Elizabeth might think more kindly toward him. He would win Miss Elizabeth's favor and convince her that his love is true. He would give her the proposal she deserved, and she would accept it.

"I do not believe you, Anne. What possessed you to speak now when you have been quiet these past two days?" Aunt Catherine asked, pulling Darcy out of his castle in the sky.

"My maid overreacted when she went to fetch my earrings for dinner. Before I could stop it, word had spread through the house. It was so uncomfortable, and I sought to clear the misunderstanding with you, but I could never find the right moment."

Darcy's head reeled. So convinced was he that Aunt Catherine had used the stolen earrings to manipulate him, he could not believe the instigator to be Anne. What motive did she possibly have to hide her own jewelry?

Aunt Catherine scoffed. "What? Is it so difficult to say? Am I that difficult to talk to?"

Darcy agreed that Anne should have set everyone straight days ago, but he also recognized that Aunt Catherine was not the easiest person to talk to.

"If you do not believe me, then I will fetch them myself," said Anne, now pale again.

Richard spoke then, "Perhaps it might be wiser to have your maid fetch them?"

Darcy hoped she accepted. In her current state, she would never make it up the stairs.

Sitting back down, Anne asked for Hortense to be brought before her.

"Hortense, I want you to go into my room. In my writing desk, there is a drawer where you will find my earrings inside their velvet pouch. Will you retrieve them and bring them here? Here is the key."

The maid turned to complete her task.

Aunt Catherine called out after her. "Nobody is fetching anything of value alone in this house. Mrs. Jenkinson, will you go with her? Anne will sit quietly until you return and should be no worse for your brief absence."

Mrs. Jenkinson patted Anne's hands, and joined Hortense.

The clock in the corner ticked the seconds loudly.

Seconds turned to minutes, and the minutes grew longer with each tick.

Darcy looked questioningly at Anne, but she looked just as curious as he did as the time crawled by. They should have returned by now.

Richard, too, fidgeted in his chair. So much rested on Anne's claim that the wait grew heavy on them.

"What is taking them so long? If the diamonds are where you say they are, they should have returned by now," complained Aunt Catherine. She pointed her finger to Darcy, "I know very well who is responsible for their disappearance, and I plan to take action. I am through waiting for you."

Finally, the door opened, admitting a grave Mrs. Jenkinson and a timid lady's maid.

"I regret to inform you, Miss Anne, that the earrings were not where you said they would be. There was nothing. Hortense only found the empty velvet case."

The lady's maid held up the satchel. It lay flat in her hands. Empty.

# CHAPTER 20

Charlotte sat in the chair facing the window, looking without blinking toward the front gate. Alternating between wringing her hands and sighing, her worry filled the room and made everyone else in it tense.

Elizabeth wanted to help her, but she understood the consequences too clearly. If Mr. Collins offended Lady Catherine, the stability Charlotte enjoyed would come to an end. She would be the wife of a parson without a parish. One unfavorable word against him from Lady Catherine and his future in his profession was in shambles. His foolishness and nearsightedness could cost them everything. For Charlotte's sake, Elizabeth prayed that all would end well. Although it was difficult to imagine. Lady Catherine did not strike her as the forgiving, forbearing sort.

"Oh, Lizzy, it is the waiting.... This dreadful,

everlasting waiting." She looked at her childhood friend for comfort.

Elizabeth had to agree with her. "Let us talk of other matters to help with the passing of time. Do you plan to walk into the village today?"

"Yes. I would have gone already, but for this." She waved her hand toward the window overlooking the lane.

"Who do you plan to call on?"

"I want to visit the Thatchers. They welcomed a new baby to their family only last week, and I knitted some little things for her. Then, I need to go to Mrs. Baxter's shop to return the magazine."

Elizabeth looked at Maria. Surely, by now, she had told Charlotte. Maria rocked herself in her chair, looking at the floor. Whether it was because she had said nothing, or because she was ashamed of her mistake, she did not know. If Maria had said nothing, then she would.

"And all is well with the magazine?" Elizabeth asked tentatively, needing to know, but not wanting to upset Charlotte more than she already was.

With a sigh, and another look out the window, Charlotte said, "Yes, of course. I will simply return it and no harm will have been done."

Maria ceased her rocking and looked thoughtfully toward her sister. "Thank you, Charlotte. You cannot know what a relief it will be when everything is set right."

Charlotte smiled softly to her. "Think nothing

more of it. You have suffered enough for your mistake, and I will not add to your misery."

Elizabeth nodded at Maria. So, she had talked to Charlotte. What a relief.

Sitting up like she had been struck by a bolt of lightning, Charlotte said, "He has returned." Unable to remain seated, she opened the door to receive her husband.

Holding her breath, Elizabeth took in every detail of Mr. Collins' demeanor. His shoulders were slumped as he trudged slowly into the room. He took off his hat and fiddled with it in his hands.

Charlotte placed her hand on his arm. "Please, tell us what happened. I have been in agony all this time." Pulling on his arm, she led him to a chair.

He sat dangling his hat between his knees until the maid took it and his coat from him.

"I think that I had best leave the investigation in Lady Catherine's capable hands. Her superior knowledge in handling such delicate matters will soon set affairs straight. It turns out that I acted in haste and her ladyship, in a display of superlative beneficence, sent me away with a mild rebuke."

Elizabeth let out the breath she had been holding, though she imagined that more than a mild rebuke had been administered. Charlotte placed her hand over her heart and smiled in relief. Maria resumed her rocking.

"What a blessing that she should consider you worthy to continue as her rector." Charlotte fluttered her fingers over her heart.

"Yes, her ladyship is magnanimous in her forgiving nature," said Mr. Collins, wiping his damp face.

Elizabeth choked back a chortle. She never would have granted the great lady that particular quality.

She wanted to ask more, but she did not think she could bear to hear it from Mr. Collins. He would draw out ever nonessential and dull detail and babble on profusely about the superiority of Lady Catherine and how honored he was to be the recipient of her generosity. She would wait to ask more details from Charlotte later.

She wondered if Mr. Darcy had been there. Had he intervened on behalf of Colonel Fitzwilliam? Had he influenced his aunt to show kindness toward Mr. Collins? After meditating all morning on the contents of the letter, she would expect nothing less of his noble nature. How horribly she had misjudged him. Her cheeks burned in shame as she remembered the words she had spoken when she refused him. She had been so forceful. So certain. If only she had known...

She looked at Mr. Darcy in a new light, analyzing his actions and comments with her newfound knowledge.

Mr. Collins regaled Charlotte with a circuitous narrative of the morning's meeting, giving Elizabeth sufficient time to ponder. She had to admit to herself that there were times when Mr. Darcy spoke in a way that defied social norms, but now it was easier for her to forgive him for it. How would she have felt in the same situation? Would she want to dance and be merry not long after rescuing a sister from a disastrous fate? Even with her love for gaiety and dancing, she had to admit that she would have difficulty feeling merry after such an event— especially if she were the guardian of an only sister who did not have the advantage of a mother's guidance.

She considered the actions of her family and shivered in her seat.

Only five days remained of hers and Maria's stay at Hunsford. They would leave as quietly as they had come, and the de Bourgh household could solve the mystery on their own. Of hers and Maria's innocence, she had no doubt. If anyone had stolen anything, it was a member of Lady Catherine's own household. Colonel Fitzwilliam, in light of the information Mr. Collins shared, did look suspicious. But he did not seem to Elizabeth to be the sort to steal... and certainly not from his own cousin.

She prayed that word did not get back to Lady Catherine of Maria's theft. Otherwise, the girl would appear guilty. Had Elizabeth not known Maria's character to be contrary to that of a criminal and had she not been at her side the entire time they were at Rosings, even she would suspect her.

Outside of the household staff, that left the Collinses, who were above suspicion in Elizabeth's eyes— Charlotte, out of love, and Mr. Collins, out of his foolishness. He was incapable of delivering a sermon without bumbling the words, much less committing a crime and lying about it. Elizabeth narrowed her suspicions to Miss de Bourgh and her companion, Mrs. Jenkinson. Only, why would Miss de Bourgh steal her own jewelry? It made no sense. She was sickly, but only in body, not in the head. Mrs. Jenkinson had been in her room only a brief time, and it was unlikely she would steal the earrings from under Anne's nose while she was in the same room. Why would she risk her position when she led a comfortable life?

Frustrated that she had made no more progress than before in her inquiries, she let her mind cross the distance to Rosings. What was Mr. Darcy doing at that moment? Had he made more progress than she had? Could he find it in his heart to forgive her?

\*\*\*

Freeing themselves from Aunt Catherine and escaping to the safety of the library, Richard asked, "You do not suppose Aunt Catherine thinks I did it, do you?"

Shrugging his shoulders, Darcy shook his head, "I have no idea what to think right now. It lies with us to find out who is responsible. Has Anne said anything to you? What was all that business about the earrings not being stolen in the first place?"

Richard shuffled his feet. "I am not at liberty to say, though I wish to with all my heart."

Frustrated at not receiving a clear explanation, Darcy pressed, "Now is not the time for secrets.

You do not suppose that Anne is protecting someone, do you? Or could she have faked the theft for some reason?" His questions fell flat.

How did Anne stand to benefit from stealing her own earrings? It was nonsensical.

Richard looked at him sideways. "I think you know the answer to that. She would never do anything to cause upheaval with her mother. Still, it might be a wise course of action to question her. Maybe she knows a vital piece of information which could put this problem to rest." He puffed out air.

Darcy, feeling the need to lighten the mood, asked, "Are you happy now that you made me stay when we should have gone before all of this mess?" He tried to keep the I-told-you-so tone out of his voice, but he failed completely.

Richard rolled his eyes. "Darcy is always right. I will remember that from now on and defer all important decisions to your superior choice."

"Sarcasm does not suit you, but I thank you for the compliment." His smile faded as his thoughts turned toward the guests at the parsonage. "We should communicate with them somehow," he said.

"Who?" asked Richard, though Darcy thought the answer quite obvious.

"Miss Bennet and Miss Lucas. They are not completely out of danger, and there is the chance they have learned something valuable."

"Right. Yes, you are correct, of course. Although, knowing Miss Bennet, she is well on her way to solving the case. She has the sort of keen wit that would make her the ideal investigator." He chuckled and raised his hand up to his chin.

It annoyed Darcy that Richard should feel that he knew Miss Elizabeth. How well did he know her? Had he called on her more often than Darcy was aware of?

Moved by jealousy, Darcy suggested, "I will walk by the parsonage to see if opportunity grants me enough time to talk to Miss Bennet." Darcy realized that he ought to have mentioned Miss Lucas too, not merely Miss Elizabeth, but fumbling over his choice of words would only draw attention to his preference. And that was a mistake he was unwilling to make in front of Richard. Continuing, he said, "You should stay here and keep an eye on Aunt Catherine. I do not trust her. I still think she knows more than she lets on."

Richard looked like he would object, but he said nothing. Darcy went up to his room to change his coat before his cousin could protest.

# CHAPTER 21

Elizabeth sat alone in the front parlor. Resting her forehead against the cool glass, she closed her eyes and listened to the breeze rustle Mr. Collins' prized rose bushes in the front garden. It was the one day she wished Mr. Darcy would call, not that she would know what to say to him if he did. His letter, along with Jane's, had changed everything. But were he to stand directly in front of her, she would not know how to begin to express her remorse. Of course, remorse was not what a man like Mr. Darcy would seek. He did not want her groveling. Then, what did he want?

She tried to imagine how she would feel in his place. Why would she put into writing an explanation that could potentially compromise one of her own sisters? For that was precisely what Mr. Darcy had done. Were she to share the contents of his letter, his sister, Georgiana, would be ruined. Elizabeth could not think of one person with whom she could confide something so precious. Not even Charlotte. Yet he had shared it with her.

The grinding of gravel under footsteps caught her attention, and she opened her eyes. Had her thoughts conjured the gentleman?

Before her stood none other than Mr. Darcy. He peered through the garden just outside the gate and raised his hand to wave when he noticed her at the window. Dropping his hand abruptly to his side, he stood looking at her. He had come to see her. But it was not for a social call. His stance was too stiff, and no trace of a smile adorned his face. More was the pity. Surely, he bore bad news.

Rising from her seat, she wrapped her shawl around her and met him at the gate.

"Good afternoon, Miss Bennet. I hope you are well?" He looked around her and toward the house, as if he meant to ask if anyone else was at home.

"Good afternoon, Mr. Darcy. I am well. Maria has hidden herself away upstairs, and Mr. Collins went with Charlotte into the village." She purposely left out the reason why her friend accompanied her husband into Hunsford. Since Charlotte left, Maria had quit to her room to ponder the consequences of her misstep and determine to do better.

"That is convenient, for I wish to speak to you privately without causing any offense," he said cautiously.

Did he think she thought he came to propose again?

"I have been hoping for an opportunity to thank

you for your letter, sir. It has changed things." She clasped her hands together, giving him opportunity to speak.

When he stood stunned, she quickly added, "I am happy to share with you that Jane is well in London. It seems that Mr. Bingley was unaware of her presence, and thanks to you, he paid her a call." Words were not enough to express her gratitude on behalf of her dearest sister.

Mr. Darcy raised his hand to stop her. "Please, Miss Bennet. I only righted a wrong committed unintentionally. I do not deserve your thanks."

He held his breath and clasped his hands together in front of him. If speaking of the letter made him uncomfortable, she would say no more on the subject.

Looking down the lane, then back toward the house, he asked, "Is there somewhere we can talk freely? I have some information about the missing diamonds."

Her curiosity piqued, Elizabeth opened the gate and led him to the orchard behind the house. The door leading to the kitchen was open, providing some sort of a chaperone in the form of the cook inside. At least it would have had Elizabeth cared to see if the cook was there.

She led Mr. Darcy to a wooden bench under the shade of a tree and motioned for him to sit.

Their knees touched as he miscalculated the distance between them.

"My apologies," he mumbled as he moved away.

Elizabeth opened her mouth to object, but bit her tongue instead and moved her legs over. Her skin tingled at his touch, however brief and accidental. She wondered if he felt the same effect, then censured herself for her vanity. Flirtations were lost on Mr. Darcy, and she should not do anything to toy with his emotions when she had refused him only days before. She had no right.

Too aware of him, of sitting alone with him so closely, Elizabeth tried to think of him as she had before. Arrogant, rude, and taciturn. She focused on his weaknesses to better control her own emotions, but as she looked up to his eyes, her determination melted away. The kindness with which his warm eyes regarded her thawed her cold judgments, so that she looked down at her hands in shame. Would she never learn? She could no longer think of him as she once had. Nor would she attempt to do so. She had mistaken his character so completely, and instead of rebuking her, he had entrusted her with information that could ruin him if she were so inclined. How well he knew her! She would never betray his trust. She was incapable of it… and he knew it.

"Miss Elizabeth," he said in a voice as tender as his eyes.

Elizabeth looked up again, shocked and pleased that he addressed her by her Christian name.

"I do not yet believe you free from my aunt's suspicions. She will lay the blame where it best suits her, and I thought it appropriate to warn you to remain watchful."

Elizabeth shook her head. It had occurred to her that she would be a prime suspect, not being well-liked by Lady Catherine for speaking her opinions so freely.

"I had hoped that you might have discovered something," he said, looking at her in a disarming way.

Uncomfortable and unsettled, Elizabeth chuckled. "Perhaps I should have taken greater care to keep my opinions to myself. Unfortunately, they often run in direct conflict with your aunt's views, making me the bane of her dinner table. I will share what I know if you will do the same."

Mr. Darcy's lips curled up on one side. "My aunt believes herself to be the authority on all things. She gives advice freely and without warrant. She is not accustomed to meeting gentry who do not bend to her will, or who defy her opinions by refusing to be intimidated by her."

Elizabeth smiled at the compliment. Though it did not remove the difficult situation she found herself in, it eased her conscience. There was someone who appreciated her outspokenness.

"You are not intimidated by her either, Mr. Darcy. I had thought you similar to her in manners before, yet I find that you are not the arrogant man I believed you to be. How do you spend so much time in her company? Were it me, I would go mad."

A full smile covered Mr. Darcy's face, and his

eyes twinkled in mischief. It was a look Elizabeth had not thought him capable of, and the effect on her was disconcerting. Her heart played a game of skip rope in her chest.

"I would have left already had it not been for this business of Anne's earrings. Aunt Catherine did not trust the constable, him being a simple blacksmith in the village," he said sarcastically, "so she insisted that I stay."

"And you stayed? Merely because she asked?" She could not believe that he could so easily be swayed to do something he was opposed to.

He considered her for a long time, his smile giving way to a more serious look. His eyes searched her face and settled on her lips. She licked them self-consciously.

With a sigh that sounded painful, he turned his head to face the trees. He said, "That is correct." He looked at her, gluing his gaze to her eyes for a long time as if he would expand on his explanation but thought better of it and chose instead to remain silent. Elizabeth had hoped for more, but she should have known better. Mr. Darcy had never been one to mince words. He seemed to communicate much better in writing.

"I am happy you stayed," she said. She meant it.

Instead of a smile, she was met with such a look of pain, she immediately sought to cheer him up.

"After all, had you not stayed, you would have deprived us of, not only your company, but Colonel Fitzwilliam's as well. He is one of the most polite gentlemen of my acquaintance." She hoped her smile and the compliment to his relative would smooth Mr. Darcy's furrowed brow, but it had the opposite effect.

"My cousin has the advantage of happy manners and easy conversation. He makes friends easily," he said in a low voice.

Trying again to lighten his mood, she said, "Yes, and I take pride in being one of them. It must be nice to have such a man as your cousin and co-guardian to your sister."

At the mention of Miss Darcy, he brightened. "It would bring me great pleasure for you to meet her. She does not often have the opportunity to mix with other young ladies, and I am sure she would welcome a change."

"I would like that. My uncle and aunt have promised to take me with them to the Lake District in the summer. My aunt grew up in Lambton. Is that near your estate?"

Brightening further at the mention of his home, Mr. Darcy said, "It is a comfortable walking distance, especially for you. I wonder if she knew my parents."

It would have embarrassed Elizabeth to reveal that she had already asked for information about Mr. Darcy and his family from her aunt. Noncommittally, she said, "Most likely. I shall ask in my next letter."

Mr. Darcy's smile faded considerably. Had her mention of a letter reminded him of the contents of his? He had been honest with her. He deserved as much from her. Taking a deep breath, she began, "Mr. Darcy, I apologize for drawing the conversation away from the topic you wished to discuss. You asked if I knew anything pertinent to the missing diamonds. Let me tell you what has recently happened here. It bears no light on the identity of the thief, but should Lady Catherine learn of it, Miss Lucas would have to fall on her mercy." She told Mr. Darcy about the magazine, confiding her concerns about Maria and her absolute faith in her innocence to him. He would care for their secret as well as he did his sister's.

He listened patiently, not once interrupting to ask any questions. Then again, she made sure to leave no detail unmentioned.

When she finished, he sighed. "Miss Lucas looks every bit as guilty as Richard. Yet, as conclusive as the evidence is against them, I cannot believe either of them capable of doing such a thing. Surely, they cannot both be guilty, and so I am led to believe that neither of them is responsible. You know of Mr. Collins' visit and accusations, but there are more details…"

Elizabeth listened closely as he described the conversation he had recently witnessed. Miss de Bourgh's admission that the earrings had not been stolen brought some measure of relief to Elizabeth, until it was discovered that the earrings were, in fact, gone.

She sat back against the bench, contemplating

everything he had told her. It was all so confusing and contradictory.

Deep in thought, they sat in silence. Though the missing jewelry should have held her attention, she found it increasingly difficult to keep her thoughts focused on them when Mr. Darcy sat inches away. She imagined having the freedom to talk freely with him and imagined the things they would discuss. When a sigh escaped her lips and she felt her cheeks tighten with a smile, she tried think of the matter at hand. She did not want him to think she did not take his warning seriously.

"I have kept you long enough," he said amidst her struggle of concentration. Rising from the bench, he turned to leave, but turned back. "Please, be cautious, Miss Elizabeth."

She nodded. "You too," was all she could think to say.

Together, they walked up the incline to the front of the house, but she held back as they neared the house to let him walk a few paces ahead. Maria may quit her room to wait for Charlotte downstairs, and it would be improper for her to be seen walking alone in a secluded area with Mr. Darcy.

As she went around the corner of the house, Charlotte stood just inside the open gate. Mr. Darcy's figure retreated in the distance. Had she seen him leave?

\*\*\*

Darcy walked away as quickly as his dignity allowed. Elizabeth, his Elizabeth, clearly admired Richard. How he wished she could think like that about him.

Leaving the gate behind, forcing himself not to look at his heart's desire, who followed him at a distance, he almost ran into Mrs. Collins. She looked as agitated as he felt.

"Pardon me, madam," he heard himself say. She nodded off his concern, which was just as well. He was in no mood for pleasantries.

Were it not for his need to talk to Anne, he would not have returned to Rosings. The last person in the world he wanted to see was Richard. He would only bother him with his playful banter and cheerfulness. Darcy did not want cheerfulness. He wished the clear sky would cloud up and drench him in rain. Then, at least, he would have an excuse for his poor mood. He would blame it on the rain.

# CHAPTER 22

"What is this?" asked Charlotte, her hands on her hips and her face flushed. She pointed behind her in the direction Mr. Darcy had set out.

Her harsh tone raised Elizabeth's defenses. Raising her chin and crossing her arms, she said, "Mr. Darcy called about a matter of importance. His stay was brief."

"Did anyone see him come alone?" Charlotte insisted.

"I do not think so. Mr. Collins is still away, and Maria has not left her room since you departed."

"So, you felt that it was acceptable to entertain a single gentleman alone, while a guest in my home?"

Elizabeth stepped back, dropping her arms to her side. She had never seen Charlotte so angry.

"Charlotte, what is wrong? Have I offended you?"

"Have you offended me? I wonder how you have the audacity to ask such a question when you openly flirt and encourage the attentions of a gentleman you have told me you severely dislike! And, now, I find out from none other than Mrs. Baxter that my own sister, whilst in your company, did not purchase the magazine from her shop. She stole it! How do you suppose that made me feel? As my friend, you should have told me, Lizzy." Charlotte's eyes swam in tears.

Elizabeth could have borne Charlotte's wrath, but not her disappointment.

Stepping forward, she implored Charlotte with open arms, "I had thought that Maria had confessed her error to you. Charlotte, had I known otherwise, I would have told you myself." Oh why, oh why, had she trusted Maria?

Charlotte stepped away from her, snatching her skirt away lest it brush against hers. "And this is your response? You lay the blame on Maria when you should apologize?" She shook her head and scoffed. "And you were so quick to deem Mr. Darcy proud. Have you looked at your reflection in the mirror lately?"

Reaching out again, her eyes burning, Elizabeth said, "Charlotte, please, let us talk about this."

Instead of the meek demeanor she had grown accustomed to with her best friend, she was met with an unforgiving stare. "Do you not realize what you have done by remaining silent when you should have talked to me? You have known Maria since birth! She is not the sort to speak up, but *you* are. *You* should have told me before I unwittingly exposed my family to criticism. Mrs. Baxter knew the magazine was gone, but she could not prove who had taken it. Thanks to you keeping me in ignorance, she now has proof. Mrs. Baxter intends to send a message in with Lady Catherine's housekeeper. She will tell Lady Catherine of the crime committed against her by the sister of her rector's wife. She will call into question our moral character, Lizzy. We could very soon be without a living."

Elizabeth was stunned speechless, her limbs too heavy to move or call out to her friend as she brushed past her to enter the house.

She stood by the rose bushes, thinking that she was the most horrid person in the world. First, she accused a man worthy of her affections of being the worst sort of interloper, and now, she could very well have caused her friend to lose her home by trusting Maria. She ought to have known better. Lady Catherine would not recommend Mr. Collins to another parish. Her horror intensified as visions of Mr. Collins, dragging along a disappointed Charlotte, would be forced to fall on the hospitality at her home in Longbourn until her father met his end. It would be the death of him to see no way out of extending hospitality to his homeless cousin, and inheritor of his estate, when it became known how his own favorite daughter had caused their removal from Hunsford.

Her vision grew blurry, but she made her way back to the bench that only moments ago, she had shared with Mr. Darcy. She sat where he had been, hoping to feel the comfort of his warmth, but the breeze gave her a chill which no matter of wrapping her shawl around her could eliminate.

Dropping her face into her hands, she let the tears pour through her fingers. What a mess she had made. She would find a way out of it, she was determined. But first, she would allow herself to feel every bitter emotion. It was her punishment, her penitence for acting thoughtlessly.

When her weeping turned into sobs, then into a whimper, she pulled out her handkerchief. The soft linen soothed her swollen eyes. She caressed it to her cheek, inhaling the scent of the lavender Jane had wrapped in it as a keepsake. Thoughts of Jane, like the smell of lavender, evoked calm, and it was enough for Elizabeth to gain control of herself. Folding the handkerchief and returning it to her pocket, Elizabeth raised her face. The breeze cooled the heat in her cheeks and dried the last of her tears.

She needed to find a way, first and foremost, to ensure that Mr. Collins kept his position at the Hunsford parish. Charlotte had married him for the security he offered, and Elizabeth could not deny her friend her one desire. If she must, she would seek out an audience with Lady Catherine. Perhaps, if she explained the circumstances surrounding the wretched magazine, she could move the great lady to extend mercy to Maria. With Maria forgiven, Charlotte's position in her home remained secure.

Elizabeth rose and returned to the house. She would not seek out Maria, though now she understood why the foolish girl hid in her room. Instead, she directed her steps to her room to pen a letter to Jane where she would pretend that things were well and only show her happiness for her sister and her change of circumstances. How she wished Jane was at Hunsford with her, but such thoughts were selfish. Jane needed to be in London where Mr. Bingley could continue to court her, not in Hunsford where she would be a witness to Elizabeth's manifestation of her worst flaws. She wished she could talk to her father. He would not fix the problem, but he would have fruitless words of wisdom to share, which would at the least put a humorous slant to her worries and make her laugh. As it was, she walked up the stairs to her room and set pen to paper, hoping that the joy she expressed would seep into her being and her normal lightheartedness would return to her.

A soft, irregular knock sounded at her door just as she bid farewell to her dear sister, who would never have refused a man such as Mr. Darcy in the first place. Jane most certainly would not have offended Lady Catherine so that she was at the top of her list of suspects of thieves either.

Opening her door, she saw a downcast young lady standing with her arms drooped at her sides and her head sagging as a tear dropped onto the floor, soaking into the wood.

"Come in, Maria," Elizabeth invited her. She had little pity for her after the lie she had told, but she had grown up near the penitent young lady, and she would not cast her out of her company so easily.

Maria looked up in surprise. "You will see me?" she asked quietly.

"Of course I will," she said as the girl sat down in the chair in the corner, and Elizabeth perched on the end of her bed to face her. "Maria, what you did was wrong, and I do not understand why you lied about it to me. And to your own sister. Why did you lie? Please tell me, for I dearly want to understand."

Tears streamed down Maria's cheeks of their own volition. She did not sob, and they did not choke her throat to render her speechless.

"I came to explain. I hardly understand myself, but maybe in speaking of it with you, I can see clearer how to set things right. I have made a horrible mess." She picked at her fingers in her lap.

"Why could you not tell Charlotte what you had done? Why did you lead me to believe you had told her?" asked Elizabeth in her most patient voice.

"I was afraid," she mumbled. Looking up, she continued, "Some part of me hoped that if I ignored what I had done, then it would go away."

"Like an ostrich burying its head in the sand," muttered Elizabeth under her breath. In a louder voice, she asked, "Have you talked with Charlotte since she returned?"

Silently shaking her head, Maria resumed picking at her fingers.

"Well, it is for the best. Charlotte needs time to

calm her indignation, but you ought not to wait too long. It could be that, together, you can think of a way to rectify the situation. And it might be a good idea to attempt to do so before Mr. Collins returns. I cannot imagine that he will be more reasonable than Charlotte." Nothing in her past dealings with Mr. Collins suggested that he would show the slightest amount of common sense or reason.

Sitting up in her chair with a determination about her, Maria said, "Until now, I have acted like a coward. I must do my best to set things right. I will go to Charlotte and tell her everything. I realize that there will be consequences to me for my actions, but they could not possibly be worse than what I have unintentionally done to my own sister."

"That is the mature way to see things, Maria, and I applaud you for thinking of how your actions have affected others rather than wallowing in your own misery."

"I have done enough of that, and what good has it served? Charlotte has quite possibly lost her home, and Mr. Collins will make her miserable. He will never forgive her because it was her wretched sister who caused him to lose favor with Lady Catherine. Oh, Lizzy, I do not know how I will live with myself if they are cast out of Hunsford on my account!"

She said the words with such depth of feeling, Elizabeth expected another onslaught of tears. But none came. The well had dried.

Setting her hand gently on Maria's shoulder,

Elizabeth tried to think of what she would need if she were in the same situation. "The first step is always the hardest, and you have already taken it by admitting your error and allowing yourself to see the consequences. Now, go, talk to Charlotte. Do not let another moment pass."

With a firm nod, Maria left the room. Elizabeth heard her tap on Charlotte's door. She hoped her friend would be understanding. It had been difficult to receive Charlotte's wrath out in the garden, and Elizabeth did not know if Maria could bear it. Elizabeth was not one to cry easily, but Charlotte had brought her to tears.

Elizabeth knew that it was wrong to listen, but she could not help herself from trying. But, try as she might, she heard nothing. It was a consolation that there was no shouting or yelling voices to make the eavesdropping easy. The silence made her optimistic that Charlotte and Maria would make peace.

Elizabeth went downstairs to Charlotte's sitting room. There, she would try to find something to do to pass the time and think. Charlotte's sewing box loomed in the corner. Elizabeth had not done any stitching since arriving in Hunsford, and she was not about to begin now. That task was better suited to Maria, who spent countless hours with her white work by the small window in the corner.

A book lay on top of a small, circular table by Charlotte's chair, but it was not the sort of book that interested Elizabeth. Best to ponder the advantages of spinsterhood.

Perhaps she should return to her room. Or she could go for a walk. She should let the fresh air and open space cast their magic on her restless, guilt-ridden mood. Only, she could not leave Charlotte so upset.

Unsure what to do, but sensing she must stay in the parsonage, she curled up in the warm window seat in the front room and waited. She had an imaginary conversation with Mr. Darcy. He spoke of books, poetry, and all the things they had in common. She held his presence close to her, letting the memory of his soothing voice wrap around her like a velvet cloak.

# CHAPTER 23

Two sets of footsteps creaked down the stairs. Elizabeth resented the interruption to her exquisite daydream until she remembered why she waited downstairs.

She searched Charlotte's face, looking for some kindness in her friend's eyes as she passed by, and she was not entirely disappointed.

"Maria has told me everything," said Charlotte, taking her place in her chair by the window. "Unless Mr. Collins already knows what Maria has admitted to me, I do not think it wise to tell him yet. If we can keep him ignorant for as long as possible, we might be able to sort this out amongst ourselves."

Gone was the anger and anxiety, and in its place was a strategic determination that eased Elizabeth's spirits to see.

"We look guilty, Charlotte. What do you propose

we do?" asked Elizabeth, who had pondered the same question over and over.

"As my husband quotes: 'In the multitude of counselors, there is knowledge.' Let us put our heads together and try to find Miss de Bourgh's earrings ourselves."

"How do you suppose we do that? We cannot march into Rosings to search for them," said Elizabeth, curious to see if Charlotte could come up with any ideas she had not thought of already.

"No, we cannot do that. Her ladyship would never approve of us poking our noses into what she considers to be her business, and her business alone— even though she has the audacity to point a finger at us and expect us to go down without a fight. Well, I, for one, will not wither before her accusations." Charlotte crossed her arms and looked pointedly at her little sister.

Raising herself up to her full height, Maria said, "Neither shall I."

Elizabeth added without hesitation, "Then, we are in this together. I have made no secret of my differences in opinion with Lady Catherine. I see no need to start now. She is wrong, and I am only grateful that no formal accusations have been made thus far."

Charlotte leaned forward to grasp Elizabeth's hand and squeeze it. "I love your loyalty, Lizzy, but we need to vow our innocence. If one of us is the thief, we should admit it here and now." She looked at her sister, whose eyes had widened to twice their size.

Maria shook her head vigorously from side to side. "No, Charlotte. I know that I took the magazine, but I would never take something so valuable as Miss de Bourgh's earrings. Besides, I have not set foot in her room. Lady Catherine can say what she will, but I know the truth. And the truth is that I did not take the jewelry," Maria said, her face growing red in her insistence.

Elizabeth added, "Maria and I were together the entire time we played the pianoforte in Mrs. Jenkinson's room. I can attest to the veracity of her words. As for me, I know that Lady Catherine would like nothing more than to send me away in disgrace, but I did not do it."

Charlotte, placing her hand over her heart, said, "I did not steal them either. I have yet to set foot upstairs."

It was time to think of solutions. Elizabeth said, "I had thought to speak with Lady Catherine privately to convince her of Maria's innocence. After all, a magazine full of fashion plates hardly compares to a set of diamond earrings. But I fear it would only be a waste of breath. She has proved herself to be unreasonable and irrational. I think that is why Mr. Darcy came to warn me earlier today."

Charlotte looked stricken. "That was why he was here?"

"Yes. After Mr. Collins left, there was an upheaval at Rosings, and he thought it best to warn

us. So, you see, there is another person who
believes that we have nothing to do with the
disappearance of Miss de Bourgh's earrings.
Otherwise, why should he bother?"

"I am sorry for doubting you, Lizzy. I spoke
rashly, and I deeply regret it." The tears pooling in
Charlotte's eyes convinced Elizabeth that all was
well between her and her friend.

"Think nothing of it. You had every reason to be
cross with me. I should have spoken more openly
with you earlier, and so much of this could have
been avoided. It is I who should apologize to you."

"We are even, then." Charlotte reached over to
squeeze Elizabeth's hand again, and Elizabeth
squeezed back.

Maria, who had sat quietly through the emotional
exchange, suddenly spoke, "Did Mr. Darcy only
mean to warn you? Or did he mean to include my
sister and me?"

Elizabeth thought back. He had not mentioned
the other members of the parsonage household, but
surely he would understand that she would take his
warning to include them. Or would he?

Doubt crept in enough that Charlotte could read
it on her face, though she said nothing. "It is in our
best defense to assume that Mr. Darcy did not mean
to include us. We do not want to pretend that we
have more allies than foes. It would only work
against us. Now, I believe that each of us is clear of
guilt, which begs the question: Who stole the
jewelry?"

Elizabeth had considered the subject in depth and was quick to share her thoughts. "The more Lady Catherine insists on our guilt, the more I suspect her of stealing them just to be rid of us."

Charlotte sat bolt straight in her chair. "Why? She has shown nothing but the most gracious condescension toward Mr. Collins and me. Why would she force us to leave under these circumstances when she could simply ask us to go and give us a recommendation securing our living elsewhere? What does she stand to gain?"

It was Elizabeth's turn to look uncomfortable. "Do you remember the day I stayed behind while you went to tea at Rosings?"

"Yes, you had a headache," Maria contributed.

"That was so. And, indeed, my head pounded by the end of the evening much worse than it did before you left. I must swear you to silence before I continue. Will you promise me that you will not say a word of what I am about to tell you? Not even to me after it is spoken!" she added, to show the import of their silence.

After securing their promises, she continued, "Mr. Darcy called to propose while you were away."

Charlotte exclaimed, "Oh, Lizzy! Imagine, you engaged to Mr. Darcy! But why did you not say anything? This is happy news and could very well mean our salvation. When it is known by Lady Catherine..." she stopped and added in a much more subdued tone, "...when it is known by Lady Catherine, she will suffer a fit of rage because she believes Mr. Darcy to be engaged these many years to her own daughter."

"That is so. I refused him, believing his character to be much different from what I have since learned it to be."

She could see the sorrow in Charlotte's eyes. "You always did judge easily," was all she said, but she may as well have stabbed Elizabeth in the gut with a dagger.

"It is the reason I have to suspect that Lady Catherine hates me and might do anything to get rid of me, punishing my friends in the process" she said, bringing the subject back to her purpose.

Charlotte squinted her eyes in thought. "It is a possibility, but Mr. Darcy does not seem to me to be the sort of man to air his failures. How would she know unless someone told her? The proposal happened in my home, yet this is the first I have heard of it." Leaning forward, she added, "And it will be the last I mention of it, Lizzy. You need not worry."

"Thank you, Charlotte. I do not know how she might have heard. Nobody was about."

"My suspicions lie elsewhere. I know that everyone likes Colonel Fitzwilliam. Before you told me of Mr. Darcy's proposal, I rather thought he fancied you. He is one of the most agreeable gentlemen of my acquaintance, but might that not mask something darker? I cannot help but think him capable of committing such a crime," said Charlotte to the disbelieving ladies in the room.

"Surely not the colonel," said Maria, aghast.

Raising a finger, Charlotte continued, "There are several points against him. For one, he has access to Rosings and the rooms. And with what Mr. Collins learned, we know that he was in need of money. He could have done it out of desperation. Men have done worse things for lesser causes."

Elizabeth struggled to maintain an open mind, and her immediate reaction to come to the colonel's defense without listening to Charlotte's reasons unnerved her. Could it be?

"However, Mr. Darcy covered his debt and came to his aid. I doubt he would have done so if he believed his cousin to be a thief. I cannot trust my own judgments, but I trust Mr. Darcy. Of anybody, he is the one individual who rises above suspicion." Now that her defenses were down, it was easier to see the good qualities he possessed. There were several.

"There is that," Charlotte acknowledged. "But I still think that we should keep an eye on him." Looking to her sister, she asked, "What of you, Maria? Whom do you suspect?"

Hesitantly, Maria said, "I know that you will not agree with me. Even in my own ears, it will sound preposterous. But could it be that perhaps Miss de Bourgh has been lying? And let us not forget Mrs. Jenkinson. She is always with Miss de Bourgh and could very well know much more than she lets on."

It was easier to imagine Miss de Bourgh fooling

everyone than it had been to imagine the colonel guilty.

"Why would she lie? What could she gain from it? They were her earrings," asked Charlotte.

"I am not sure, but maybe she stole them herself for the money she would need to flee from home?" suggested Maria timidly.

"Why would she flee? She leads a comfortable existence at Rosings and needs the constant medical attention Lady Catherine arranges for," dismissed Charlotte.

"How would you like to live as she does? She is so pale and weak, and it seems to me that she ought to try a different doctor. Is that not what you would do if you were constantly ill and never improved?"

Maria had a good point. Elizabeth had thought it before. Why did Lady Catherine only employ one doctor when her daughter's health did not improve? If she had a daughter, she would search until she found a doctor who could offer a treatment she would respond well to. Could it be that Miss de Bourgh yearned to escape, but she got caught taking her own earrings before she could get away?

Elizabeth asked, "You mentioned Mrs. Jenkinson. We have overlooked her, but she has been at Miss de Bourgh's side this whole time. Could she be responsible?"

Charlotte and Maria looked at her like she was mad.

"What? She has access to Miss de Bourgh's room. What if she took them?"

"The question we need to consider is: what motive does she have? She has a comfortable position as a companion in a household which, no doubt, suits her needs very well. I find it difficult to believe that after all her years with the de Bourghs, she would steal from them. They would cast her out, and where would she go? No, Lizzy, the risk is too great for her."

Maria added, "I think she would only assist Miss de Bourgh if it came to that. But I agree with Charlotte: I do not think she would act of her own accord. She stands to lose too much. At her age, why should she risk it?"

Elizabeth chewed on her bottom lip. There was so much to think about. Missing diamonds, livings in jeopardy, confessions, the ache she felt in her stomach every time she thought of Mr. Darcy. Was it guilt? She had felt a lot of that particular emotion that day, but it felt different. More like misery mixed with bliss.

# CHAPTER 24

The first matter of business Darcy attended to on returning to Rosings was to seek out Richard. He was the last person in the world he wanted to see, but he needed to ascertain if anything had happened in his absence.

He found him in the library with a periodical spread out before him, his legs flopped over the side of a chair, nursing a drink.

Coming up from behind him, Darcy shoved his feet off the seat, causing Richard to nearly fall from his perch.

"What?" he found his footing and turned to see who had disturbed his comfort.

Forcing himself to smile, Darcy stood still and waited. It never took long. Besides, it helped ease the jealous monster taking root in his heart to cause Richard discomfort. The brotherly love he treasured with his cousin would never allow him to do anything more.

"What in the infernal blazes possessed you to startle me like that? I nearly spilled my drink. And we know what Aunt Catherine would say if her carpets smelled of spirits." He looked like a ruffled up rooster prancing about, his face red in agitation.

Darcy could not explain why he had done it, other than a need to follow his impulse and break through the tension that swept over him when he set foot in the house. It was such a drastic change after the lightness and calm he felt with Miss Elizabeth. He could imagine her laughing beside him that very moment. She had the most adorable laugh. Like what sparkling stars would sound like if they danced.

With a shove at his shoulder, Richard came to his amiable senses. Darcy stepped back with the force Richard pushed him, but he only chuckled. He deserved it.

"You looked much too comfortable draped over the chair as you were. I only meant to assist you," he said mischievously.

"You, Darcy, are a pest. Where have you been that has put you in such a playful mood?" His face lightened up as he remembered. "Ah, so this is what happens when you pay a call on Miss Bennet. Did you find her well?" he teased.

"Miss Elizabeth is the sort of lady to find sunshine and laughter where there are only clouds."

Richard looked at him with a cheeky grin. "You like her, admit it!"

Growing serious, Darcy answered, "I have no

reason to deny it. I daresay she is liked by a good many people."

Looking at him askance, Richard said, "You are only one of several admirers? Your admiration is merely friendly?"

Darcy did not like where the conversation led. "You certainly must be one of them," he tried to say carelessly. Being a poor actor and hating disguise in any form, he knew he failed. His words had come out sounding exactly as he meant them— as a resentful grumble which Richard would use against him at every opportunity.

Laughing out loud, Richard said, "I will say no more on the subject. I much preferred you when you were in a merry mood and will do nothing to spoil it further."

Darcy moved around to the other side of the chair Richard had sat in. "Has anything of note happened since I left?"

"You are determined to find out what has happened, then?" asked Richard, rubbing his palms against his breeches.

He had Darcy's interest. Richard may not have stolen anything, but he most certainly was hiding something.

"As you should be. You have always held a high sense of justice. Could you stand by while one you know to be innocent is condemned for an action she did not commit?"

"You assume that it was a woman who stole her jewelry?" asked Richard.

"Unless we can prove otherwise, all that matters is that Aunt Catherine is convinced of it. Besides, the only gentlemen to have any access to Anne are you, me, and Mr. Collins. Do you think one of us did it?" asked Darcy sarcastically.

Richard rubbed his chin. "Mr. Collins... hmm... No, I cannot say that I believe him capable of carrying off such a farce. He would have to be a master of deceit coming here the way he did to accuse me, only to have stolen them himself. No, I do not think he could."

"I agree. That leaves the women, but I cannot believe Miss Bennet responsible."

"Nor I, Darcy, though I admit that I do not know her well enough to give proof of my belief."

"What can you tell me of Anne? Do you know why she said that the earrings had not been stolen?" The question had bothered him since that morning, but he had not had opportunity to ask, feeling it more urgent to warn Miss Elizabeth of the goings-on at Rosings. That, and he had wanted to see her. Needed to see her.

Richard cleared his throat. "I am privy to some information regarding Anne, but I am not free to reveal it just yet. Please, believe me that it has nothing to do with the theft of her jewelry. I did know, however, that she had hidden the earrings for a short time. Of their theft, I know as little as you." He stared steadily into Darcy's eyes, willing him to let the subject drop and accept his reassurance for the time being.

"If I can get no more information from you, perhaps I should speak to Anne." He watched Richard closely for any sign of nervousness. There was no time to play these games.

Richard exhaled deeply and sat back in his chair. Opening his hands wide, he said, "That would be for her to decide. If she deems it necessary to talk, then that is her affair. I do not like these secrets and can only handle so much."

Relieved at his cousin's openness, Darcy asked, "Whom do you suspect?"

Richard rubbed his hands over his face. "Do you want to know the truth? I suspect Aunt Catherine has a great deal to do with this whole business. I think she is desperate for you and Anne to marry, and she contrived this means to keep you here. Otherwise, you would have gone."

"You forget that it was you who asked me to stay another couple days."

"You would bring that up. If you must revel in how I was wrong and you were right, then let me oblige you. I admit it. I was wrong." He waved his arms in the air theatrically, making Darcy chuckle.

"Why did you want to stay in the first place? Can you tell me that?"

"I had hoped not to have to ask you for a loan. I had another prospect nearby, but in the end, the deal fell through. It was my way of maintaining my dignity before my richer, handsomer cousin. Can you blame me?" Richard shrugged his shoulders and grinned.

Darcy did not like comparisons between Richard and himself— even when made in good humor. From his point of view, he would come out the loser in a competition. What good was wealth when he had been unable to convince the one woman whose opinion mattered to marry him?

Losing no time, he inquired if Anne could join them in the library, but she was indisposed, thus delaying his conversation with her.

With dinner fast approaching, Darcy readied himself for another meal in the company of his imperious aunt. He wished to speak with Anne privately and hoped to make arrangements to do so the following morning. However, Aunt Catherine could not know of his requesting an interview. She would expect him to propose, and it would only make her increasingly strong insinuations about him doing so all the more unbearable.

Dressing and descending the stairs to wait until dinner was announced, he saw his opportunity. Mrs. Jenkinson would be present when he spoke with Anne, not only as a chaperone, but as another person who was aware of the events which occurred the day the diamonds went missing. She might have recollected a helpful detail, and Darcy meant to find out.

Aunt Catherine and Anne were engaged in conversation, leaving Mrs. Jenkinson off to the side to feign as if she was not listening. Aunt Catherine, who had been in a snappy mood all day with Darcy, hardly acknowledged him as he walked in.

Richard followed closely behind him, and the distraction proved to be enough for Darcy to sit down on the other side of the couch, next to Mrs. Jenkinson.

In a voice loud enough for Aunt Catherine to overhear, he said, "I have some questions I should like to ask you. Might I speak with you in the morning at your earliest convenience?"

Mrs. Jenkinson's cheeks crinkled up, pushing up her eyes until only slants appeared on her face. "Of course, Mr. Darcy. What delicacy of manners to ask about my convenience. That is very kind of you, when you know very well that if you ask to meet early, I would have to acquiesce."

Darcy smiled kindly at the woman. He did not know much about her history, but she had been in Anne's company ever since she no longer required a governess. Living in the de Bourgh household could not be easy for her.

Aunt Catherine resumed talking about whatever it was she was talking about with Anne, and Darcy added under his breath, "I wish for Anne to be there as well. Could we meet in her sitting room at eight in the morning?"

He chose that hour knowing that Aunt Catherine was never disturbed from her slumber before the hour of nine. That should give them plenty of time to discuss matters and for him to depart before anyone noticed. He would not have Aunt Catherine believing that he had proposed to Anne.

With a fleeting glance behind her, Mrs. Jenkinson

said with a twinkle in her eye, "That suits me well, and when I tell Miss Anne, she will be pleased to know your reason for calling."

Darcy's face fell. How could she possibly know his reason for calling? Unless she thought he was coming to propose. He shook his head and opened his mouth to clarify, but could utter no words without causing an unnecessary scene. The butler announced that dinner was ready, and he had no further opportunity to talk with Mrs. Jenkinson.

Aunt Catherine had a good deal to discuss with them at the table during the course of the meal.

"I received a letter today from Mrs. Baxter. She is the owner of the shop in town. Apparently, my suspicions were well-founded about Miss Lucas and Miss Bennet. They robbed her of one of her most expensive magazines after Miss Lucas artfully flustered Master Baxter with her coquetries. Mrs. Collins returned the magazine as if nothing awry had transpired, which was all the proof Mrs. Baxter needed. She saw fit to inform Mrs. Collins of the transgressions of her house guests, and she wrote to me that Mrs. Collins appeared to be sincerely ignorant of the goings-on of her own household. In my mind, that is just as grave an error. I take it as my responsibility to know everything transpiring in my household and in Hunsford. It is my duty to be aware and give counsel where needed."

Darcy noticed every pause and intake of breath as his aunt spoke. He asked no further questions, as Miss Elizabeth had already told him in much greater detail what had transpired. "What do you intend to do with this new information?" he asked when she had finished her rant.

"Conduct such as this, especially from family and friends of my parson who is to be an example in morality, cannot go unpunished. I have decided that it is time that we call at the parsonage on the morrow. They must know who they answer to or else risk losing their place at the Hunsford parsonage."

Never mind that a parson was answerable to God. Aunt Catherine would make sure they understood where their loyalty and devotion lay.

He swallowed a mouthful of wine. "At what time do you intend to call?"

"Certainly not before ten. Though what I have to say is of great importance to them, I would not hasten to bear ill-tidings."

"Ill-tidings?" asked Darcy, his sense of foreboding increasing by the second.

"Of course. Depending on what we find tomorrow, they will have to leave. I will not have a thief on the property."

"You do not think that Mr. or Mrs. Collins stole the diamonds, do you?"

"Of course not. But I have made it no secret to you that I highly suspect their guests of committing the crime against me. Though I dislike Miss Bennet's outspoken character, I think that the fault lies with Miss Lucas. A fashion magazine seems too frivolous for one as plainly dressed as Miss Bennet.

If we find Anne's earrings on the premises, then they would have housed a criminal in the home I graciously improved for them to live in. I could not in good conscience or my fair sense of justice allow them to continue dwelling there when there are others more worthy to fill the role of parson in my parish."

"Find the earrings? Do you mean to search the house? Was Mr. Collins' search not enough?"

"Initially, I trusted Mr. Collins to do a thorough job of searching his home. But that was before I had reason to doubt his loyalty. Perhaps his wife has tainted him to believe that he should seek out her advantage rather than that of his patroness. His lack in judgment will not go unnoticed by me. Or unpunished. No, Darcy, we must conduct the search ourselves to ensure that it is done properly. My reaction will depend a great deal on our findings."

"I can go with your housekeeper and save you the trouble," he suggested.

Before he had time to hope, she answered. "Absolutely not. The search must take place under my direction and instructions. If the earrings are found, I will waste no time in dismissing Mr. Collins from his position and Miss Lucas shall be sent to the constable to be dealt with properly."

The food on Darcy's plate lost its flavor. They would not find the earrings at the Collins' home. Of that he would bet his fortune. But he had to accompany Aunt Catherine while she insisted that their home be searched. Any trust Miss Elizabeth had in him would be lost. She would see him as the villain coming to accuse her and her friends of a crime he knew none of them could have committed. Still, he could not let Aunt Catherine go alone.

# CHAPTER 25

Darcy walked on the balls of his feet down to the door of Anne's sitting room. Aunt Catherine would not awaken for another hour. However, he did not trust her not to catch him entering Anne's room at the worst possible moment, thus increasing her expectation and making his refusal to propose even more awkward.

He had spoken to Richard after dinner, and they had decided that one of them needed to talk to Mrs. Baxter about what had happened at her shop. Since Darcy was to go to the parsonage that morning, Richard volunteered to go into the village.

The door was open and Mrs. Jenkinson stood by the door, ready to receive him.

"How glad I am to see you, Mr. Darcy. I have been waiting for this moment too many years. Her ladyship will be pleased." Her congratulatory smile made Darcy feel guilty that he could not correct her misunderstanding the night before.

"I am afraid that you mistake my reason for calling. I have not come to propose, but rather to inquire about Anne's missing earrings."

Mrs. Jenkinson raised her hand to her mouth, and her eyebrows bunched together in confusion. "Oh, dear me. I apologize, sir. I had assumed…" she lowered her hands, wringing them in front of her. "I had assumed that, after all these years of waiting, that…. Well, never mind what I thought. It is of little import." She turned abruptly, leading him to the seating area where Anne was comfortably settled on her couch.

As her companion of many years sat beside her, Anne reached out to take her hands, holding them between her own. "My dearest Mrs. Jenkinson. You have been so good to me, but there are some things I prefer to keep to myself. However, it is time that you know that I have no intention of marrying Darcy. I do not love him, nor does he have affection for me."

Darcy could see the multitude of questions coursing through Mrs. Jenkinson's mind, but she knew her place too well to ask them. Only one question did she allow herself the indulgence to ask, "What will her ladyship say when she finds out?" Her voice was a low hush.

Raising her head, Anne said, "You leave Mother to me. All I ask is for your support."

Patting Anne's hands and taking a deep breath, Mrs. Jenkinson nodded resolutely, "You know that I will do whatever you bid me. You have become like the daughter I never had, and I would do nothing to jeopardize your happiness."

The women smiled at each other, and it brought comfort to Darcy to know that his cousin had a friend in the household. Aunt Catherine would not take kindly to their news. Not that they ever were engaged, but in Aunt Catherine's mind, their marriage had been eminent since Anne's birth, and she had thought of the scheme.

Darcy cleared his throat. Now that the misunderstanding had been clarified, he had some questions for Anne. "I requested to see you because of what you said yesterday. You said that your earrings had not been stolen; that it was all an unfortunate misunderstanding. What did you mean?"

Anne looked down at her lap, then all around the room— anywhere but at him.

"It was true. At the time, my earrings had not been stolen. I had… misplaced them." She looked up at him, willing him to ask no more, which, of course, only made him all the more curious.

"Misplaced them? Anne, please do clarify."

"It happens all the time. I am rather careless sometimes," she said in a rush.

"Why did you not say anything?"

"I tried to, but once Mother had heard and alerted the whole household, it became increasingly difficult to set matters straight. When all of these horrid accusations mounted, I spoke up only to find that my earrings really were gone! Mrs. Jenkinson and the maid searched where I indicated to them. Just to make sure, I also searched on returning to my room."

"They really are stolen, then?" he asked.

"I hate to say it aloud, but it is so. They are gone."

"Whom do you suspect?" asked Darcy.

Anne's eyes grew large. "I really have no idea."

Darcy sighed. "I am to accompany Aunt Catherine to search the parsonage today. Do you have any reason to suspect any of its residents?"

Anne considered, her face growing long as a thought struck her. "Miss Bennet and Miss Lucas were here with me when my maid found my earrings. I had misplaced them as I am wont to do, and Miss Lucas found them. Hortense put them away that instant."

Darcy looked through the doorway. Anne's jewelry box was arranged on top of her chest of drawers in the corner of her room just visible through the frame of the door. But the jewelry case was not where Anne had sent her maid to look for the earrings.

"If your lady's maid put the earrings in the case, why did you instruct her to look for them in your desk?" he asked, looking between Mrs. Jenkinson and Anne.

Mrs. Jenkinson shrugged her shoulders and looked to Anne.

Anne picked at the lace trimming on her long sleeves. "It was foolish of me, and I know it. I had every intention of speaking plainly to Mother, but could not find the appropriate opportunity to do so. She has been incredibly agitated of late. So, I hid them where nobody would look until I could speak to her."

"Nobody knew the earrings were in your desk?" he asked for confirmation.

"It is a locked drawer. Not even Hortense or Mrs. Jenkinson knew. I do not see how Miss Bennet or Miss Lucas could possibly have known they were there— much less stolen them without the key."

Darcy was well-aware that Anne left out some details. He could only pray that they were unnecessary. Surely, she would not allow someone innocent to take the blame. Why could she not speak plainly? What was she hiding?

Exasperated, he asked, just to be certain, "Did anything in Miss Bennet or Miss Lucas' manners make you think that either lady is capable or desirous of stealing an article of value?"

"No. I enjoyed their visit whilst waiting for the doctor and, had my health allowed it, I would have made more of an effort to become friends. Miss Bennet has the kind of outspokenness and ease of opinion which I admire greatly. Miss Lucas is a sweet girl, who I suspect does not get away from Hertfordshire much." Anne smiled at the mention of the girl. Darcy had to agree with her and, with the exception of illness, could see several similarities between her and his cousin.

Mrs. Jenkinson nodded in agreement with Anne. "The two young ladies have been a welcome

addition to our usual company, and I would hate
for anyone to defame their name. I cannot freely
share my opinion in front of her ladyship, but I find
it difficult to give much credence to her suspicions
toward them. Unless the earrings are found in their
possession, I would not give much credit to it."

Darcy was happy to hear that others doubted
their guilt.

"Very well." He slapped his hands against the top
of his thighs to stand and take his leave.

He had not fully abandoned his chair when
Anne's door opened from the hallway without so
much as a knock. When he saw who stood there, he
almost fell back into the cushioned seat.

Aunt Catherine had her hands clasped at her
breast, a calculating smile on her face. "And so it
has finally come to pass!" Entering the room, her
stiff silk gown swishing with every step, she gave
Anne a kiss on the cheek. Her display of parental
affection startled Anne, and Darcy inwardly
groaned.

She next took him by the hands, holding them
between her own, the stones of her rings digging
into his flesh. "We can talk to Mr. Collins about
reading the banns. He will be happy to oblige, and
given his precarious position here, he will be
overjoyed to have an opportunity to render service
to me."

Darcy could not let her continue. "I have not
come to propose, but rather to ask my cousin and

Mrs. Jenkinson some questions regarding our visit to the parsonage this morning."

Withdrawing her hands as if she had touched unwashed linen, her smile vanished into a cold countenance that bode ill for the day.

"Oh. I see. You did not see fit to alert me to your intentions, but you thought it best to sneak around, so that I would not know what you were up to?" She looked between him and Anne, dividing her blame evenly between them.

Anne wilted in her chair, blanching where only minutes ago she had beamed contentedly at her mother's kiss. Darcy had not seen Anne smile since he had spoken with her and Richard in the garden. Had she enjoyed the same healthy glow to her skin as Miss Bennet, she would have been noted in all of Kent for her beauty.

"I had every intention of discussing our conversation here with you once you were awake and seeing people." There was truth in that, though he had hoped that she would not find out about his visit at all. He had hoped to avoid the scene which was presently transpiring in Anne's sitting room.

"Mother, I feel a headache coming on. Will you please excuse me? I must lie down." Anne departed, followed by Mrs. Jenkinson.

Alone in the sitting room with his vexed aunt, Darcy clenched his fists at his side. The anger he felt toward the woman standing before him choked the words he might otherwise have spoken. So, he stood— angry and silent.

"Have you nothing to say for yourself? I am horribly displeased with your conduct in my home during this visit. You give every indication that you mean to propose, yet you refuse to do so. Why have you prolonged your visit if it was not to spend more time with Anne? Why would you arrange to meet her, and secretly I might add, if you have no intention of declaring what you know very well it is your duty to declare?" Aunt Catherine's icy eyes bore into him, demanding answers he could not give her. No matter what she would threaten him with, he could not marry her daughter. His heart belonged to another.

"Do you ask in earnest, or is this another attempt to get what you want through the implementation of the guilt you suppose I should feel?" he asked slowly, measuring each word before he spoke. He would not risk any more misunderstandings.

She sniffed and lifted her chin.

"I wish Anne great happiness, but she will not find it with me. She has made that clear, and I suggest you take more of an interest in her wants than in forcing her to bend to your will. As for me, my heart will not be denied. I love one woman, and I shall love her until my last breath, though she would not have me."

Aunt Catherine stepped back, horror stricken. "You would waste your life and your fortune on someone so undeserving as to refuse an offer from you? Why would you want such a woman as a wife?"

Thanking the stars above that Aunt Catherine had not asked who the object of his affection was, he said, "I cannot give up hope that I might win her heart yet. She is worth the struggle." Before she could ask anything further, he bowed. "If you want to leave at the assigned hour, I must attend to some business." Never mind what business that might be, but it needed attention. He was done answering her questions, and he would not degrade Miss Elizabeth by speaking of her to someone who did not appreciate affairs of the heart. It was only wasted breath against a brick wall.

# CHAPTER 26

It came as no surprise to see Lady Catherine's opulent coach with her family crest emblazoned on the side stop in front of the parsonage.

Mr. Collins yelled from his book room facing the road, "She has come!" He came out of his study — the happy, self-satisfied smile of a man ignorant of the goings-on of his own house covering his oblivious face.

Charlotte looked up from her knitting. She was finishing a pair of socks for baby feet in an ambiguous yellow color. Elizabeth had not thought to ask them who they were for until that moment, then felt guilty for allowing her thoughts to be so distracted that she had not thought to do so until the worst possible moment. She would ask later.

Maria, who had neglected her white work the past day, set aside the novel she had attempted to read between dreamy-eyed stares out of the small window and her audible sighs.

Elizabeth put away her quill and papers, setting them on top of the table near the sewing box in Charlotte's sitting room.

Standing up in unison with her friends, they went into the front parlor. Charlotte looked nervous, as did Maria. Mr. Collins knew nothing of the stolen magazine, and Charlotte had hoped to keep it from him.

One look at Lady Catherine's face as she descended from her carriage with the help of Mr. Darcy increased her anxiety all the more. She squeezed Charlotte's hand on one side, and Maria's on the other.

Mr. Darcy appeared grave indeed.

Mr. Collins opened the door before they could knock, such was his eagerness to receive his beloved patroness.

"What an honor that you should call at my humble home, Lady Catherine. Such a privilege is worthy of the finest refreshment we are capable of offering, though it be nothing in comparison to the bounties proffered at your table." Calling the maid, he ordered that she bring in some tea and the little bit of sugar he allowed himself to indulge in for the benefit of one who had little appreciation for their frugality. Not once had he offered sugar for their tea at the breakfast table.

Sitting in the chair he normally sat in, Lady Catherine said, "Some news from Hunsford has been brought to my attention, Mr. Collins. It seems that you have not taken care to oversee your household in the manner expected of one in your position." She stopped to breathe, her manners agitated.

Mr. Darcy continued before she could. "Our inquiries of the household staff are complete, and it only befits a thorough investigation to question the remainder of those who have visited Rosings since the diamond earrings went missing. That has led us here."

Lady Catherine glared at Mr. Darcy, but Elizabeth could not help but rejoice at how effectively he had cut her off. She looked down at the floor in an attempt to hide her smile. She was certain that one lady in the room would find it incredibly inappropriate.

Feeling someone's eyes piercing into the top of her head, she looked up when she had regained her composure. Lady Catherine glowered at her as she continued, "As my nephew pointed out, we have come to investigate. Now, Mr. Collins, I know that you effected your own search recently, so I know that you will have no qualms when I recommend another one. When your maid returns with our tea, I will instruct her to search each room along with my most trusted housemaid under Darcy's watchful eye. I will remain here until the search is complete." No doubt enjoying her tea and sugar as the house was ravaged yet again in a search for something that would not be found.

Elizabeth looked at Mr. Darcy. He hid it well, but the tips of his ears had turned red. So, she was not the only person in the room to be shamed by her family. This newfound discovery comforted her, and when he met her glance, she smiled encouragingly to him. It was how she would have preferred he react before the crass comments of her mother, the excruciating indifference of her father, the over-exuberant displays of poor instrumentation by Mary, and the blatant flirtations of her two youngest sisters. She would be kinder than he had been, for though he witnessed the worst her family had to offer, he still saw fit to respect her and Jane. He had misunderstood Jane, but he was not so proud to have refused her correction, though poorly given. His honor and sense of justice had set the problem right. All of this, and Elizabeth had no doubt that he had come with Lady Catherine not only to offer his assistance in the investigation, but to soften her cantankerous blows to those who would be most affected by them. Elizabeth's respect for him grew as surely as her breath escaped her in his presence.

Charlotte said, "Mr. Collins, I suggest that we let Miss Elizabeth accompany the maids as they look upstairs. Maria and I shall remain with you as you entertain our guest. Do you mind, Miss Elizabeth?"

Elizabeth knew what Charlotte was about. Several times in Meryton, she had suggested that Mr. Darcy preferred her, and she knew of his proposal. If Lady Catherine suspected any such thing, she would surely object. But she did not. She seemed to be glad that she would not have to endure her company any longer than necessary.

They entered the first room— her own— and Mr. Darcy spoke, "Miss Elizabeth, I must apologize for my aunt's behavior. She is convinced that we will find the earrings here today. She has even ordered an older carriage to wait outside so that her own coach might not be corrupted by having a thief transported to the village constable in it. She shall leave here disappointed."

The thought of her bringing two carriages was so ridiculous, Elizabeth tried to stifle a giggle. Not completely successful, she covered her mouth to keep the noise down. She did not want to get Mr. Darcy into trouble by drawing Lady Catherine's attention upstairs.

Under Lady Catherine's maid's watchful eye, Betsy searched everywhere. Mr. Darcy, too, watched but had the delicacy to turn his back when she got to certain articles of clothing, saying that he trusted the maids' judgment when they declared that nothing was found.

"If I ever am tempted to steal valuable jewelry, Mr. Darcy, I shall know where to hide it," Elizabeth teased, trying not to feel awkward standing in the room where she slept. She knew that— considering the gravity of the situation— she ought not to make light of it, but she could not help herself.

With his lips curled upward, he said, "You ought not say such things, or else I will suggest that Aunt Catherine conduct the search herself."

Raising her hands up, she said, "Pray do no such thing. I am not afraid of her, but Charlotte would be miserable." The mention of her friend's name and the seriousness of Mrs. Baxter's accusation against Maria made Elizabeth ask, "Has Lady Catherine's opinion of my cousin and Mrs. Collins changed in any way lately?"

Mr. Darcy's smile melted away to show his concern. "Mrs. Baxter sent her a message. I surmise you know what she wrote."

Elizabeth nodded. "It was a foolish mistake made by a silly girl offered more freedom than she is accustomed to. She has learned her lesson, and she is not the kind to repeat the same mistake."

"Do you think Miss Lucas capable of stealing worse?" he asked.

"Absolutely not. She is a girl who has never stepped off the straight and narrow path. When opportunity and temptation collided, it proved to be too much. But I can tell you in all truthfulness that her conscience has tormented her since. The experience startled her so greatly, she will never allow herself to stray again. I believe that with all my heart."

That seemed to be enough to convince Mr. Darcy. As they moved to Miss Lucas' room, the search continued in the same manner. Attention was given to every detail— not that there was much to give with the room's simple furnishings.

After some moments in nervous silence, as they oversaw the search of Miss Lucas' room, Elizabeth asked, "Mr. Darcy, do you think your aunt has any inclination toward dismissing Mr. Collins from his responsibilities as the rector? I have been quite anxious on the subject of late." Wringing her hands, she waited longer than she had hoped for him to respond.

She wanted him to reassure her that nothing was amiss; that his aunt, for reasons unknown to anyone else, would act like a friend toward her cousin and his wife; that her worry was unheeded. But no such reassurances came.

His silence answering more clearly than any words he could have pronounced, Elizabeth pursed her lips to keep her tumult in check.

Turning toward her, he reached out as if he would touch her gloveless hand. He stopped himself just in time, leaving Elizabeth's fingers twitching. She clasped them together.

"Miss Elizabeth, I do not for a moment believe that the earrings will be found here. Thus, your friend's home is secure. It is, and has been, my firm opinion that the earrings are merely a ploy used by my aunt to keep me here. Otherwise I should have left a week ago."

He had proposed a week ago. Regret filled Elizabeth's heart as she saw the hurt in his eyes, the same expression he wore before stepping out of the front parlor. He remembered too. Would she answer differently now? Now that she had cast her own prejudices aside to see the man as he really was? The speed with which she had accepted others' gossip and snide remarks shamed her, and she felt the heat rise in her cheeks. She was glad he had stayed and honored that he cherished her good opinion enough to explain his actions in a letter. But, he would have gone…

Her throat felt tight, but she asked the question, "You would have gone? So soon?"

Mr. Darcy's head rose to give her his full attention; his expression was one of hope.

Lady Catherine's maid pronounced firmly, "There is nothing here, sir. Shall we inspect the master's room next?"

Mr. Darcy nodded, never once looking away from Elizabeth. She felt warm from the intensity of his gaze.

She tried to pay attention to the actions of the maid, but it grew increasingly impossible not to look at Mr. Darcy. He did not even attempt to distract his gaze, his mouth open like he wished to say something but was uncertain how to proceed. Elizabeth, unlike herself, found that she had no words either. So much could be said, but how to begin? This was hardly the time or place, and there were other matters which demanded their complete concentration.

Her attention was caught as Betsy held up a collection of baby bonnets, gloves, socks, and gowns on a chair on Charlotte's side of the bed. There was enough there for a newborn.

As realization hit, she reached out and smacked Mr. Darcy across the arm in her shock. How had she not seen it before? "Oh, I do apologize. The realization hit me rather violently," she tried to justify. She could not help but appreciate how solid he felt under her touch.

Mr. Darcy rubbed his arm and chuckled. "Thank you for the reminder that I ought not stand so close." Dramatically taking a large step away, he smiled and continued rubbing where she had hit him.

Playful banter felt much more comfortable at that moment than the serious thoughts she had entertained over the past few minutes. She embraced the humor wholeheartedly.

"It is the best of news, and now that I see the evidence, I wonder why I did not see it before. Look at the clothes on the chair."

Mr. Darcy nodded with a happy smile. "The only way to be certain is to confirm it with Mrs. Collins herself. It is all the more reason to end this search and this nonsense with my aunt so that Mr. Collins' position is secure and no harm is done to your friend's security."

Conspirators in their newfound knowledge, they returned downstairs of lighter heart than when they had gone up.

The Rosings maid looked to them for instruction, clearly wanting her work to be over, so that she could attend to her normal tasks.

"Since it is the ladies whom her ladyship suspects, let us go into the sitting room," suggested Elizabeth once they stood in the front parlor.

Curious faces looked toward them. All except Mr. Collins, who soliloquized on the advantages of raising their own pig over buying butcher meat. Lady Catherine appeared bored and ready for any interruption on the subject on which she had advised Mr. Collins several times. As if she were an expert on raising livestock.

Mr. Darcy was left no option but to interrupt Mr. Collins to inform them, "We have found nothing, nor do I suspect we shall."

Lady Catherine harrumphed, and Mr. Collins continued, switching from swine to his precious rose bushes in the front garden.

Charlotte's room being small, and having little besides some chairs, a table, and her sewing box to occupy it, the maid did her work quickly. Not that anybody besides Lady Catherine thought she would find anything.

The great lady, growing tired of the one-sided conversation in the parlor, soon waltzed into the room to admire the recent improvements she had given the space. She inspected the paper on the walls and set about telling Charlotte how better to arrange the room.

"I wonder why you should choose this room in the back of the house for your use. The light is not so good as the front, and I wonder how you are able to do any needlework, reading, or writing in here," she commented, unconcerned with the fact that she was the one responsible for the positions and proportions of the rooms.

"Mr. Collins needs the daylight much more than I do for his reading. That is why I chose this room for my own particular use. However, I do spend a good deal more of my time in the front parlor. The window seat you added was such a lovely detail," said Charlotte smoothly.

Satisfied, Lady Catherine continued about the room. "Darcy, are we done? There are other matters which require my attention at Rosings."

The search was being called to an end. Glory be!

Interrupting Elizabeth's high humor at Lady Catherine's attitude toward the Collins, the Rosings maid said, "There is only the sewing box in the corner to check."

The maid, determined to complete her assigned task no matter how fruitless, moved Maria's white work draped over its lid and flipped the top open to rummage through the bits of lace and thread neatly arranged in their compartments. When she reached the buttons, she froze. She looked as if she had come upon a cockroach hidden in the buttons.

"What is it, Betsy?" asked Charlotte, thus sending her housemaid over to see what the fuss was about.

Betsy peeked into the box, then backed up against the wall, speechless.

Everyone stood fixed in place, wondering what could have affected the women so greatly.

Elizabeth, unafraid of unsightly insects, walked over to the box and her heart felt like it would leap out of her chest. Mixed into the buttons, she saw a set of sparkling diamonds.

# CHAPTER 27

"What is it, Lizzy?" asked Charlotte. Elizabeth heard her steps crossing the room to join her.

Spinning around to face the audience, which now included every inhabitant of the house as well as their visitors, Elizabeth reached into the box to grab the earrings with one hand and held her other out to stop anyone from nearing.

With one regretful look at Mr. Darcy, she addressed Lady Catherine. "I know where the earrings are, but I will not give them to you until I have your promise that what I am about to reveal to you in no way affects the inhabitants of this parsonage."

Lady Catherine balked. "Whose white work is that on top of the case?" she asked.

Ignoring her question, Elizabeth repeated, "Do I have your promise?" Trying to add more weight to her negotiation, Elizabeth held the earrings out in front of her, pinching the tops so that the delicate diamond drops dangled and cast rainbows against the wall. Everyone admired her find, but she pulled her arm back so that they were out of reach. She would not risk them being snatched away until she had secured Charlotte's home.

"Elizabeth—," started Mr. Darcy, his hand held out as if he would help her.

How she cherished hearing him call her by name, but it was a dreadful mistake.

Lady Catherine, her face red, looked between the two of them. "I see," she hissed.

A hush pervaded the room. Elizabeth watched as the heat in Lady Catherine's aspect chilled. In a voice as cold as ice, she asked, "Do you really think that you have the power to negotiate? It is obvious to me who took the earrings and hid them away in her sister's sewing box. You have made it clear through your speech and example that you possess none of the accomplishments a lady capable of doing fine white work has." She cast a withering stare at Maria, who did her best to disappear in the corner she stood in.

Raising her head and steeling her voice, Elizabeth said, "Yet, I am the one holding the earrings. On my honor, I will not give them to you until I have your promise that the Collinses' position under your patronage remains unchanged."

Mr. Darcy stepped toward his aunt. In a calm voice, he said, "The earrings are worth much more than the price of this harmless promise. You have no doubts about the devotion of Mr. and Mrs. Collins."

The color of her complexion soothed, Lady Catherine, never one to give up the final word, said, "I will promise that Mr. Collins continues here with his wife so long as word of the events of the past few days does not spread. There is something particular I should like to discuss with you and him." Her eyes glinted in satisfaction at Mr. Darcy. Looking overly pleased with herself, she said, "I have a carriage outside to haul the thief to the village constable. Darcy, be so kind as to escort Miss Lucas out to the carriage."

Worry filled Elizabeth. What scheme had Lady Catherine conjured in her mind, so that she agreed so easily? Elizabeth sensed that she had complicated matters for Mr. Darcy. Oh, when would she make a decision that did not lead to disaster? She clutched the earrings in her hands.

Maria, as white as her neglected embroidery, sunk to her knees before Mr. Collins, who stood next to her, could react. Mr. Darcy helped her into a chair. It was all Elizabeth could do to not allow her eyes to linger on him. She had a horrible presentiment that he was lost forever to her. That would please her ladyship.

Forcing down her anxious thoughts, Elizabeth focused on Charlotte. Her dear, sweet friend of many years held a handkerchief to her mouth as tears ran down her hands.

Elizabeth begged Lady Catherine, "Why do you

assume Miss Lucas committed the crime? It could not possibly have been her doing."

"I am not a fool, Miss Bennet, and I thank you not to insult my intelligence. I know that Miss Lucas stole a valuable magazine from Mrs. Baxter's shop. I know she had access to Anne's room and was present when her diamonds were put into her jewelry box. She knew where to find them, and she hid them in a place so open to the other members of the parsonage, they were sure to remain undiscovered unless I insisted on this search. That, Miss Bennet, is why she must go to trial to pay for her crimes against me. Now, hand over the diamonds." Her words came out like the crack of a whip, and Elizabeth flinched every time the lady pronounced her name with such derision.

Maria rocked back and forth in her chair, weeping loudly, unable even to defend herself. Charlotte, Elizabeth could see now, had rallied her strength and would soon make her stand against her patroness in defense of her sister. Elizabeth could not let her fall into disfavor with Lady Catherine— not at the price of her home when she was convinced that her friend's family would have a new member before the end of the year. Not while it was in her power to prevent it.

"No!" she exclaimed over the weeping and exclamations in the room. "You cannot send Maria away when it was me who stole the earrings. It is me you should send away, not her!" Her chest heaved, and she blinked her eyes furiously to hold the tears back. She would not cry in front of Lady Catherine.

Mr. Darcy stepped forward, his hands out, but he stopped himself short, the emotions on his face changing as quickly as Elizabeth could feel them in her own breast. She whispered so low, only he could hear. "I am sorry."

Lady Catherine's arm extended, her fingers pulsing up and down in expectation. Elizabeth thrust the odious earrings into her waiting hand.

In a calculating voice, Lady Catherine asked, "You openly confess before the witnesses in this room that you are the thief?" She inspected the earrings in her grasp and slid them inside the velvet pouch she had brought in anticipation of their discovery.

Elizabeth nodded. She would not say the words unless forced to.

With a haughty sneer, Lady Catherine asked, "When did you take them? How did you do it?"

"I took them the same day Miss de Bourgh's doctor came. It was not difficult, nor shall I bore you with the details." She did her best to keep the waver out of her voice. Never in her life did she think she would have to convince someone of a lie like this.

"Why are you admitting to something it is impossible for you to have done?" asked Mr. Darcy.

She loved him all the more for coming to her defense, but she could not allow it at the expense of her friends. Her eyes never wavering from his, she said, "I am known to be careless and not take things so seriously as I ought to. I can only hope that, if given another blessed chance, I would have reacted differently." She watched him closely. Did he understand her meaning? Could he save her from the agony she felt, trapped as she was between despair and hope? Was she worth the bother?

"Take her to the carriage, and see that she is kept under the constable's watch. Mr. Collins, I will send for you later. There are some plans we need to discuss." With that said, Lady Catherine stormed out of the parsonage.

Mr. Darcy assumed control once she had gone. Everyone was in such a state of shock, they could have heard a pin drop.

"Mr. Collins, will you accompany Miss Elizabeth and myself into Hunsford? Mrs. Collins, perhaps you could stay here with Miss Lucas? She looks like she needs some sisterly reassurance. I will send the carriage back for Miss Elizabeth's trunk. Can you please see that her belongings are packed?"

Elizabeth felt sorry for Maria. Had Mr. Darcy not helped her into a chair, there was no doubt that she would still be in a crumpled heap in the corner of the room. As it was, she reminded Elizabeth of the dolls she and Jane had made their younger sisters out of stuffed bits of fabric. She sagged in her chair, unable to even hold her head up.

Between sobs, she muttered, "I am so sorry. I am so sorry," over and over.

Elizabeth rested her hand on the girl's shoulder.

"I know you did not do it, Maria. As for me, I will have to trust that the real thief is found before a trial is arranged." She looked imploringly at Mr. Darcy, lingering over his features, so that she could remember every detail. If anybody could find out who was responsible, he would. Not that it mattered much. Even if she were granted freedom, she feared he was lost to her.

The muscles at his jaw and temples tensed, and the determination on his face was unmistakable. It brought her comfort.

Charlotte, silent tears flowing down her cheeks, grabbed Elizabeth, hugging her so violently, she struggled to keep them on their feet.

"Oh, Lizzy. What have you done?" With a kiss on her cheek, she backed up to stand at arm's length.

"Nothing more than you would have done. Of course, you would have had more sense than I have shown and would have avoided this mess completely, I daresay." Elizabeth tried to smile.

"You would laugh at a time like this," Charlotte said through a choked voice.

Mr. Collins cleared his throat. "My dearest Charlotte, why do you not sit in the front parlor with our sadly repentant sister? I will order some tea to be brought in for you."

Elizabeth, who had started toward the door to the carriage, paused mid-step. She looked at her cousin— the same man whose false humility and absurdity made him the cause of ridicule to many, including herself. Yet, there he stood, reaching out to take Charlotte's hand to tenderly caress it. Elizabeth had not seen any affectionate exchanges between the newly married couple before this, but the tender display he showed his wife in that moment, and her sweet acceptance of it, made her think kindlier toward Mr. Collins. Her sacrifice seemed more worthwhile somehow.

Her noble thoughts lost their strength the closer they got to the carriage. No longer could Elizabeth enjoy what she had helped her dear friends gain, as the implications of her rash action trickled in.

Mr. Darcy sat opposite her with Mr. Collins at his side.

She did not have it in her heart to regret what she had done. Her loyalty to her friends was too strong. But it did not prevent the regrets of all she had lost from tormenting her.

Wanting to break the silence— to do anything to distract herself from her own imaginings, she opened her mouth to speak. But what could she say?

"I am sorry, Mr. Darcy. I think I may have complicated things further for you."

Mr. Darcy looked at her much the same way he had the day she had mercilessly and unjustly accused him of the worst evils she could cast against his character in her eyes.

"It is nothing I cannot manage. My aunt will have to learn to live with her disappointment," he replied with a melancholy smile.

"Cousin Elizabeth, I..." Mr. Collins began.

For a man who never suffered from a lack of words, his pause caught Elizabeth's attention more than a sermon would have. She pulled her eyes away from Mr. Darcy and braced herself for the lecture which was sure to come.

"...I want to thank you," he finished. "There are details which I will get clarification on from Charlotte upon returning to my home, but I do realize what you did for us today. Thank you for securing my living. We expect a little olive branch in some months, and I despair to think what would have happened to us had we been cast out of Hunsford."

So, she had read the signs correctly. The joy he and Charlotte would experience brought a bittersweet smile to her face.

"Thank you, Mr. Collins," she managed to say through the lump of lost hopes balling up in her throat.

Mr. Darcy said nothing at all. She did not sense disapproval from him. His frequent glances in her direction bore no judgments. Still, she wished he would say something. Anything.

They arrived in short time to the blacksmith's shop. He worked outside, pounding on a chunk of red hot metal. He waved and smiled as Mr. Darcy got out of the carriage.

Elizabeth did not expect Mr. Darcy to assist her—a confessed criminal— but he did. In her haste to leave, she had forgotten her gloves. The touch of his skin against hers sent chills up her spine and through her limbs. She gasped at the current running through her.

The blacksmith, appropriately named Mr. Smith, dunked his metal in a bucket of water, set it to the side, and came over to greet his visitors.

"Good day, Mr. Darcy. Miss Bennet," his look grew in confusion as he acknowledged the third passenger of the Rosings carriage. "Mr. Collins," he nodded. Mr. Smith looked at the group before him.

Mr. Darcy stepped forward and spoke in a tone low enough for only them to hear, "Mr. Smith, I apologize for troubling you. We have come to you about a matter of the utmost delicacy. Might you have some minutes to spare?"

"Aye, Mr. Darcy. I would nary refuse you." He stood with his feet planted widely, clearly expecting the discussion to take place in his open shop on the main lane running through the village.

Looking around him for onlookers, Mr. Darcy asked, "Might we go where we will not be overheard?"

Slapping his hands against his work-worn trousers, Mr. Smith slid the heavy, leather apron over his head and hung it on a hook. "Let us go to the house. The missus will be glad to offer you what we have in the way of refreshment." He turned and led the way to the small residence behind his shop.

Laundry hung on lines peeking out from behind the house. Mrs. Smith, her hands red and chapped, came bustling up to meet them at the call of her husband.

"Nelly, be so good as to bring out some of your small ale for our guests, will you, love?" he asked.

She curtsied to everyone and exchanged welcomes to her humble home before she hurried to the kitchen.

Mr. Smith closed the door, standing in front of it with his thick arms crossed after everyone was seated.

Elizabeth sat on a wooden bench with room enough for herself and Mr. Collins. Mr. Smith insisted that Mr. Darcy sit in what must be his chair. It was larger than the rest.

"What is the reason for your visit, Mr. Darcy?"

Mr. Darcy scooted forward in his chair so that his long legs jutted out. "It is unpleasant business which brings us here, I am afraid. You may have heard about Miss de Bourgh's missing diamond earrings?"

Mr. Smith nodded once. "Everyone in Hunsford has heard."

Mrs. Smith came out with a tray with assorted mugs. Accepting her offering with thanks, Elizabeth sipped at the ale without tasting it.

"They were found today, and Miss Bennet, with the most honorable intentions, admitted to taking them when she is, in fact, innocent of the crime."

Mr. Smith raised one calloused hand up to rub his face. "I see. I take it that Lady Catherine believes Miss Bennet's false confession?"

"She does. As such, we had to bring Miss Bennet here as you are the village constable, but my hope is that she might be treated more like a guest than a prisoner until I can get to the bottom of this wretched mess."

Elizabeth swallowed hard. She had expected nothing but consideration in Mr. Darcy's treatment of her, but experiencing it when she felt so completely helpless was almost more than she could bear with the weight of her confession freshly on her shoulders. It was clear to see that Mr. Smith respected his word above that of Lady Catherine's.

"That should not be difficult, Mr. Darcy. My home is a humble one, but you may rest assured that Miss Bennet will receive the best we have to offer and will be treated with as much care as one of my own children."

Elizabeth heard the sounds of children playing outside. The older children would be out working in the fields.

"Good. Might I have a word with Miss Bennet and Mr. Collins?" Mr. Darcy asked. Mr. Smith dismissed himself, and Darcy sat looking at her pensively.

Elizabeth had so much she wanted to tell him, but most of it seemed entirely inappropriate at that moment. How could she tell him that she would give him her heart? She had been blind to their similarities. He understood her in a way too few did, and she could help him see the humor in life when he grew too austere. How could she tell him that she would respond differently were he to ask her the same question he had asked only a week ago?

She clasped her hands together for what she wanted most to tell him was difficult. Her desire to set things right was stronger than her pride, so gulping in enough air to guarantee that she could utter the words in one breath, she said, "Mr. Darcy," at the same time he said, "Miss Elizabeth".

She appreciated the use of her name. Perhaps, when all was said and done, he could think of her as a friend, though she craved so much more.

Ever the gentleman, he insisted that she continue.

Curious about what he had to say, she kept it brief, "I must apologize. I misjudged you completely, letting my misguided prejudice taint my attitude toward you. I am sorry. It has weighed on my mind, and I wanted you to know that my opinion of you is quite changed and even more favorable since our last discussion. You truly are a gentleman." She gave no concern to Mr. Collins sitting with them, ogling back and forth between the two.

Darcy's eyes softened as he looked straight at her. "Thank you," he said. "You are not the only one seeking forgiveness. Had my manners been those of a gentleman, we could have avoided this misunderstanding all together. After my pride allowed me to see past my outrage, your words brought me to my senses. You helped me see myself as others do, and there were things I did not like in that unflattering reflection. Can you forgive me?"

Abashed that he saw fit to apologize, she answered without hesitation, "Of course. How could I not when I, too, have wronged you so badly? And I am not in a position to change the offenses done against you. My family will remain as you know them."

Mr. Collins cleared his throat, but she ignored him. What she had to say needed to be said. Continuing, she said, "I chose to believe a man I hardly knew when he maliciously lied about your character, thus causing me to snub you when given the opportunity. And now, I have forever ruined my name. I would ask for your forgiveness, but it would feel presumptuous to do so under the circumstances."

In a low voice, tender in its sincerity, he said, "But I do forgive you."

They looked at each other for quite some time. There would be no more declarations of love, but she felt better that he accepted her apology and saw it in his heart to let go of any pain she had caused him.

Elizabeth felt lighter, though her problems were far from over.

"Miss Elizabeth, why did you do it? I am convinced of your innocence, yet you took the blame for Miss Lucas."

"It seemed to be the right thing to do at the time,"

she said with a shrug, in an attempt to sound more at ease with her decision than she presently was.

"You could have chosen an easier solution," suggested Mr. Darcy, his gaze piercing through the layers of her soul.

"If there was an easier way, I could not see it. It was my choice of taking the easy path that complicated matters for my dearest friend and cousin. I remained silent about Maria's mistake when I should have done what was right by ensuring that Charlotte knew about it earlier. That decision would have ruined the security of my friend at the worst possible time."

Mr. Collins sniffed, his downcast face full of gratitude.

"What you did took great courage, though how you manage to act both admirably and fool-hardily is something I may never understand," Mr. Darcy said as he shoved a hand through his hair so that a forelock curled down to touch his brow.

"Nor I, Mr. Darcy," Elizabeth agreed wholeheartedly. How her father would shake his head at the quandary she had trapped herself in.

Clearing his throat, Mr. Darcy asked, "Who has entered the parsonage since the earrings went missing?"

She forced her mind to focus on the business at hand. "Aside from the Collins and Miss Lucas, we have only received Miss de Bourgh and Mrs. Jenkinson. As always, their visit was brief."

"Where were they received?" he asked, growing agitated and shifting in his seat.

"In the same room in which the earrings were discovered." She knew what he thought, but she could put no faith in it.

"Anne and Mrs. Jenkinson," Mr. Darcy pondered aloud. Looking back up to her, he asked, "Have you any reason to think either lady resents you or Miss Lucas?"

She had gone over motives, possible motives, and extravagant, imaginary motives since she found the earrings sparkling up at her in Charlotte's sewing box. "I have never felt any animosity from either lady. Mrs. Jenkinson has been gentle and kind to Maria and me— even in her room as we practiced the pianoforte. Unless she acted on behalf of Lady Catherine..." Hmm, now that was a possibility. She could see from Mr. Darcy 's reaction that he thought similarly.

Mr. Darcy's knee bounced in place. Like her, he was not one to languish in one attitude for long. He was a man of action, and she was grateful that he wanted to help her.

A knock at the door interrupted their conversation. Mrs. Smith came out of nowhere with a stunning velocity to open it.

# CHAPTER 28

"Colonel Fitzwilliam, what a pleasure to see you here. I know Thomas thanked you already, but I want to add my thanks as well for your help mending our roof. Thomas is capable with his hands and can create anything with a bit of metal, but he is all thumbs with our thatched roof," Mrs. Smith said with a chuckle as she opened the door wider to receive the colonel.

"Think nothing of it, Mrs. Smith. It is always my pleasure to help Aunt Catherine's tenants and neighbors in any way I can," he said with a smile before he looked incomprehensibly at the grim occupants of the room.

Elizabeth had always thought favorably of the colonel, but learning of his thatching skills was surprising. She doubted such things practical to one responsible for an estate was taught to soldiers in the army.

Mrs. Smith started to move the wooden bench

closer to their group, but both gentlemen in the room pounced to her assistance.

"Very well then, I still have work to do. If you require anything, please just shout for me," she said, wiping her hands on her apron as she walked toward the back of the house once again.

Elizabeth could not imagine any of the three gentlemen present shouting her name aloud, though it was a common practice in her own home at Longbourn. The smile in her heart tightened as she thought of her home and her family. Homesickness, brought on at the very real certainty that she might never see them again, choked out the flicker of happiness their memory brought.

Sitting down, Colonel Fitzwilliam said, "I saw Aunt's old coach outside and thought to see what was going on. I had an interesting discussion with Mrs. Baxter. She admitted that, outside of Miss Lucas' lack of judgment on taking one fashion magazine, she would not have thought the young lady capable of doing any worse. She admitted to writing more severely than necessary to Aunt Catherine in the hopes of sending the young miss away and out of the view of her son, who is of the age to drool over anything in a skirt." He chuckled at Mr. Darcy, but soon remembered that there was another lady in the room. "Oh, I do apologize for speaking so plainly, Miss Bennet."

"Think nothing of it. I am happy to have my young friend's innocence reaffirmed." She tried to look cheerful and reflect the gaiety of the colonel, but it was growing increasingly difficult to do so as consequences crashed around her.

"Miss Bennet, if I may be so bold, what are you doing here?" he asked.

Mr. Darcy stood. "I will explain all on our return to Rosings. It is imperative that we act swiftly and decisively, as Miss Elizabeth has been charged with the robbery of Anne's diamonds."

Colonel Fitzwilliam nearly fell backward off the bench. "You cannot be serious," he exclaimed.

"I will be back shortly to ensure that all of Miss Bennet's belongings make their way here," said Mr. Darcy, signaling to Mr. Collins that it was time they depart.

"Take care of the lock on the trunk. It is broken." Elizabeth wished the ground would swallow her whole, or that she could think of something better to say than to warn the gentlemen of her faulty latch. She choked the tears back, but she had held them back for too long, and they threatened to betray her.

Mrs. Smith mercifully chose that moment to see Elizabeth to what would be her room during her stay. Elizabeth turned back, hoping to catch another glance or comforting word from Mr. Darcy, but all she heard was the jingle of coins as they transferred from Mr. Darcy to Mr. Smith's hand and the sound of the men's voices as they walked toward the waiting carriage.

Elizabeth appreciated the privacy the Smiths allowed her more than she could express. Not one to allow herself to feel defeated for very long, she did permit herself some measure of grief. She finally understood the depth of feeling her mother and Lydia gave to most events, which she felt fully under her current circumstances. She might never see her family again— not if she was allowed to continue living. She might never see Mr. Darcy again. The threat of death hovered over her like a raincloud. It was not unheard of, and caused quite the sensation in the papers when a poor gentleman's daughter met her end after she was sentenced as guilty for some blunder on her part. Blunder. That was exactly what she was guilty of. She should have told Charlotte of Maria's mistake instead of assuming Maria had confessed. Maria would have been angry with her, but that was nothing in comparison to the guilt she would have for the rest of her life knowing that her sister's best friend had sacrificed herself for her. Maybe it was wrong, but Elizabeth liked to think that the girl would suffer from some discomfort of conscience every now and then on her behalf.

A knock broke through her despair. Straightening her shoulders, arranging her hair, and dabbing her eyes with the wadded handkerchief in her hand, she opened the door to Mrs. Smith. The woman glanced over her shoulder, her fingers entwined in her apron. She looked like she bore bad news.

Then Elizabeth heard her. A shrill voice in front of the house insisted, "You will tell Miss Bennet that I have come to see her."

Mrs. Smith squeezed Elizabeth's fingers before rushing over to the door to greet Lady Catherine. She curtsied as her ladyship breezed past her and into the middle of the front room.

"Where is Miss Bennet?" she demanded, searching the small space with her squinting eyes until she saw Elizabeth standing in the open doorway outside her temporary room.

Charging over to her, Lady Catherine said, "You can be at no loss, Miss Bennet, to understand the reason of my call. Your own heart, your own conscience, must tell you why I come."

"Indeed, you are mistaken, madam. I have not been at all able to account for the honor of seeing you here." Though she suspected it had everything to do with her nephew Darcy.

"Miss Bennet," replied her ladyship, in an angry tone, "you ought to know that I am not to be trifled with. But however insincere you may choose to be, you shall not find me so. My character has ever been celebrated for its sincerity and frankness, and in a cause of such moment as this, I shall certainly not depart from it. Have you formed an attachment with my nephew, Mr. Darcy? Though I saw evidence of it with my own eyes, I know it must be a scandalous falsehood, and I would not injure him so much as to suppose the truth of it possible."

Full of disdain at Lady Catherine's rude behavior toward Mrs. Smith and her insults to her person, Elizabeth said, "If you believed it impossible to be true, I wonder you took the trouble of coming here.

What could your ladyship hope to accomplish by it?"

"At once to insist upon having such a report contradicted."

"Your coming to call at my place of imprisonment will rather be a confirmation of it, if indeed, such a report exists," said Elizabeth, resolved to sound as cool as her ladyship had when she accepted her confession and sent her away like a common criminal.

"If! Do you then pretend to be ignorant of it? Have you not industriously designed to entrap my nephew?"

"I have sought to entrap no one, much less Mr. Darcy."

"And can you likewise declare that there is no foundation for me to suspect an attachment?"

"I do not pretend to possess equal frankness with your ladyship. You may ask questions which I shall choose not to answer." She crossed her arms in front of her, more to keep her hammering heart in her chest than for any protective barrier from the adversary before her.

Exhausting her calm, Lady Catherine shook in rage. "This is not to be borne. Miss Bennet, I insist on being satisfied. Has my nephew made you an offer of marriage?"

"Your ladyship has declared it to be impossible." She would never give her the satisfaction of a direct answer. Were her manners any less grating, she might have obliged.

"It ought to be impossible unless he has lost his powers of reason. But your manipulative arts and allurements may, in a moment of infatuation, have made him forget what he owes to himself and to his family. You may have drawn him in."

The nerve of her ladyship accusing her of acting manipulatively toward Mr. Darcy— even going so far as to question his sanity! "If I have, I shall be the last person to confess it."

"Miss Bennet, do you know who I am? I am not accustomed to such language as this. I am almost the nearest relation he has in the world and am entitled to know all his dearest concerns."

"Be that so, you are not entitled to know mine. Nor will such behavior as you have demonstrated ever induce me to be explicit."

Dropping her voice to a hiss, Lady Catherine said, "Let me be rightly understood. This match, to which you have the presumption to aspire, can never take place. No, never. Your confession ensured that as securely as your deal that I keep the Collins at the parish. Besides," she said with her nose in the air, "Mr. Darcy is engaged to my daughter. Now what have you to say?"

Refusing to show how Lady Catherine's words hurt her, Elizabeth said in as steady of a voice as she could, "Only this; that if he is engaged to Miss de Bourgh, you can have no reason to suppose he would make an offer to me."

"The engagement between them is of a peculiar kind. From their infancy, they have been intended for each other. And now, at the moment when the wishes of his relatives would be accomplished in their marriage, I see it threatened by a young woman of inferior birth and of no importance in the world! Do you pay no regard to the wishes of his family? Are you lost to every feeling of propriety and delicacy? Have you not heard me say that from his earliest hours he was destined for his cousin?"

"Yes, and I had heard of it before. But what is that to me? You did as much as you could in planning the marriage, but its completion depends on others. If Mr. Darcy chooses not to marry his cousin, why is he not permitted to make another choice? And if I am that choice, why may not I accept him?" She restrained herself from furthering her attack, though she dearly wanted to cut the pompous woman before her.

"Your alliance, not that one is possible anymore, would be a disgrace. After today's events, your name will never even be mentioned by any of us. Now, tell me once and for all, are you engaged to my nephew?"

She dearly wanted to remain silent, but she desperately wanted the interview to end. Swallowing her pride, she said, "I am not."

Pleased, Lady Catherine pressed, "And will you promise me never to enter into such an engagement?"

As if such a miracle were possible. Still, not all the fight had left Elizabeth. "I will make no promise of the kind."

Highly incensed, Lady Catherine said, "Selfish girl! Do you not consider that a connection with you would disgrace him? You are nothing more than a criminal; a low-born daughter of a nobody. In every way you have proved yourself to be nothing more than an obstinate creature bent on ruining Darcy's happiness. Do not imagine, Miss Bennet, that your ambition will ever be gratified. I came to try you. I hoped to find you reasonable, but, depend upon it, I will have my way in the end."

With a final huff, her ladyship turned toward the door and marched out of the house. Elizabeth made it back to her room and closed the door before hot tears full of anger and disappointed hopes poured down her cheeks.

# CHAPTER 29

Disturbed silence fell over the coach after Darcy recounted the events Richard had missed that morning.

"I do not understand it," Richard shook his head slowly back and forth.

"She did it to protect the Collinses and prevent Miss Lucas from experiencing the unpleasant imprisonment she is presently suffering."

"I see. So, we are going back to Rosings to find the real culprit? Are you certain the villain is to be found there?" he asked, not so concerned with Miss Elizabeth's current state as Darcy had expected him to be.

"From the beginning, I have believed this merely a scheme of Aunt Catherine's to prevent me from leaving, thus forcing me to propose to Anne. However, I now know for a certainty that she is not acting alone. Someone is helping her, and I aim to find out who it is."

"Excluding the residents and guests at the parsonage, that leaves me, Mrs. Jenkinson, Anne, the maid, and the doctor." Richard counted on his fingers as he mentioned each person.

Darcy had not considered the doctor, and he had already spoken to the lady's maid enough to convince him that she was clueless. She was too afraid of losing her post to risk it.

"The real question is: Why? What motive would any of those individuals have? What do they stand to gain by blaming Miss Bennet for the theft of the earrings?" asked Richard, mulling over the facts in his head as he spoke aloud.

"The thing that stumps me is that it was not Miss Bennet who was blamed. She took that on herself out of loyalty to her friends. It was Miss Lucas who looked guilty. Why would someone act against her? She is too timid to cause much trouble. Unless their intention was to see the Collinses out of the parsonage, I do not understand it."

Mr. Collins looked ash white against his black coat and hat.

"Then why involve Aunt Catherine? She has been content with Mr. Collins until these recent events. She could not possibly be involved if that was the goal." To Mr. Collins, he said, "She would miss your praise and compliments too much."

Darcy sank back against the cushions. What Richard said was true, and they arrived all too soon at the parsonage.

The door opened, but Mr. Collins did not move.

"Mr. Collins, we are at your home. Do you wish to disembark?" asked Richard.

With a large puff of air, Mr. Collins squared his shoulders and said, "I should join you at Rosings. I have some information which will help my selfless cousin and, be it to her ladyship's approval or not, it must be revealed. My conscience will be uneasy until I have freed myself from this wretched burden I carry."

Darcy breathed out, "More secrets." Just what they needed.

Wishing he had more information with which to plan an attack, Darcy had to continue on nothing more than instincts and trust that what Mr. Collins had to say would help Elizabeth. The truth needed to be told today, or else he would forever lose her. Her comments proved that her attitude toward him had changed. He could not be sure if she could overlook his faults so much as to love him, but he would hate himself eternally if he did not try. His jealousy against Richard had fallen flat at their exchange at the Smiths'. Either they were both superb actors, or there were no special feelings between them.

"You do realize why my aunt wants to consult with you and me later, Mr. Collins? Will you comply with Aunt Catherine's order to read the banns against my wishes?" Darcy asked.

"We shall see. My place here rests on shaky ground, and I recoil from acting contrary to her wishes."

"One word from me would see you comfortably into another living. If you help Miss Elizabeth, you are helping me, and I would be in your debt," Darcy said, intent on the clergyman. He would listen to a lifetime of sermons from the dullest gentleman of his acquaintance if it meant he had a future with Elizabeth.

"I assure you that I will do what I can, Mr. Darcy," said Mr. Collins in quite possibly the shortest sentence uttered by him in their acquaintance.

Not wanting to waste any time, Darcy told the coachman to take them on to Rosings.

Aunt Catherine was out when they arrived. Darcy did not recollect seeing her on the road. It brought Darcy no comfort when Simmons told him her destination, but it also meant that she would not be away long. He said a silent prayer in his heart for Elizabeth.

He rallied forces in the library, sending for Anne and Mrs. Jenkinson to join them. Darcy asked Simmons to request a meeting with Aunt Catherine as soon as she arrived. It was urgent.

Darcy paced the room, watching the lane leading up to the house from the window. Richard spoke quietly with Anne, Mrs. Jenkinson sat with her fingers laced in perfect repose in a nearby chair, and Mr. Collins gesticulated in his seat, apparently practicing his speech before it must be given to his most unforgiving audience. The occupants of the library understood their purpose in being there and prepared themselves. Darcy did not need to say anything.

After the passing of a quarter hour, Darcy saw the coach make its way up the drive. Another few minutes after that, Simmons called them into the drawing room. Silently, saving their words for when they were needed, they walked through the antechamber and into Aunt Catherine's lair. She sat in her usual spot, to be flanked on one side by Anne and Mrs. Jenkinson, and by a mural of Marc Anthony and Cleopatra on the other.

Mr. Collins sat across from them, somehow managing to postulate from a sitting position. The man had talent.

"What is this? I arrive home only to find myself surrounded by all those who have disappointed me and set themselves up for mockery," said Aunt Catherine, causing Mr. Collins to break out in a fresh layer of sweat as his face burned red.

Nodding encouragement to the clergyman, Darcy motioned for him to speak.

Through his noted embarrassment, Mr. Collins bowed his head before her, saying, "It is so, your ladyship, and I thank you for your magnanimity toward myself and my wife. I will seek never to disappoint you again, once I have confessed the wrong I have done against those who looked to me for protection as my guests and blood relations. As a man who upholds high morals, I can do no less than admit my fault and throw myself upon your abundant mercy, if you should deem me worthy of your consideration."

Aunt Catherine sat taller in her chair, rather enjoying being treated like a god. Darcy shivered at the imagery in his mind. Aunt Catherine would be a horrible deity. Her stubborn nature and exalted opinion of her own importance prevented her from empathizing with others, much less extending forgiveness. Darcy cringed at the similar tendencies he shared with her. Elizabeth had seen them. He would fight them. Or he would not deserve Miss Elizabeth. For her, he would change. He had changed. He would do everything in his power to keep her happy and put her needs and desires above his own. He would do everything to prove himself the opposite of Aunt Catherine.

Mr. Collins looked up at him. Fear covered the clergyman's face. It took Darcy a moment to realize that his nervous reaction was in response to the firm determination at his vow to himself. He must look stern and unyielding. So, he made a concerted effort to soften his expression. He thought of Elizabeth as he took a seat near Mr. Collins. Richard sat next to him too, balancing the two sides on either side of the yellow target on the rug.

To further reassure the clammy parson, Darcy added, "It is an admirable quality and a true display of humility to admit one's faults. I hope you are blessed with the ease of conscience which often accompanies a confession of the truth."

Mr. Collins stopped squirming at that and bowed

his head in his thankfulness. "I do hope so, Mr. Darcy. Thank you for your kindness. It is in moments like these where one most appreciates the traits which emanate from families of high birth."

Darcy refrained from rolling his eyes. Flattery repulsed him, but it was a smart maneuver on Mr. Collins' part to make reference to Aunt Catherine's aristocratic connection. She never let anyone forget that she was the daughter of an earl, and thus, exalted above her richer relations.

She waved her bejeweled fingers in the air impatiently. "That is enough, Mr. Collins. You have come with a purpose, and I insist you get on with it."

Scooting forward in his chair, Mr. Collins said, "I hope that you are gracious enough to understand that my motives in doing such a thing were born from the purest intention. My mission in life is to glorify God to the good people in and around Hunsford, thus improving their spirit— their very nature— so that they might prove worthy of living and representing the noble family on whose estate they live…"

Would the man never get to the point? He rambled on and on about how great the de Bourgh name was, second only to the royal family themselves, and first in his thoughts. Darcy's understanding deepened as he continued. His aunt had acquired a worshiper to adore her. Unless his adoration diminished in time, his position was as secure as his aunt's need for admiration. But even she had a limit to her patience.

Interrupting after a few minutes, where Darcy had been lulled into tedium to the sound of Mr. Collins' monotonous tone in the background, she said, "Mr. Collins, you say you have come to confess, yet I hear nothing untoward. Pray tell what you have done."

Darcy looked over at Richard, who sat up in his chair and shook his head as if recently waking. He jutted out his chin to keep from smiling. He did not want Aunt's focus to stray away from Mr. Collins. Mrs. Jenkinson fanned herself and Anne in an effort to remain alert.

Mr. Collins slid forward in his chair again, until Darcy thought he might run out of cushion and fall to the floor. But he stopped himself just in time. How had Elizabeth endured his attentions when they had been focused on her? The man had a lot of nerve, or he was so blind to their differences that he could not see how unsuited they would have been for each other. Most likely, the latter. The slick skin and constant wiping of his sweaty palms against his black breeches contradicted any amount of bravery.

Clearing his throat, Mr. Collins continued, "Now that you are fully aware of my high regard for you and your family, as well as my unshakable loyalty, please let me repeat only one time more that my motive in going along with it was entirely for your benefit." After receiving an impatient nod, he continued with a glance over to the couch where

Anne sat, "It was communicated to me that there was a threat to your plan that Mr. Darcy marry Miss de Bourgh."

Darcy's attention focused fully on Mr. Collins.

"It was pointed out to me by one who also holds your interests as a priority that a visitor in my home was a distraction. The intent was not to accuse anyone of a crime. Of the young lady's innocence, I can attest. However, our motivation came out of a desire to separate the two individuals of whom I speak and thus promote a happy union between the Darcys and de Bourghs— as it should be, your ladyship."

"Of which young lady do you speak, Mr. Collins? Which of your guests would dare go against my plans for my daughter's match?" Aunt Catherine spat out the question before Darcy could ask who Mr. Collins' partner in crime was.

He looked toward Anne during the ensuing pause in which Mr. Collins collected his thoughts, but Anne looked just as confused as he did. Mrs. Jenkinson fanned her face and patted her hand as she always did, occasionally glaring at Mr. Collins for upsetting her mistress so much. Richard appeared as ignorant as Darcy himself and only shrugged his shoulders at him when their eyes met.

Surely, Aunt knew the answer, but she sought confirmation of her suspicion.

"My cousin, Miss Elizabeth Bennet," Mr. Collins responded, his head bowed in shame.

Lifting her chin high, she asked, "What proof do

you have of this horrid accusation against my nephew?"

Darcy felt the hair on his arm stand on end. She saw it as an insult that he found love with a lady she deemed inferior, when in every way, Elizabeth was far superior to her. Elizabeth did not like Lady Catherine any more than Lady Catherine liked her, yet Elizabeth would never seek to raise herself on a pedestal at the cost of another's dignity. Nor would she openly spew insults before her own relatives. No, Elizabeth was a lady, unlike the woman before him who merely bore the title.

Biting his tongue so as not to distract Mr. Collins more than he already allowed himself to be, he buried his feelings until a more opportune time. He would wait.

Everyone stared at Mr. Collins, who evidently struggled with the shame he felt toward his cousin and his admiration for her. At least, that was what Darcy hoped. He would give the clergyman the benefit of the doubt, especially if he could clear her name. He had said that he could attest to her innocence.

"About a week past, your ladyship was gracious to condescend to invite myself and my household for tea. My cousin, unfortunately, was suffering a headache and chose to remain behind. It is suspected that during this time, in which Mr. Darcy was also absent from tea, he called on her while she was unattended. There have been other instances where they have been seen walking together through the lawns in the park."

Aunt Catherine turned on Darcy, her eyes fuming and red-rimmed. "Is this true? Did you knowingly call on an unmarried woman?"

Darcy, annoyed with the use of so many words to reveal so little, as well as the implication that Miss Elizabeth was too low for his attention, spoke clearly and plainly. "I did call on Miss Bennet. I proposed to her."

The gasps in the room were so dramatic he would have burst out laughing had the matter not been so serious. Richard did not have the same delicacy. He clamped his hand over his mouth and shook in merriment.

Aunt Catherine stood up from her chair, her hands shaking so violently, Darcy stood to assist her should she topple over. "You are engaged when you are promised to another? How dare you act so perversely whilst a guest in my house?" she shouted.

With all the calm he could muster, Darcy answered, "She refused me. I am not engaged — more is the pity." He refused to look at Richard, who surely was in fits of laughter by now. Darcy hoped he would choke on his tongue.

Sitting back down, Aunt Catherine said, "Then she is more sensible than I had believed her to be. We shall keep this amongst ourselves, for I will not have you compromised and thus be forced to marry her."

"I still love her, Aunt. I shall marry none other than her," he said, still standing.

He looked at Anne. She smiled at him, bit her lips together like she would weep, and fluttered her hand over her heart.

Before Aunt Catherine could exclaim the cutting retort on the tip of her tongue, Anne stood, drawing everyone's attention. Mrs. Jenkinson heaved herself out of her place to keep her hand at Anne's elbow. Richard moved to get up, but Anne stopped him with a shake of the head.

"Mother, there is something I wish you to know. I am in love." She stopped to smile. She looked lovely with happiness adorning her face.

"Of course you are in love— with Darcy!" exclaimed Aunt Catherine.

Her sweet smile still illuminating her with peace and joy, Anne stepped toward Richard and extended her hand.

"I am ashamed of my cowardliness in keeping silent so long. All of this could have been avoided had I overcome my fear. Would I could be more like Miss Bennet in that regard," she said.

Richard took her offered hand, caressing it between his own with a tenderness Darcy had not thought Richard capable of. With a touch of his lips against her fingers, Richard rose to stand by Anne.

Silence consumed the room.

# CHAPTER 30

It was the closest to an apoplexy Aunt Catherine had ever come to Darcy's knowledge. She clutched the arm of her chair like an angry cat clawing at the furniture. Her knuckles looked shockingly white against the purple of her dress and the red blotches on her face.

"How dare you betray me! You, of all people, Anne. My own daughter! I shall disinherit you!" she threatened. Darcy did not doubt that her anger would last long enough to carry out such a drastic measure. He looked at Richard and Anne in worry. Could their love for each other stand through the trials Aunt Catherine would heave in their path?

Neither wavered. Anne clasped all the more firmly onto Richard's arm, and he pressed it into his side, resting his free hand on top of hers. Whatever they had to face, they would face it together. It was a pleasure to see. Darcy wanted nothing less for them.

He heard Anne's breath shake before she spoke,

but there was no doubt in her voice. "Richard has taken measures to see that our estate earns more money, Mother. The tenants love him, and he has developed a good rapport with our land steward. In fact, he has a plan to help you in your endeavor to beautify the park even further without the added cost of hiring an architect. We think you will be pleased."

The mention of money certainly got Aunt Catherine's attention. "But Richard has no money! He brings nothing to the estate like Darcy can!"

Darcy grimaced. Aunt Catherine made it painfully clear that she valued his monetary worth far more than the man he was.

"Did you not listen to me, Mother? I just told you that Richard can help the estate earn more money, and he has wonderful ideas to help us cut costs..."

Aunt Catherine balked. She would rather go destitute trying to keep up appearances than be forced to spend less and sacrifice the excesses she had grown accustomed to. "I will not send away any of the servants! I will not change my habits in the slightest, so you can put to rest your plans to save money."

Richard spoke up, "I would never suggest that you send away your servants. There are good families who depend on this estate for their living. I would no more recommend that you dismiss them than you would."

Aunt Catherine harrumphed, but she kept her objections to herself. After a moment, she lowered her stubborn chin and looked at Richard out of the corner of her eyes. She was curious.

Taking that as encouragement, Richard continued, "Have you never noticed how your estate has provided more in the past few years than in the previous? Are you not at least a little curious to know what I have been up to? Would you not be interested in hearing what ideas I have for increasing your income? Surely, that is to your advantage as well as Anne's." Palms up, he implored her to do what she seldom did— to listen.

She snorted derisively, but she cast no more judgments toward the couple now standing before her. Perhaps shock had set in.

Now Darcy understood Richard's actions better. He had thought that he merely sought to take advantage of the large space to ride— an activity Richard enjoyed. Instead, he had been riding over the property and making friends with the tenants and steward. Even Mrs. Smith had thanked him for helping with their roof. All this time, Richard had been making improvements and learning how to care for an estate, so that he would make a worthy husband of Anne. Pride for his cousin filled his breast. Only he could conduct such a maneuver, subdue the dragon, and rescue the maiden from the tower of seclusion she had lived in her entire life. Looking at how Anne glowed that moment even convinced Darcy that love would work its miracle and ease the malaise which had wasted most of her youth. Richard was giving her a second start in life.

It made him want to storm the blacksmith's walls on his white steed and rescue his own damsel in distress.

The connection hit him like a brick to the head. Looking at Anne, he said, "Your earrings were not stolen, were they? *You* gave them to Richard to help him with his debt."

Anne smiled sheepishly and Richard's face turned scarlet red.

Bunching up his chin in his willful way, he said, "I could not accept them."

Shaking her head, Anne said softly, "You and your foolish pride. Would you have taken them like I begged you to, we could have bought them back once you paid them off. I know you would have done so."

Before the conversation could become distracted again, Darcy turned to Collins, who sat quite forgotten by everyone else in the room. "You said that you know for a certainty that Miss Elizabeth is innocent of taking the earrings? Please explain yourself."

Mr. Collins took in a large breath, no doubt to speak a good amount of vocabulary without saying anything at all.

"In few words," Darcy added for good measure.

Exhaling, Mr. Collins looked deflated, but he soon recovered enough to say, "I know she did not take them because I was the one who put them in Charlotte's sewing box to be found during the search of my home."

Darcy lurched forward in his seat. "It was you?" he exclaimed.

"I did not steal them, of course. I would testify before the Almighty Himself that my motive in doing so was only to protect the interest of her ladyship. I did not know, however, that Miss de Bourgh's affections lay elsewhere or else I might not have acted against my own household as I did. I am ashamed." Mr. Collins bowed his head.

Darcy voiced the question he had pondered since Anne's admission. "If you did not steal the earrings, Mr. Collins, then please be so kind as to tell us who did."

Mr. Collins said nothing, but his eyes darted to the couch where one lone figure sat. Mrs. Jenkinson— who looked like she wished she could disappear.

Anne gasped, "But of course! What a simpleton I have been." Leaving Richard's side, she went to the couch and sat next to her companion of many years. "Why did you do it?" she asked.

"I found your letters, Miss Anne," she said softly.

Anne nodded in understanding and looked up at Richard.

"When Mother sent you up to my room with the maid to retrieve the earrings I knew were in the compartment?" she pressed.

"Yes. I understand why you would have put them there. Nobody would look in that part of your desk, knowing it was not to be disturbed. But I saw what you had hidden, and I sought to protect you from yourself. I thought you would ruin your future, and I could not bear it."

Aunt Catherine, who had been abnormally quiet, found her voice, "For goodness' sake, speak plainly, Mrs. Jenkinson. What did you see, and why did that make you do what you did?"

"I saw packets of love letters tied with red ribbons addressed to Miss Anne from Colonel Fitzwilliam. There were dozens upon dozens of them. I saw with my own eyes that theirs was no passing fancy, and I even suspected a secret engagement. So, I pretended to drop my spectacles on the floor by accident to distract the maid, and I snatched the earrings until I could speak with Mr. Collins."

"Why not simply speak to me? Mrs. Jenkinson, you have become a close friend to me. Why did you not trust me?" asked Anne.

Mrs. Jenkinson patted Anne's hand as she always did. "As much as I esteem your friendship, my attachment to her ladyship is even stronger. She saved me from the workhouse after my husband died and left me with nothing. I owe her my life, and I could not bear for her to suffer disappointment when she learned that you were in love with someone other than Mr. Darcy."

Aunt Catherine quietly smiled. She was a striking woman anyway, but Darcy saw an inkling of humanity in her at that moment.

That explained why she acted the way she did toward Anne, but it did not explain her involving Mr. Collins. "Why did you confide in Mr. Collins?"

Looking accusingly at him, she answered, "I saw you leave the parsonage the afternoon Miss Bennet had stayed at home from taking tea with Lady Catherine and her hosts. Anne needed some air and felt well enough to ride out in her pony and cart. We had just passed by when you came walking out of the house. Why else would you enter the parsonage when you knew the only person home was Miss Bennet?" She paused to catch her breath. "I saw the longing in your eyes when you looked at her, and I noticed how you paid her particular attention when she played the pianoforte after dinner. You found praise where there should have been none. Only the rose-colored tint of love could have cast its partial glow to the noise she produced from the instrument. I wanted her gone so that you could pay attention to Miss Anne! That was my reason in choosing Mr. Collins to take into my confidence. His loyalty to the de Bourgh family is as great as mine."

It was Anne's turn to soothe the elderly woman. Anne was far more sympathetic than he was. He glared at the woman who was the cause of Elizabeth's wrongful imprisonment. Fortunately for Mrs. Jenkinson, he would have little say in her punishment.

Addressing Mr. Collins, he asked in disbelief, "You went along with her? What could have possessed you to act in such a manner against your own cousin? And do not forget that it was Miss Lucas, your sister by marriage, who looked guilty.

Were you willing to cause unrest in your own home just to please your patroness?" He shut his lips in disgust, Mr. Collins' actions growing more detestable in his mind as he thought about them.

Mr. Collins stuttered, "I did not know about Miss Lucas'... error. To be fair, Mrs. Jenkinson promised me that she would merely encourage her ladyship to send the ladies away. Once they were gone, things would return to normal."

"Were they not planning to leave in less than a week anyway? What could you possibly stand to gain by allowing your own cousin and sister to leave in shame?" Darcy insisted, growing increasingly impatient with the clergyman.

Mr. Collins had the decency to blush crimson. "It is nothing I am proud of. I will admit that I wished to knock my haughty cousin down a peg or two. I never sought to do her any lasting harm. I only thought it would do her good to be put in her place for once."

Everyone in the room knew she had refused him. It was Aunt Catherine who had encouraged him to take a wife from amongst one of his cousins at Longbourn.

Never in Darcy's wildest dreams would he think to retaliate against Miss Elizabeth for refusing him. His distaste for the man seated next to him grew and only calmed when he reminded himself that it was Mr. Collins' uneasy conscience which had revealed so much in the past few minutes.

"Your resentment might very well cost Miss

Elizabeth a good deal more than her pride. What do you think of her character now— after witnessing the lengths she went to for you? She took Miss Lucas' place and ensured your living at Hunsford out of her sense of responsibility and friendship to your wife." A woman who felt so deeply for her friends would be the best ally in life. Darcy dreamed of them dealing with the challenges brought their way, knowing that she would not shrink back. She was the bravest woman of his acquaintance, and his respect for her grew the more he understood her. Had he only known how much better than himself she was, he never would have insulted her with his poor excuse of a proposal.

He would come to her aid. He would be the champion she needed. Whether she could return his love or not, Darcy would strive to be the gentleman she deserved. If Elizabeth would concede to love a man who had wronged her so badly, he would live every day trying to prove himself worthy of her.

"If there is anything I can do to make it up to her, I am determined to do so," stated Mr. Collins. Miraculously, he uttered nothing more.

About to retort that he had done enough already, another idea occurred to Darcy. There *was* something Mr. Collins could do for her.

"I should like to meet with you in the library in a few minutes, Mr. Collins. There *is* something you can do for Miss Elizabeth which will mean a great deal to her, and I can promise that I will make it worth your while."

# CHAPTER 31

More than anything else, Elizabeth hated the waiting. If she knew what her future held, good or bad, at least she could prepare herself for it. Instead, she found herself forced to hope that others would care as much about her fate as she did, while preparing herself for the worst to happen. The state of limbo without the advantage of clearing her mind by taking a walk outdoors filled her with a desperation which she fought for what felt like endless hours.

Mrs. Smith was good enough to allow her out of doors, where the smaller children played, as she rooted the weeds out of the garden. Elizabeth had knelt beside her to help, needing to do something— anything to distract her mind and make the time pass. But Mrs. Smith would have none of Elizabeth staining her dress in the dirt. If only she knew the liberties Elizabeth was allowed to take at home.

With a sigh, her thoughts carried her to Longbourn and her family. She had failed them miserably. One whisper of her predicament, and her mother's hopes that her daughters make brilliant matches would be shattered. Nobody would marry into the family of a criminal. Not even Mr. Bingley would dare.

Not able to do anything else, she prayed with all her heart that her family not be made to suffer too greatly for her error. She could not bear it if they did.

Mrs. Smith, smacking the dirt off her hands and wiping them on her apron, came over to sit by her.

"You have had a rough afternoon, miss. Is there anything I can do to ease your heavy heart?" she asked.

With a weak smile, Elizabeth thanked her. "You have been too kind already, Mrs. Smith. You have made me feel at home in your house as any proper guest could be when, for all you know, I am nothing more than a common thief."

Mrs. Smith laughed. "I think not, miss. Whatever would you steal Miss de Bourgh's earrings for? No, there has been a storm brewing for too many years at Rosings, and it is about time that Lady Catherine comes to terms with it. Miss de Bourgh is a grown woman, and contrary to the limitations her mother places upon her, she will not forever succumb to being treated like a child."

Both curious and agreeable to distracting conversation, Elizabeth asked, "You think that Miss de Bourgh is not so sickly as Lady Catherine thinks? Whenever I have been in her company, she always looks so pale and fragile."

"Aye, that she is. You would too if you had some fancy doctor bleeding you every week of the poison. You ought to see the scars on her arms. Granted, I have not seen them with my own eyes, but my niece is a housemaid, and she told me how Colonel Fitzwilliam quarreled with Lady Catherine about that overpriced charlatan killing Miss de Bourgh slowly."

"It is good that Miss de Bourgh has a champion to fight for her. She seems too weak to defend herself."

"Tis so. We have come to look forward to the colonel's visits. He takes an interest in the tenants and is well-liked by all in the village. Mr. Darcy is an honorable gentleman as well, but everyone knows that he cannot take much of an interest in his aunt's affairs lest he encourage her to think that he will propose to her daughter. Anyone can see how ill-suited they would be. Miss de Bourgh and Colonel Fitzwilliam, however... That is a match I should like to see."

Elizabeth had never considered the possibility, but her skin tingled in excitement as she pondered it. "Why would they make a good match?" she asked.

"Colonel Fitzwilliam has a strong personality and a sense of humor. He is not afraid of Lady Catherine. She would soon enough be put in her proper place. With his experience in maneuvers and battles, she would not even know it had been done until it was too late for her to complain!" She laughed with her hand covering her mouth, eyes darting around, as if even from the distance between that spot at the back of her home and Rosings, Lady Catherine might overhear her unflattering comments.

They chatted more and Elizabeth's mood cheered. The more she thought about Colonel Fitzwilliam and Miss de Bourgh, the more she believed it to be a possibility. And then, it struck her.

Elizabeth remembered the debt which made Mr. Collins suspect that Colonel Fitzwilliam had been the one to take the earrings. Putting herself in Miss de Bourgh's position, how would she react if the man she loved had a debt she could easily help him with? She would not hesitate. She would have given him something of value which he could use to cover the amount. Not able to base her suspicion on anything more than Mrs. Smith's ramblings and her own imagination, she bit her tongue. But her legs fidgeted in her anxiety to speak with someone about it. Oh, would Mr. Darcy never return? She could talk to him with impunity. He would know what to do and could soon allay her suspicion or pronounce her correct. The longer she dwelt on it, the more certain she grew that the latter was the case. It fit too well. Had not Mr. Darcy said that it was implied that the earrings had not been stolen in the first place?

Elizabeth, filled with hope once again, waited. The time passed no more quickly for her change in attitude, but it was bearable.

The crunch of hooves in the lane made both women look toward the front of the house. Most likely, it was work for Mr. Smith, but the logical thought did not prevent Elizabeth from walking through the house to look through the open door.

To her relief and surprise, she saw Mr. Darcy dismounting his horse and hand the reins to Mr. Smith. Mr. Collins was with him, astride a horse she had not seen before.

She bounced forward before she remembered to calm herself. Clasping her hands together to keep from gesturing too wildly in her excitement, she said with a rushed curtsy, "Mr. Darcy, Mr. Collins, I believe I may know what might have happened to Miss de Bourgh's earrings!"

Mr. Darcy looked taken aback, but Mr. Collins only shrugged his slumped shoulders.

"I would be pleased to hear what you have to say. Perhaps we might discuss this inside?" suggested Mr. Darcy.

They had hardly sat when she began. "In conversation with Mrs. Smith, she mentioned Colonel Fitzwilliam and how he would make a perfect match for Miss de Bourgh." She paused, hoping to have her suspicion confirmed, but as usual, Mr. Darcy's expressionless face revealed nothing, and her cousin wiped his forehead with a handkerchief, covering most of his face in the process.

Continuing, she said, "We all know of the predicament Colonel Fitzwilliam was in not long ago. No details are needed or applicable on that account, so I will not speak of them. However, if a lady who loved him was aware of his situation, she would gladly give him something of value to help. I would not hesitate to do so, and if my suspicions are well-founded, neither did Miss de Bourgh."

She stopped, having said what she needed to say, and waited.

Mr. Darcy looked at her in that disconcerting way she had grown accustomed to in the months of their acquaintance. Soon enough, the corners of his lips twitched up, and the relief it brought her had no limit. She was right! She had solved the crime—which was not a crime at all!

"You are correct in part," he said, his eyes brilliant with elation. "Unbeknown to anyone, my cousin has been courting Anne for several years now. In fact, we left them to deal with my aunt only minutes ago. He is not one to easily lose his resolve, and Anne has grown stronger than I ever thought her capable of being with his rock-like support. I think they will make each other very happy." Melancholy flickered across his face, dulling his countenance ever so slightly.

"Is it possible? How did Lady Catherine react?" she asked, a rush of questions on the tip of her tongue.

"It has happened and my aunt, though initially furious, is making the best of it. It turns out that Richard has a solid head for business and can increase her income. Also, Anne was smart and learned the conditions of her inheritance. According to her deceased father's will, she is to inherit when she marries."

"I wish them happy," agreed Elizabeth politely, craving for his smile to return. Surely, he was content. Was he not?

A carriage passed through the yard. Elizabeth leaned forward to peek through the door, but she could not see enough to confirm what she could only hope.

Clearing his throat, Mr. Darcy said, "Yes, well, we came to see you safely back to the parsonage. We must not delay any longer. Mr. Collins and I have business in London. We must make haste if we are to make any progress before nightfall."

Elizabeth cocked her head to the side, confused and wanting answers.

"I am free to go?" she asked, just to ensure she had not dreamed the last exchange.

"You are free, and as far as anyone knows, you merely visited Mrs. Smith while her husband fixed the broken clasp on your trunk."

Elizabeth had been outside most of the afternoon and had not paid much attention to her surroundings. There, in the shade of the door, sat her trunk with a new clasp on it.

Once again, Mr. Darcy had thought of everything. He had protected her reputation by giving her an alibi, so that no one in the village would dare call her character into question.

"Thank you," she whispered, desperate to read his heart. He was free from his engagement, but was he free to love her as he had once claimed that he did?

His smile returned.

Mr. Collins fanned himself with his damp handkerchief. He mumbled some words which Elizabeth did not try to hear. She did not want to look away from the man in front of her. How she wished she could have more answers, but it was not to be.

A footman stood in the doorway, and everyone sprang to action. Elizabeth thanked the Smiths for their hospitality and company while Mr. Darcy arranged for her trunk to be transported back to the parsonage. He handed her into the carriage, ensuring she was comfortable before he mounted his horse to follow the distance to Mr. Collins' home.

It took just minutes for her trunk to be returned upstairs to the room in which she had spent the past month. The dust had not yet settled, and the coach was gone along with Mr. Darcy and Mr. Collins.

Questions swarmed in her mind, the foremost of which was: What urgent business did Mr. Darcy have with Mr. Collins in London? Who had stolen the earrings and allowed her to take the blame? Was Charlotte's place in her home safe? Why did Mr. Darcy have to leave? Did he still love her?

Turning to the house, Charlotte and Maria welcomed her with embraces and kisses. She would ask Charlotte what she could.

# CHAPTER 32

"What has happened?" Elizabeth asked Charlotte once she felt calm enough to ask.

"Mr. Darcy did not tell you?"

"He told me about Colonel Fitzwilliam and Miss de Bourgh and that the earrings had not been stolen to start with. What I do not understand is how they were found here, in your sewing box, if they were not stolen."

Charlotte took her by the hand, leading her to the seating area. The last rays of sun peeked through the tops of the trees, lining the lane, and warmed Elizabeth. After the anxieties and nerves of the past few days, she thought she might melt into a puddle, such was her relief to be amongst her friends and free again. She planned to go on a very long walk on the morrow.

Charlotte ordered some tea, maintaining their conversation until it arrived.

"There, now that you are properly settled, I have

much to tell you... and even more for which to thank you." She rocked in her chair, already the picture of maternal bliss. Her hand rested protectively over the front of her dress. She would be a wonderful mother. A stab of envy pierced Elizabeth's soul at the lovely sight.

The whole story of the revealing conversation at Rosings was told from beginning to end by the time the contents of the tea pot had run dry.

Elizabeth sat in pensive quiet while Maria perfected the flowers on her white work, and Charlotte rocked contentedly in her chair. It was a lot to think through and make sense of.

Finally, grasping the truth fully, Elizabeth shared her conclusion. "What amazes me is how much of this could have been avoided had we trusted each other enough to confide in each other. Had I told you about the magazine, Maria probably would not have suffered Lady Catherine's scrutiny. Had Colonel Fitzwilliam or Miss de Bourgh trusted Mr. Darcy or revealed the truth of their affection for each other to Lady Catherine earlier, the earrings would not have been stolen in the first place."

"And if I had trusted my husband, he would not have involved himself as he did by inviting a search in our home. Had he trusted me, I would have helped him overcome his desire for revenge, and you would have enjoyed a more peaceful visit with us," added Charlotte.

Elizabeth sighed. "Do you think we will learn from our mistakes? Or will we forget as the time passes and continue on as we always have done?" She folded her legs up under her dress and leaned her head back until it touched the wall.

"For me, I am determined to change. The events of the past few days have been too difficult to so easily forget them. In that time, I spoke in anger against my dearest friend, displayed a lack of trust in my own husband, and allowed my sister to stray down the wide path when I should have offered her help."

Maria finally spoke. "But you did not know what I had been up to, Charlotte. How could you possibly have helped me? And Lizzy, had I openly admitted to my wrong instead of acting like a coward, you would have had no need to talk to Charlotte. I wish that neither of you would feel guilty on my account. I beg your forgiveness."

Elizabeth smiled at Maria. After all the trouble she had put her through, it was nice to hear an apology.

Charlotte stopped rocking. "It is true. I did not know what you had done. But I did notice a change in your behavior. You became more withdrawn than you normally are, and you would not meet my eyes when we spoke. You looked guilty of something, and I did not press you to talk to me. You would have told me had I only asked."

Maria nodded her head. "I have learned my lesson. Keeping a secret is miserable, and I plan to do nothing that would involve keeping one ever again. I would sooner tattle on myself and be done with the guilt."

"Speaking of secrets, Lizzy, what of the proposal you received? Mr. Collins said that Mr. Darcy almost looked proud when he informed his aunt that you had refused him. What could he possibly have said for you to reject him?"

She knew it was not the most appropriate reaction, but she smiled. Laughter soon followed. How ridiculous it all seemed now! And how very long ago it all felt.

"You must believe me when I say that it was quite possibly the worst proposal ever voiced by a gentleman. My hope is that Mr. Darcy is able to reflect on that moment with the humor that I can, for it truly was abominable. He insulted my family, my position in society, and my inferior circumstances, saying that he loved me most ardently despite struggling against those deficiencies he held against me."

Maria gasped, her mouth open as wide as her eyes.

Charlotte covered her mouth with her hand, her eyes dancing in merriment. "He did not! Oh, I should have liked to have witnessed that! I can only imagine how you replied."

At that, regret tempered her laughter and withered her smile. "I responded exactly as you might expect me to. At first, I tried to be polite, but the insults overpowered my delicacy, and I informed him that were he the last man in the world, I could never be presumed upon to marry him."

"Oh, Lizzy, were you as blind as that? You would be hard-pressed to find a gentleman so complimentary to you in disposition. I always thought that once you saw past each other's unfortunate first impressions, you would grow to like each other very much. Perhaps I was wrong." Charlotte shrugged her shoulders nonchalantly, but she glanced up too many times to successfully feign complete disinterest.

Elizabeth thought of all the ways she and Mr. Darcy complimented each other. Not everyone appreciated her sense of humor, but he understood her. People determined at a first glance that Mr. Darcy was serious and haughty. His comments only encouraged them to think so, but Elizabeth understood him better now. She had committed the same fallacy, only to find that he was everything a gentleman ought to be through his actions. By her ease and liveliness, his terse manners might improve. And from his judgment, information, and knowledge of the world, her own views stood to benefit.

"You were right, Charlotte. Only, I realized it too late," Elizabeth said softly, her eyes closed.

When no consoling words came, she sat up and stretched her legs down to the floor. She wished Charlotte would say something. Or even Maria. Something. Anything to give her some small reason to hang on to hope. But none were offered, and the conversation soon turned to Lady Catherine and the effect her daughter's revelation would have on her.

\*\*\*

The next day passed slowly. Too many times, Elizabeth found herself looking out of the window toward the lane. Her preferred occupation had become sitting in the window seat with a book in her hand. Not that she read much, but it gave her an excuse to watch for riders coming up the road.

She chose her walking paths likewise as well, never straying too far lest she miss Mr. Darcy's return. What could he have gone to town with Mr. Collins for?

Elizabeth asked Charlotte that same question, but the only response she got was a pursing of the lips and a: "You must wait to find out for yourself. You will get nothing from me."

There was nothing in her words or her manners to signify if that was good or bad.

As another day passed by, and hers and Maria's departure from Hunsford neared, she wondered if she would ever find out. She and Maria would leave Hunsford on the morrow. Yet, Mr. Darcy had not returned with Mr. Collins. Charlotte was not worried in the least but kept herself busy in her home. Maria helped her, and Elizabeth, feeling restless and hopeless, was left to her own devices. It was torture.

The evening before their departure, Lady

Catherine invited them to dine at Rosings. Still no Mr. Darcy.

Miss de Bourgh looked happier and livelier than Elizabeth could recall seeing her. She had thought her a sickly, mousy lady, but now she could better appreciate Mr. Collins' compliments to her aristocratic looks.

Colonel Fitzwilliam, always one to bring joy to the table, was twice as jolly as he had ever been. It was both a pleasure and a misery to spend hours in their company. Elizabeth was happy for anyone who was fortunate enough to marry for love, but as her prospects of ever experiencing such a blessed emotion dwindled down to nothing, she could not keep the melancholy at bay completely.

Lady Catherine was shockingly reserved. Instead of spewing unasked for advice at every turn, she limited herself to the occasional remark.

When they went into the drawing room for coffee, Elizabeth found herself seated by a glowing Miss de Bourgh.

"Let me take this opportunity to congratulate you, Miss de Bourgh. You both look so happy," Elizabeth managed to say with a smile.

Blushing and looking down at her hands before meeting Elizabeth's eyes, she said, "I feel like I am living in a dream. Even Mother seems to have come to terms with it."

"You are very fortunate indeed. I would not have thought such a miracle possible," Elizabeth said, her smile growing more genuine and less forced.

"I have learned never to underestimate myself and the people I love."

"May I ask what will happen to Mrs. Jenkinson?" Elizabeth had been surprised to see the elderly woman sitting in her usual place by Miss de Bourgh's side. If anything, she was more attentive than before.

"Of course. She has been with us for far too long to cast her off so easily, and I do believe her when she promises that she speaks kindly of Richard to Mother. She has become an ally, and I think the guilt she feels for acting as she did will guarantee her continued good behavior." Miss de Bourgh smiled at Mrs. Jenkinson, who conversed quietly with Lady Catherine. Lady Catherine, in turn, looked in surprise toward Colonel Fitzwilliam to nod in approval at whatever Mrs. Jenkinson had revealed to her.

"You see that?" Miss de Bourgh whispered to Elizabeth. "She is doing a masterful job, is she not?"

Elizabeth had to admit that she was and thought more of Miss de Bourgh for arranging things how she had done.

She kept looking toward the door, hoping that Mr. Darcy would walk through it. After all, Mr. Collins would despair to know he had missed the chance to dine at Rosings. Yet, the evening passed and soon Lady Catherine ordered a coach to convey her guests to their home.

Miss de Bourgh squeezed her hand affectionately. Colonel Fitzwilliam smiled warmly at her, but he had smiled most of the evening, so it did not signify. Mrs. Jenkinson avoided eye contact, but that was no surprise, was it? Lady Catherine looked down her nose with pinched lips whenever their eyes met, but she did invite Elizabeth to make free use of the Collins' hospitality whenever she was so inclined. As if it were hers to offer. Elizabeth thanked her for her kindness while inwardly rolling her eyes.

They arrived home without chancing upon two horsemen. Not that she expected to see anyone riding at that time of the night, but it did not stop her from looking out of the coach glass all the way back to the parsonage.

As fortune would have it, Mr. Collins did return after she had changed into her nightclothes. Unsuitable for company, she cracked her door open to listen for the smooth baritone of Mr. Darcy's voice, knowing that she would not hear it. His propriety would never allow him to call at such a late hour unless it was absolutely necessary. She wished she could be as necessary to him as he had become to her. Breath came painfully as her heart broke deeper with each passing hour away from his company.

Flipping her pillow to the dry side, she tried to sleep. She and Maria would leave early in the morning, and she would have the whole ride home to plan how she could hide the emptiness burdening her.

# CHAPTER 33

It was just as well they planned to leave at first light in the morning. Elizabeth tossed and turned all night, her dreams of Mr. Darcy indelibly imprinted in her soul. If only she had understood his character better when he had proposed. If only he had not said the very words guaranteed to provoke her. Would she could turn back time, she would forgive him his unfortunate choice... or would she? No, in her heart she knew that had she been madly in love with the gentleman at the time, she never could have accepted such a poorly executed proposal. Every fiber of her being rebelled against the thought. But she would not have refused him in such a way so as to prevent him from asking again.

A sigh escaped her, one in so many she had lost count. She should not waste her time thinking of what might have been. The past was in the past, and now she had to worry about the present— a present she could only dream would include Mr. Darcy. If only...

Shaking her head to rid herself of the torturous thoughts that needled her, she finished dressing and went downstairs.

Her trunk was carried down to sit in the front parlor. The polished metal of the new clasp gleamed in the soft morning light.

Elizabeth and Maria, traveling as they were in the Lucases' coach and expected in town by a certain hour, had to leave before breaking their fast. Charlotte had prepared a basket full of food for them to take inside the coach. Elizabeth was grateful Sir William had sent their family coach for them to travel in more comfortably. Maria would sleep most of the way, and she would be free to think about what might have been.

Holding little hope that Mr. Darcy would stop by at such an unseemly hour, Elizabeth just wanted to return home to her family. She welcomed the noise and turbulence she had grown up surrounded by. She would hug her sisters, tell them all about the grandness of Rosings, and let their laughter lift her spirits. Then, when she had had enough, she would retreat to the quiet study to warn her father of Mr. Wickham. Lydia and Kitty enjoyed the militia's attention overly much, and it would not do for them to associate with that particular officer. She might even confide in him the contents of her heart. He would answer in a manner which belied a complete misunderstanding and impractical view of her sentiments, but she might feel better in the telling. She would not tell Jane yet. She would sooner suffer in silence than diminish her dear sister's well-earned joy in her reunion with Mr. Bingley.

It was time to leave. Looking around, for she could not help it, she noticed not what was there, but who was missing. Still, she hugged Charlotte with a genuine smile.

Pulling back, Charlotte clasped both of her arms, pinning them to her side. "Lizzy, I wish you all the happiness in the world. I will write often, and I do hope that you visit us again when my confinement is done." Pinching her lips together, she added, "It is a pity you have to leave now. Can you not stay long enough to break your fast with us?"

"You know we cannot delay. I could not impose after your family so kindly lent us their carriage. Besides, we do not want to cause them needless worry if we were to arrive later than planned," she said, half-heartedly. Would that they could stay until Mr. Darcy could call. *If* he would call.

Charlotte embraced Elizabeth again, and her optimism almost made Elizabeth cry.

Mr. Collins stood next to Charlotte. Elizabeth turned to curtsy to him, but he extended both of his hands to hold hers in a gesture devoid of any selfish malice. He shook her hand between his own, and while Elizabeth thought it odd, she did not retract her hands. Somehow, it felt appropriate and she felt the gratitude in his expression.

Shuffling his feet and taking several breaths, he said, "May the angels above serve as my witnesses this blessed day of the gravity of my compunction. I must apologize to you, Cousin Elizabeth. My dear wife, who has proved herself to be much more righteous than I, helped me discern the consequences of my resentful attitude toward you. It has led me down the path of sin, and my shame is complete. I would not dare ask for your forgiveness after the wrongs I have done, but could you find it in your heart to accept my apology?"

There being nothing she could say to add to his grief, and her desire to do so lacking entirely, Elizabeth smiled. "You married the best of women, Mr. Collins. I accept your apology, and what is more, I forgive you."

Shaking her hands vigorously, he said, "I cannot thank you enough, Cousin Elizabeth. Please know that you are always welcome in our humble home. Do not forget us and pray think of us kindly when you leave for your new home."

Elizabeth, uncertain which new home he could possibly refer to, was interrupted from asking when Charlotte said, "For a certainty, Lizzy. You have been away from home long enough, Longbourn will feel new again, and I daresay you shall forget us until you fall back into your normal habits."

Shrugging her shoulders, Elizabeth chalked Mr. Collins' strange wording up to another case of misused verbiage.

Mr. Collins let go of her hands, and with one final

farewell, she walked out to the waiting coach for hers and Maria's journey home. Only, Maria was not there.

***

She looked at Charlotte. "Where is Maria? Our things are stowed away, and it is time to depart." Now that the hour to leave had arrived, an uncomfortable resignation settled over Elizabeth, and she wanted nothing more than to be on her way home. That was what she told herself anyway. She would feel better with her family, she repeated to her stubborn heart.

A shriek from the side of the house and a pink blur bolted past their group. Betsy ran after the squealing troublemaker, taking the menservants surrounding the coach with her. Only the driver remained seated to secure the horses.

"Oh, no, not again! Mr. Collins, the pig has escaped!" exclaimed Charlotte, turning to the lane.

Mr. Collins pulled her back. "Do not trouble yourself, my rosebud. You must consider your delicate condition and let the others follow in pursuit. I will help them."

Perhaps love would blossom at the parsonage after all, thought Elizabeth. She was pleased for Charlotte.

Before Mr. Collins could leave, Maria walked out of the house, slapping her hands against each other.

She froze in place when she saw the group looking at her open-mouthed.

"What?" she asked in innocence. There was a twinkle in her eye.

Charlotte laughed and sent Mr. Collins off to oversee that the escapee was caught before it intruded into Lady Catherine's manicured park.

"You do beat all, Maria," said Charlotte, draping her arm around her sister's shoulders. With a shrug, she added, "There is nothing more to it but to stay here until the pig is returned. You cannot leave without the menservants. Let us hope the little beast gives them some trouble in the catching," she said, her eyebrows raised.

Elizabeth, who would much rather have run after the animal than sit in one place, acquiesced. Looking past the coach and down the road, she soon caught sight of who she had looked for countless times across the lane.

Sensing her friends withdraw, she stood alone in the rose garden, surrounded by buds and their promise of fuller blooms to come.

As he drew closer, shouts of frustration from further down the lane reached her ears. He heard them too, bringing a gorgeous smile to his handsome face. He carried flowers in his hands.

His eyes never left hers, though there were enough distractions about. Walking through the open gate, he offered the cut blooms for her to take.

She hugged the mixture of spring blossoms and rosebuds to her bosom, burying her nose to overwhelm her senses with their sweet perfume. He had brought her flowers. He must have risen early to pick them just for her. The happy tears in her eyes blurred her vision, making the scene seem more like a dream.

"Elizabeth," he said in his velvety voice. It was real. He was real. "My dearest Elizabeth," he repeated. The sound of her name coming off his lips nearly made her swoon.

"Fitzwilliam," she said aloud, testing his name for the first time. Liking the feel of it rolling off her tongue, she whispered again to herself. "William." Now that was better.

Stepping forward, he placed his hands on her cheeks and raised her face up to meet his smoldering gaze.

"Elizabeth, let me tell you how ardently I admire and love you. From the moment we first met, you took possession of my heart, and I knew that life was not worth living if I could not share it with you. You have bewitched me, body and soul, and I must know: Will you marry me?" He rubbed his thumb across her cheek. She would float up to the heavens if he did not hold her to the earth.

She felt his warm breath caressing her forehead. "I would like nothing more than to spend forever with you," she said, leaning forward as closely as she dared, the flowers forming a well-intentioned, but unwanted barrier between them.

William heaved a sigh of relief, making her laugh.

He seemed to be such a self-assured, confident man, yet he had been nervous.

"Did you really think I would refuse you?" she teased.

"I had hoped to perform better this time around," he said through his grin. Like the rest of him, his teeth were perfect, and he gave her occasion to see all of them. She determined to make him smile thus every day.

"Let me reassure you that your second attempt is something I will relive over and over in my dreams. What is more, I vow to do my utmost to erase your atrocious first proposal forever from my memory and only remember this one."

That suited him just as well as it did her.

Out of the corner of her eye, she saw her friends through the window. Their arms were around each other, and Maria bobbed up and down in excitement. Charlotte's hand rested over her heart. Elizabeth winked to them as she turned her full attention back to the man before her.

"Let us go to the orchard," she suggested.

She did not need to ask twice.

"God bless that pig for delaying your departure," he said through his laughter. He tipped his hat at the ladies standing before the window and, arm in arm, they walked past the house to the bench settled amongst the fruit trees.

"I believe we have Maria to thank for that. Otherwise, we should have gone. And I so badly wanted to see you," she said softly, not bothering to dampen the longing in her voice.

"I would have chased you down on my horse. When I saw that there was a chance that you returned my affection, nothing could prevent me from asking again." He rested his hand gently on top of hers, sitting so close she could feel his leg against her own.

Turning over her hand and lacing her fingers through his, she asked, "Why did you leave? I was free, but the agony was unbearable."

"I cannot tell you now, but please know that everything I did, I did it for you," he said, raising her hand up to brush his lips over the top of her fingers.

Her thoughts garbled at the intimate gesture, but her tenacity prevailed. Though her heart threatened to flutter away like a butterfly, she asked, "Cannot or will not?"

He leaned forward so that their foreheads touched. He smelled so much better than the flowers, now lying beside her on the bench, and she felt that her tingling skin was the only thing preventing her from melting into a puddle as he brought his fingers up to touch her hair.

She tilted her chin up and closed her eyes, feeling her eyelashes brush against him.

"Thank the Lord and his angelic army, the pig is returned!"

Elizabeth bolted upright, the magic of the moment gone.

William, too, looked like something precious to him had been taken away.

Mr. Collins stood victorious across the orchard while a footman tossed the pig inside its pen. Closing the door with vigor, the group marched in triumph back to the house.

Elizabeth looked yearningly at William. She had to leave, but she could not make herself stand.

\*\*\*

It took every ounce of self-discipline, but Darcy stood, pulling Elizabeth up with him.

"I will return to Longbourn with you. Bingley is expecting me and your father is anxious to see you," he said.

It was adorable how her face lit up. "You spoke with my father? Does he know about us?"

There was so much he wanted to tell her, but he would not ruin his surprise. Mr. Bennet would guard his silence until their wedding day.

"So determined was I to do things correctly, I went to Longbourn seeking his blessing in case you said, "Yes."

Elizabeth laughed like the sound of jingling bells. "What did he say? How did you convince him?"

Darcy enclosed her fingers within his own, walking slowly toward the waiting carriage. "It was not easy. I had the distinct disadvantage of falling in love with his favorite daughter. But, in the end, he was reasonable." More, he would not say.

Not even her incessant questioning pried the truth from him on their journey to Hertfordshire.

*** 

True to expectations, Elizabeth's family received her with vociferous exclamations, a multitude of embraces, and a good deal of bouncing. William continued to Netherfield Park where an equally joyous Mr. Bingley awaited.

Jane had the best of news to impart. Mr. Bingley had proposed. She, of course, had accepted. Elizabeth would never tell her about the role William really played in Mr. Bingley's return to Netherfield Park and his Jane. Elizabeth would cherish the knowledge safely in her mind.

Mary was pleased to hear about the Collinses and inquired about the subjects sermonized, as well as the uplifting books to be found at the parsonage. Truth be told, Elizabeth had used her time in church to let her mind wander on other godly thoughts. Surely, pondering the good traits of thy neighbor was a godly thought— and the more she thought of William, the handsomer he grew.

Kitty and Lydia were only interested in Hunsford until they found out that, indeed, there were no officers stationed there. Then they greatly pitied Elizabeth for the lack of entertainment the regiment always brought with them and of which they had been allowed to partake freely. Elizabeth spoke to Father that very day lest their lack of sense get them in a predicament from which the whole family would suffer.

Mother went into raptures at Elizabeth's description of Rosings— especially of Lady Catherine's drawing room. Her eyes darted about her own drawing room, and Elizabeth knew she was planning how to infuse some grandness into Longbourn. Father would not be allowed much peace that day.

Father stood close to Elizabeth, but he let the others do their talking until the dust settled.

She did not know what to expect, but it certainly was not what happened. When she finally had a moment alone with him, he kissed the top of her head, and said, "I could not let you leave me were it not for such a worthy gentleman. He will make you happy, my dearest Lizzy, and I pray you cherish him as much as he loves you."

His watery eyes and utter lack of sarcasm were so out of character, she was moved to bury her face in his chest and squeeze her arms around his middle like she had done as a child. He patted her hair and, after some time, pulled away with a sniff. "It is as it should be, Lizzy. Besides, Jane will stay at Netherfield Park and I shall soon be kept away from my books with all the grandchildren they will supply me."

He did not look like he minded too much.

# EPILOGUE

He didn't want to tell her, but she eventually had her way. He simply could not deny her— a fact she was all too aware of and planned to exploit often, so long as the benefit was two-sided.

It was on the third try that he finally broke down. It was the evening before their wedding, and he had come to call. Mr. Bingley, too, was there to see Jane. Like William, he could not wait another day to see his bride.

"William, please tell me what you and Mr. Collins were up to. What good can possibly be served by keeping it from me any longer? We marry tomorrow," she implored.

He wavered, and her feminine perceptions sensed that she had gained some ground. "Does it have something to do with Charlotte, or was it only business for Lady Catherine?" she asked, batting her feathery eyelashes up at him.

"It is a surprise," he said in resignation, but with a large grin.

"That is what you keep telling me. What kind of surprise?"

He kissed the tip of her nose, in no hurry to pull away. "I find your curious nature enchanting."

"It pleases me to hear that you do not think my excessive curiosity a fault," she smiled back.

In a more serious tone, he answered as he moved close enough for their knees to touch, "Perhaps it is our imperfections that make us so perfect for each other." He looked to her for her opinion.

"And I, too, have learned your tricks. You seek to distract me through your sweet talk and kisses. Well, it will not work. Not this time."

William scoffed. "Me? When it was my lack of eloquence that provoked such a passionate refusal of my suit?"

Elizabeth laced her fingers through his and admired how well they fit together. "It was not all bad. Had you stopped after declaring how ardently you admired and loved me as you did this last time, I should have been sorely tempted to accept your proposal. Every lady ought to hear those words at least once in her lifetime. Now, you have deflected the topic once again, and I plan to stay here with you as my captive until you tell me what business you had with Mr. Collins in London." She held up their entwined fingers to emphasize the seriousness of her threat.

She waited for it, knowing it would come.

It started at his mouth. The corners turned up, flashing a dimple on his right cheek and spreading up to his eyes, illuminating his face. Then his deep laugh, which she had heard much more of over the fortnight since his successful proposal, resounded through the room. He had given so much to her, it seemed only fair that she gave him the gift of laughter. He was beautiful when he laughed.

"Very well, my inquisitive bride. I had hoped to tell you as a wedding present, but I would rather see you happy now. When Mr. Collins confessed his spiteful act toward you, he was so remorseful and eager to repair the damage he had done, I suggested that he mend family relations by agreeing to put in writing that, in the case of your father's demise, he will transfer the title deed to you."

Elizabeth's heart jumped at the news. "He gave up his inheritance? However did you manage that? I cannot believe that guilt alone could do it. What did you do?" She knew that William must have left out a big piece of the puzzle.

"In exchange for a sum of money, which he will receive when the property is transferred, your mother and sisters can stay here as long as they please."

"You arranged to buy Longbourn when you were unsure of our future? Why did you do it?" Any other man would have secured her hand before arranging for the comfort of her family.

"I had to do it. I wanted to know that, whether

you wanted me in your life or not, you would be secure. As loyal as you are to your family, naturally, I included them."

With no regard to propriety, she wrapped her arms around him and rested her head against his shoulder. His heart beat as quickly as hers did. Many tears had been shed over the past months, but they could not be stopped, for her abundant joy could not be contained.

He had tightened the embrace so that her face pressed against his neck cloth. His musky, familiar scent of sandalwood and leather made her pulse race all the more.

"You are too good to me, William."

She felt him rest his cheek against her hair and kiss the side of her forehead. "You deserve nothing less than the best I can offer you, and I intend to find ways to make you happy every day of our life together."

Her breath taken away at the intensity of his devotion, she closed her eyes and reveled in his tight embrace, resolving in her own heart to prove herself worthy of his love.

They remained so until the clock chimed, reminding them of the late hour. It was time for William to depart with Mr. Bingley to await the morrow when their life together would truly begin.

\*\*\*

Elizabeth donned her best dress, and the maid

had finished twisting the final lock of hair into place, when a caller was announced for her.

She went downstairs, unsure what to expect, but hoping it was not Lady Catherine come to protest her nephew's imprudent choice in a bride.

To her surprise, it was Colonel Fitzwilliam and his blushing wife.

Mrs. Fitzwilliam rose, her hands extended to take Elizabeth's as she crossed the room to meet her. "Oh, I am so happy we are to be cousins. I do hope that you call me Anne from now on."

She was a different woman from the wilting lily she had been only a couple weeks before, though it would take some time for her to add some flesh to her delicate frame and grow in strength.

"You look well, Anne, and I am so happy to see you. It would please me very much for you to call me Elizabeth."

The colonel, having risen when she entered the room, added, his face beaming in pride as he looked at his wife, "She is well, is she not? My first order of business was to put a stop to the incessant bloodletting and request the attendance of a new doctor with modern ideas. Anne looks more beautiful each day."

With a blush, Anne looped her arm through the colonel's and sat next to him.

"I know how busy you must be getting ready for your wedding, so our visit will be brief," said Anne as she pulled a velvet pouch Elizabeth recognized all too well from her reticule. "I felt it appropriate to lend you these." She spilled the contents of the pouch into her hand and let the diamonds sparkle in the daylight.

Elizabeth gasped at her offer. "I could not possibly. They are much too valuable."

"Nonsense," Anne said in a tone resembling Lady Catherine so much, Elizabeth could not contain her chuckle. "From the way I see it, these earrings have done more to bring us together with our perfect matches than anything. Without them, Darcy would have left Rosings much sooner, and I would still be struggling to find a way to tell Mother how much I loved Richard. You must wear them at your wedding and for the rest of this blessed day."

"But how will I return them to you?" asked Elizabeth.

Waving her hand carelessly in front of her, Anne said, "I can trust you with them until we next meet. I hope you will not be a stranger to Rosings, and it is my hope that, when I have recovered more strength, perhaps we might travel to Matlock and to Pemberley to visit you in your new home."

"And most welcome you will be!"

Looking lovingly to Colonel Fitzwilliam, who in fact was no longer a colonel, but a gentleman of property, they rose to depart. Anne pressed the earrings into Elizabeth's hand and away they went, to meet later at the Longbourn parish church.

The hour remaining before they needed to leave in the carriage with streams of ribbons tied to the back passed in a flurry.

Elizabeth waited to put the earrings on until they were in front of the church, not wanting her mother to see them and start another scene about their turn in fortune and how lucky her girls were to catch such wealthy gentlemen for husbands. It especially irked her when William's fortune was compared to Mr. Bingley's... as if her love had been bought.

The first person she saw was Jane, who had come in the first carriage, standing next to Father.

"Are those the diamond earrings?" asked Jane in a whisper.

"The very ones," Elizabeth answered in a hush.

Father took his place between the two of them, clutching their arms tightly to his sides. Just before entering the building, he kissed them on the tops of their heads in a silent blessing. His eyes misty with emotion, he received a kiss to either side of his cheeks from his favorite daughters, whom he would miss very much.

With a sniff and a stiffening of his spine, he led his girls to the altar where their grooms waited.

Father squeezed her hand before placing it on William's extended arm.

Elizabeth saw the precise moment when William noticed her earrings. At first, he looked shocked, then a large grin spread over his face.

Leaning toward her ear, he whispered, "An appropriate choice, my love."

"I only hope Anne informed the maid of her loan," whispered Elizabeth with a nervous smile.

"Nobody would accuse Mrs. Darcy of stealing anything other than my heart," he replied, playfully.

"Now that is a valuable possession indeed. What is to be my sentence, Mr. Darcy?" she teased.

"A lifetime of love and happiness," he said just before the rector interrupted their private tête-à-tête.

As she pledged her loyalty and devotion to the man who was so much more than he had appeared to be, she knew that she was the most fortunate of women.

During the weeks leading up to the ceremony, Elizabeth had been accused of theft, of overstepping her position, and of being remiss as a friend. She almost chuckled to herself. From now on, the only accusation that could possibly be made of Mrs. Elizabeth Darcy was that, from this day forward, she would be completely, perfectly, and incandescently happy.

The End

# Thank you!

Thank you for reading *Colonel Fitzwilliam's Challenge.* I hope you enjoyed reading it as much as I loved writing it. If you did, please help other readers find it by leaving a review or recommending it to your Jane Austen fan friends!

If you would like to know when my next book is available, you can:

\* sign up for my new release newsletter at www.jenniferjoywrites.com

\* follow me on twitter at @JenJoywrites

\* friend my Facebook page at facebook.com/JenJoywrites

## About the Author

When Jennifer isn't busy dreaming up new adventures for her favorite Austen characters, she is teaching English, reading, perfecting her doughnut recipe, or taking her kids to the park.

Her wish is to continue to write sweet romances with happy endings for years to come.

She currently lives in Ecuador with her husband and twins. All of them are fluent in Spanglish.

Right now, Jennifer is imagining a new way to bring our beloved Darcy and Lizzy together so that they can enjoy another Happily-Ever-After.

## Other Books by Jennifer Joy

*Darcy's Ultimatum: The Cousins Series, Book 1*
*Anne's Adversity: The Cousins Series, Book 2*
*The Colonel's Challenge: The Cousins Series, Book 3*
*Earning Darcy's Trust*

Printed in Great Britain
by Amazon